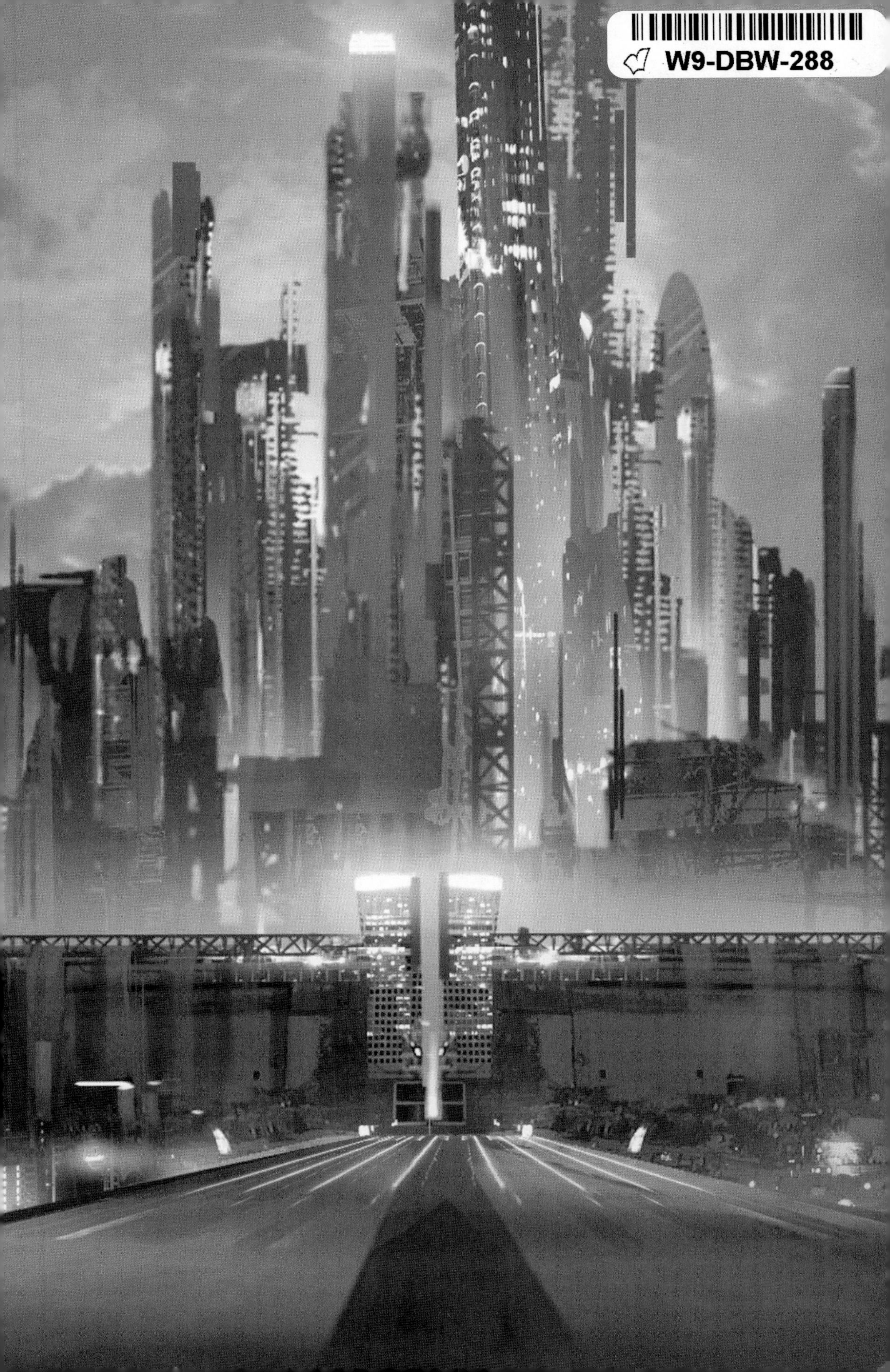

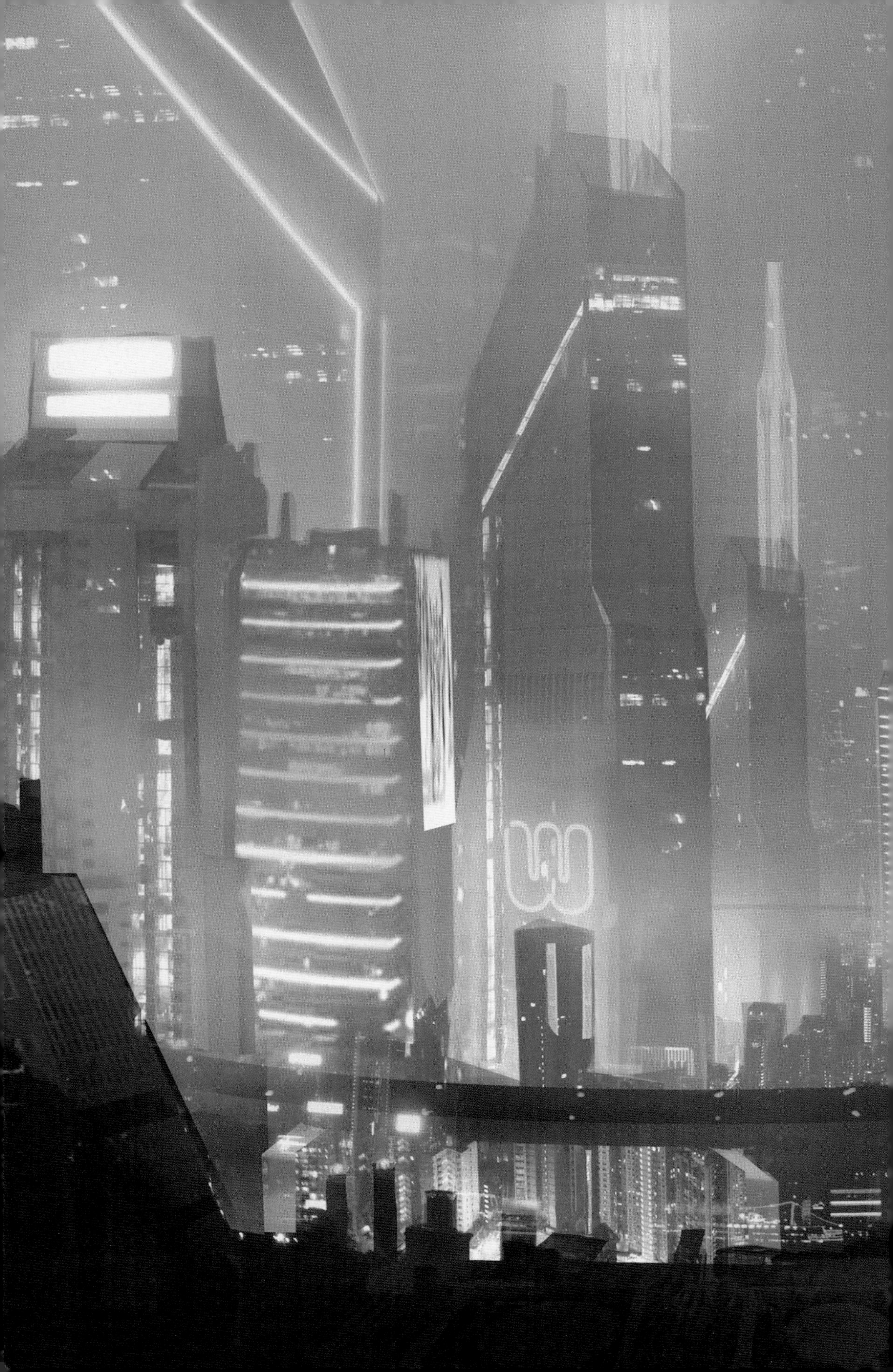

MAZE RUNNER:
THE
DEATH
CURE ™

OFFICIAL GRAPHIC NOVEL PRELUDE

MAZE RUNNER: THE DEATH CURE OFFICIAL GRAPHIC NOVEL PRELUDE,
November 2017. Published by BOOM! Studios, a division of Boom
Entertainment, Inc. Maze Runner: The Death Cure is ™ & © 2017
Twentieth Century Fox Film Corporation, Inc. All rights reserved. BOOM!
Studios™ and the BOOM! Studios logo are trademarks of Boom
Entertainment, Inc., registered in various countries and categories.
All characters, events, and institutions depicted herein are fictional.
Any similarity between any of the names, characters, persons, events,
and/or institutions in this publication to actual names, characters, and
persons, whether living or dead, events, and/or institutions is unintended
and purely coincidental. BOOM! does not read or accept unsolicited
submissions of ideas, stories, or artwork.

For information regarding the CPSIA on this printed material, call:
(203) 595-3636 and provide reference #RICH – 763860.

BOOM! Studios, 5670 Wilshire Boulevard, Suite 450, Los Angeles, CA
90036-5679. Printed in USA. First Printing.

ISBN: 978-1-60886-826-1, eISBN: 978-1-61398-497-0

MAZE RUNNER: THE DEATH CURE
OFFICIAL GRAPHIC NOVEL PRELUDE

Written by Eric Carrasco
Illustrated by Kendall Goode
Colors by Valentina Pinto
Letters by Jim Campbell

Designer Marie Krupina
Assistant Editor Matthew Levine
Editor Jasmine Amiri

MAZE RUNNER: THE SCORCH TRIALS

"THE ZEALOT"
Story by Wes Ball & T.S. Nowlin
Written by Jackson Lanzing
Illustrated by Nick Robles
Colors by Juan Manuel Tumburús
Letters by Jim Campbell

"A FATHER OF THREE"
Written by Collin Kelly
Illustrated by Nick Robles
Colors by Juan Manuel Tumburús
Letters by Jim Campbell

Editors Dafna Pleban & Stephen Christy

From the world of the 20th Century Fox Feature Film
MAZE RUNNER: THE DEATH CURE

Written by T.S. Nowlin

Based on the novel by James Dashner

Produced by Wyck Godfrey, Marty Bowen,
Ellen Goldsmith-Vein, Lee Stollman, and Joe Hartwick Jr.

Directed by Wes Ball

Special Thanks James Dashner, Wes Ball, T.S.Nowlin, Joe Hartwick Jr.,
Wyck Godfrey, Ellen Goldsmith-Vein, Eddie Gamera, Beth Goss,
Jason Young, Nicole Spiegel, Dafna Pleban and Stephen Christy

INTRODUCTION *BY JAMES DASHNER*

Hey guys. Welcome back to another graphic novel set in the world of *The Maze Runner*! You may remember some of my remarks in the last edition brought to you by BOOM Studios, setting up *The Scorch Trials* movie. I talked about the wonders of the imagination, how we can get lost in worlds that aren't our own—places like Middle Earth and Hogwarts and Gotham City. They're like playgrounds for the mind, and just like how little kids need their time on the swings and monkey bars and teeter-totters, *we* need those escapes in life that are provided through storytelling. I know that I do, and I suspect the same of you.

Also, I made the point that sometimes, it's kind of fun to allow others to play in the playground that we might have created. I say "we" because creating the world of *The Maze Runner* has definitely been a mutual effort, an unwritten contract between me and you, the reader. Although I may have worn out my fingertips writing the words of the books, they never would have blossomed into something that felt real unless you had read them, accepted them into your minds and hearts, and let the characters and world come to life. Those books, that special thing between us, will always be there, and no one will ever change them. Not over my dead body!

But then we had something wondrous happen. Something that not every author and his or her fellow partners in crime—the readers— get to experience. The movies. Wes Ball and his team took our stories and gave us their own interpretation, allowing us, in a way, to

experience the lives and adventures of Thomas, Newt, Teresa, Minho, Gally, Sonya, Harriet, Chuck, and many others for the first time again. "The first time *again*." That phrase doesn't even make sense, seems impossible. And yet we were allowed to do that.

I feel the same way about these graphic novels. Several writers and artists came together to play in our playground for a bit, giving us a chance to dive into the lives of these characters we care so much about, chances that the books could never provide. The canon is different in many respects, and that's okay. It really is okay. It's fun. It's exciting. The spirit of the books is there, fully. These *are* the characters we know and love. Sit back, relax, and enjoy the thrill of seeing your old friends again.

It honestly and truly brings tears to my eyes, quite often, when I think of what *The Maze Runner* world has become, and how much all of you mean to me. We are like a family, and these characters are our brothers and sisters. No one can ever tell *me* that they aren't real. I hope you feel the same. And what a gift that we can spend a little more time with them within these pages.

Come on in, my friends, enjoy the playground. Try not to get hurt.

—James

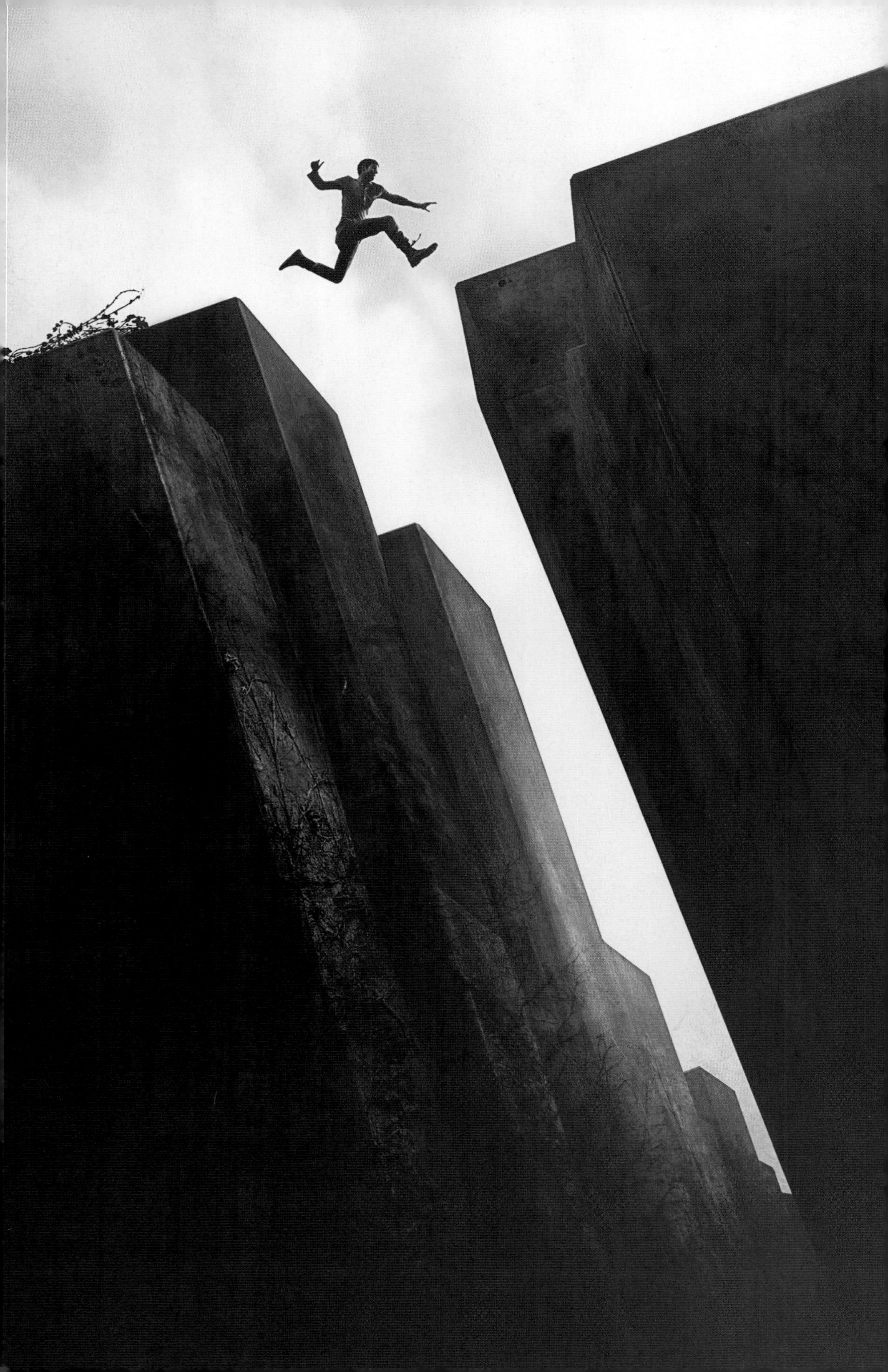

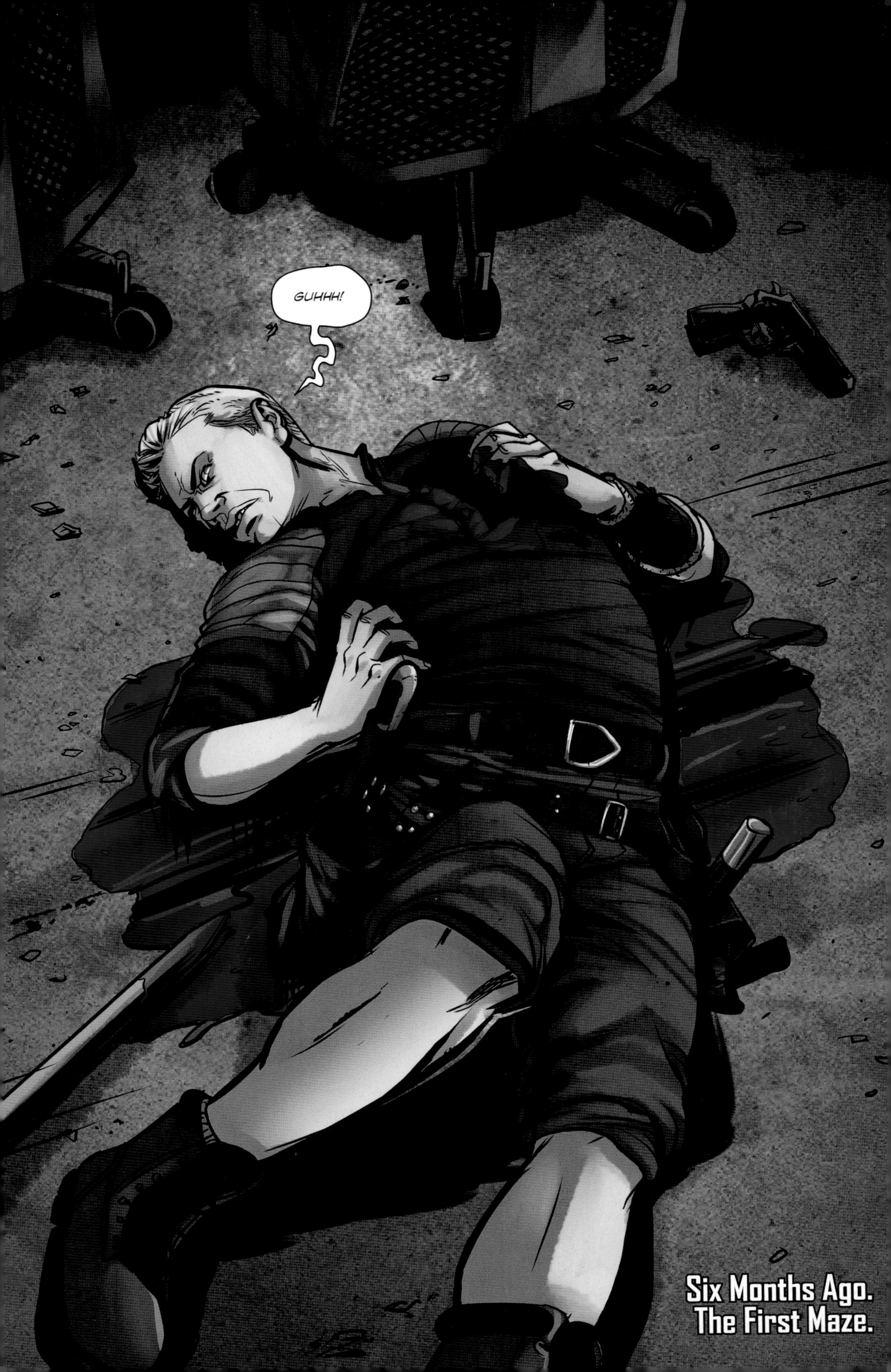
GUHHH!
Six Months Ago.
The First Maze.

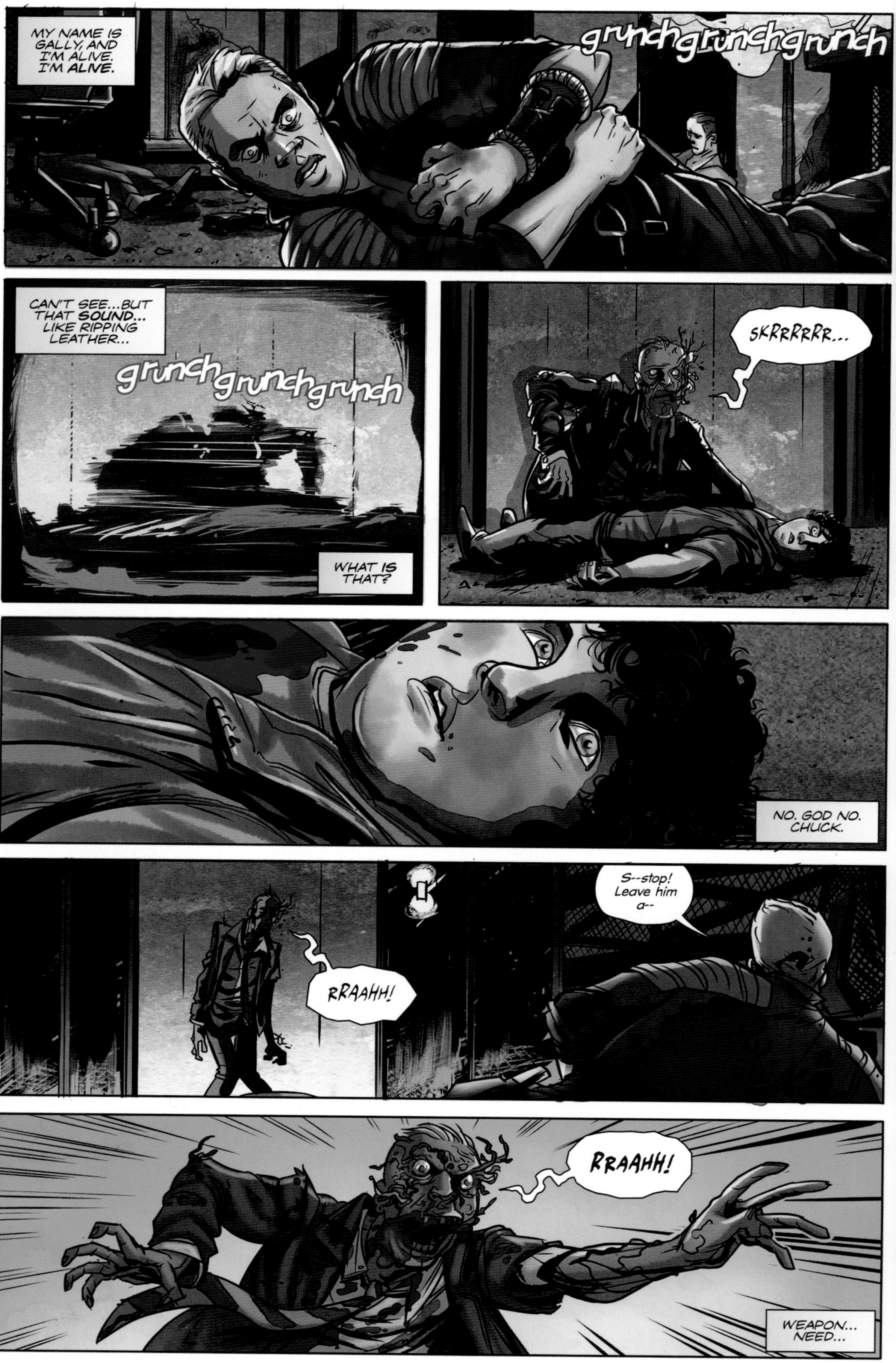
MY NAME IS GALLY, AND I'M ALIVE. I'M ALIVE.
grunchgrunchgrunch
CAN'T SEE...BUT THAT SOUND... LIKE RIPPING LEATHER...
grunchgrunchgrunch
WHAT IS THAT?
SKRRRRRR...
NO. GOD NO. CHUCK.
S--stop! Leave him a--
RRAAHH!
RRAAHH!
WEAPON... NEED...

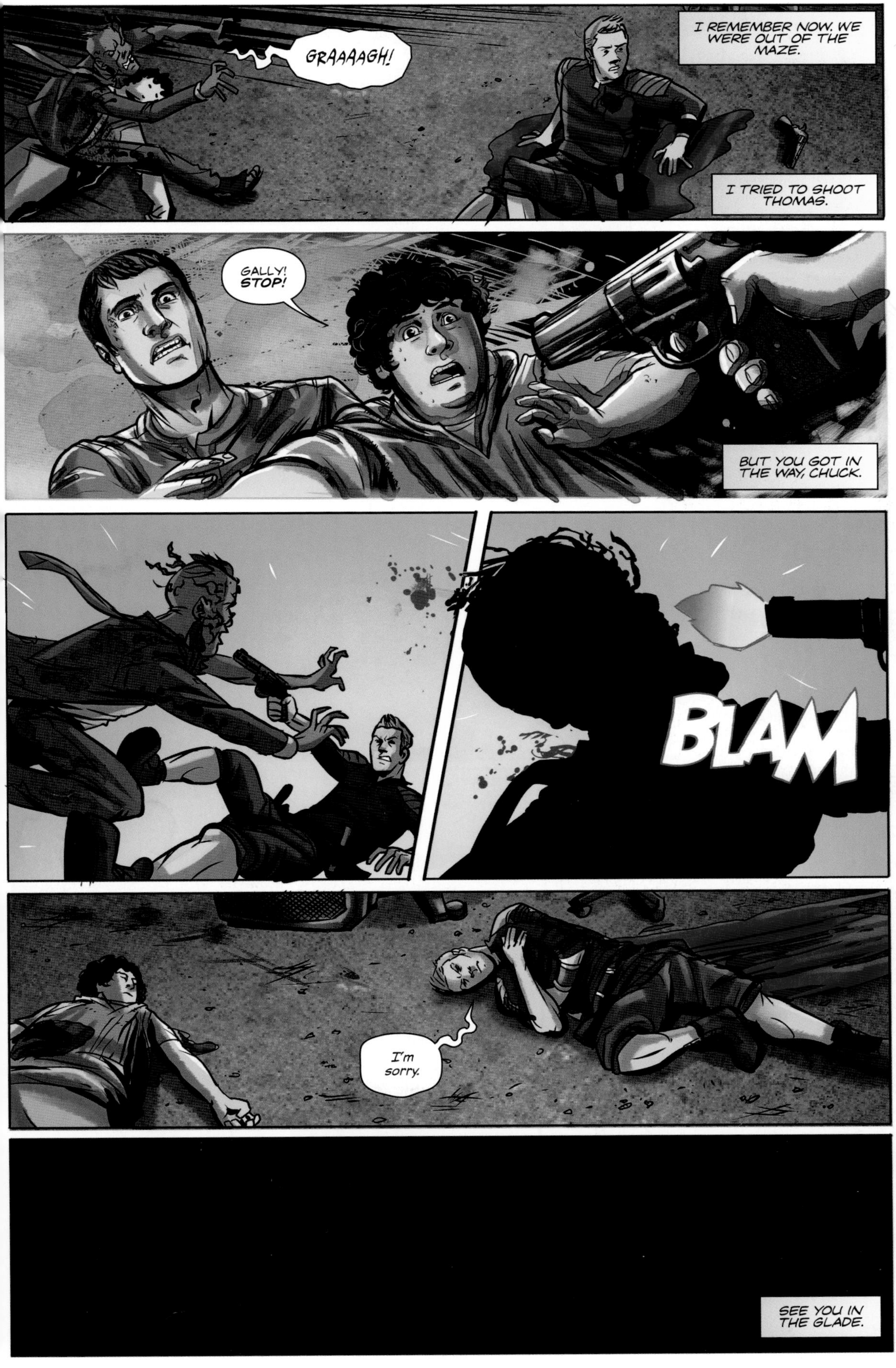
I REMEMBER NOW. WE WERE OUT OF THE MAZE.
GRAAAAGH!
I TRIED TO SHOOT THOMAS.
GALLY! STOP!
BUT YOU GOT IN THE WAY, CHUCK.
BLAM
I'm sorry.
SEE YOU IN THE GLADE.

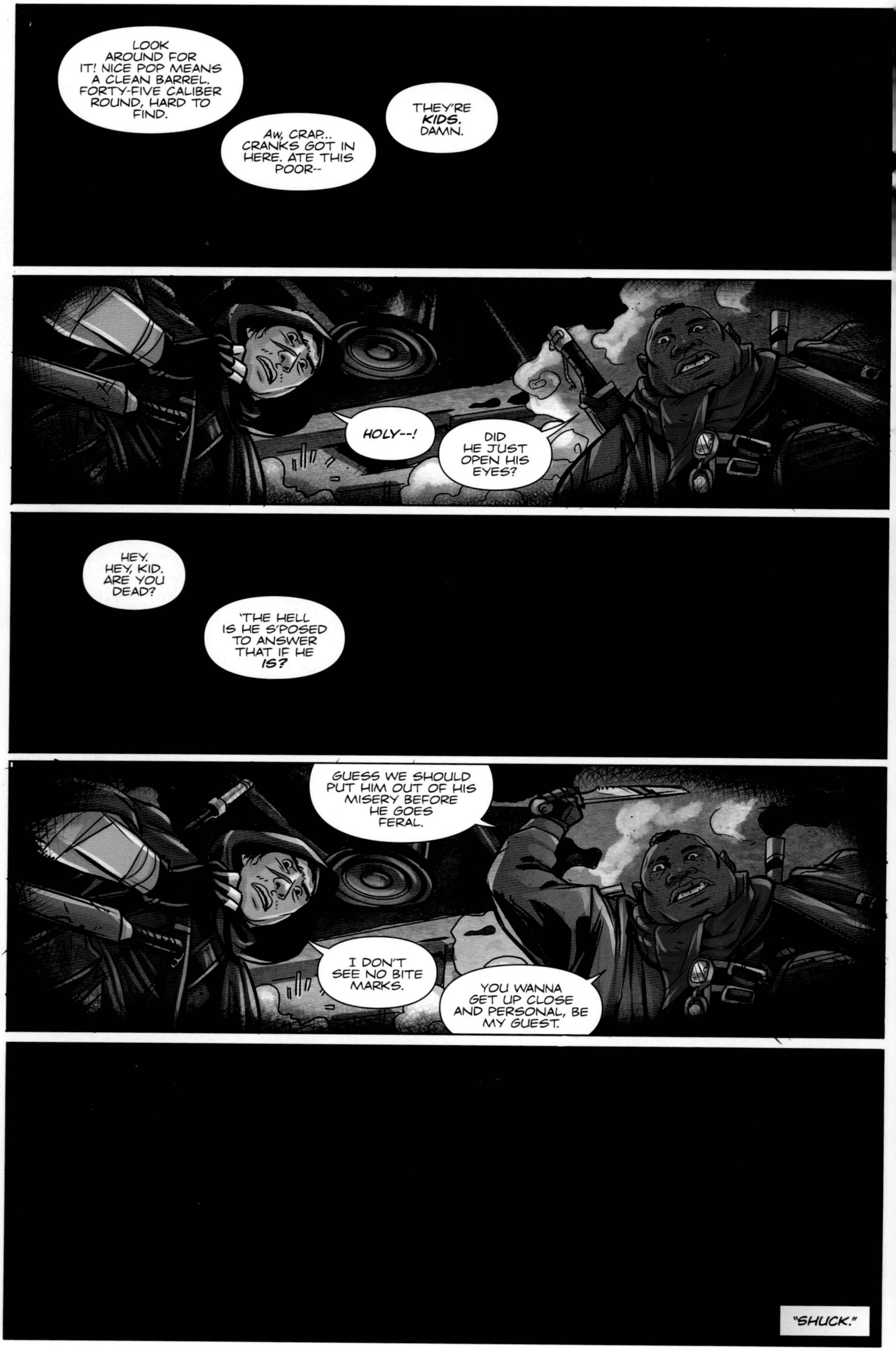
LOOK AROUND FOR IT! NICE POP MEANS A CLEAN BARREL. FORTY-FIVE CALIBER ROUND, HARD TO FIND.
AW, CRAP... CRANKS GOT IN HERE. ATE THIS POOR--
THEY'RE **KIDS.** DAMN.
HOLY--!
DID HE JUST OPEN HIS EYES?
HEY. HEY, KID. ARE YOU DEAD?
'THE HELL IS HE S'POSED TO ANSWER THAT IF HE *IS?*
GUESS WE SHOULD PUT HIM OUT OF HIS MISERY BEFORE HE GOES FERAL.
I DON'T SEE NO BITE MARKS.
YOU WANNA GET UP CLOSE AND PERSONAL, BE MY GUEST.
"SHUCK."

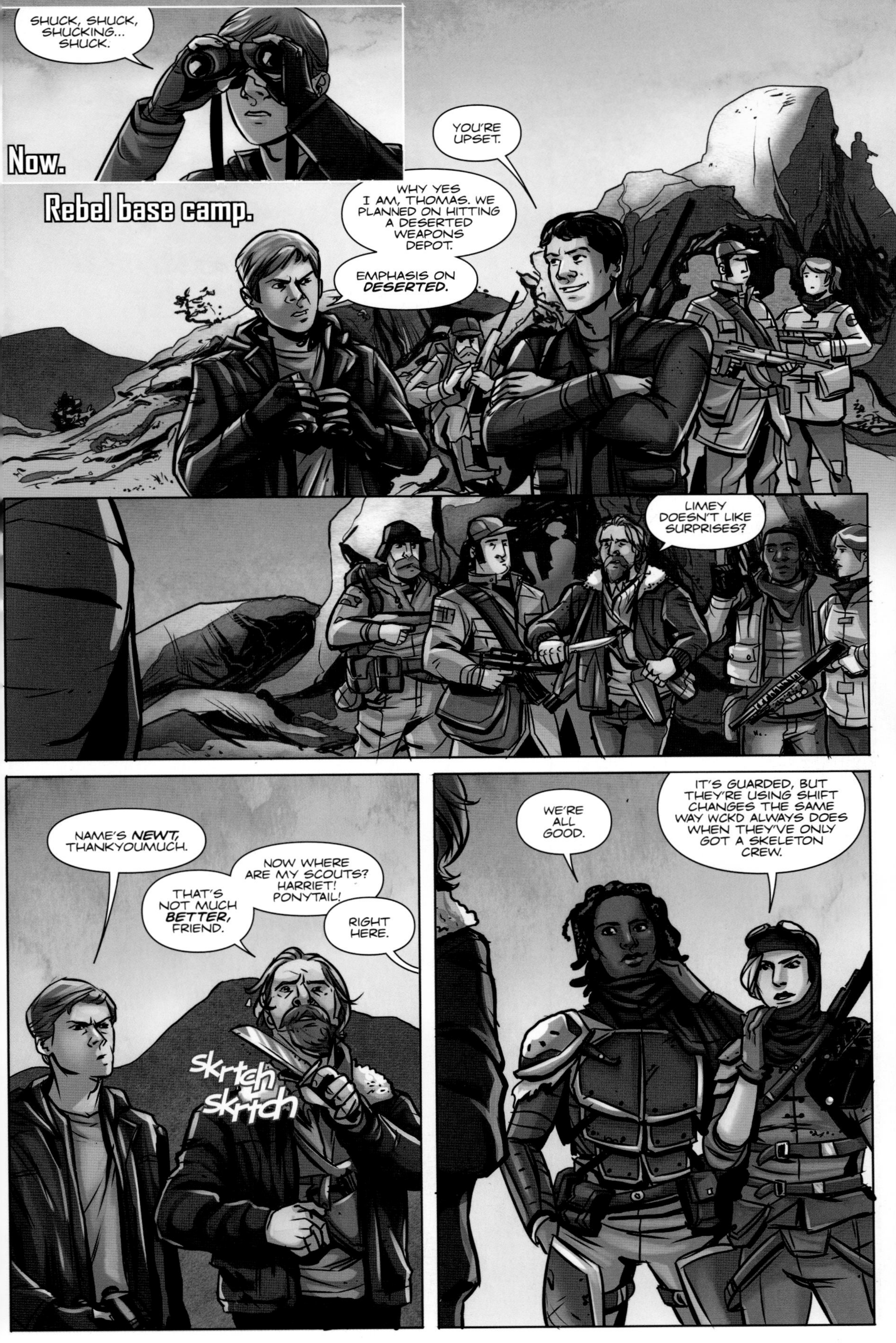
SHUCK, SHUCK, SHUCKING... SHUCK.
Now.
Rebel base camp.
YOU'RE UPSET.
WHY YES I AM, THOMAS. WE PLANNED ON HITTING A DESERTED WEAPONS DEPOT.
EMPHASIS ON DESERTED.
LIMEY DOESN'T LIKE SURPRISES?
NAME'S NEWT, THANKYOUMUCH.
THAT'S NOT MUCH BETTER, FRIEND.
NOW WHERE ARE MY SCOUTS? HARRIET! PONYTAIL!
RIGHT HERE.
skrtch skrtch
WE'RE ALL GOOD.
IT'S GUARDED, BUT THEY'RE USING SHIFT CHANGES THE SAME WAY WCKD ALWAYS DOES WHEN THEY'VE ONLY GOT A SKELETON CREW.

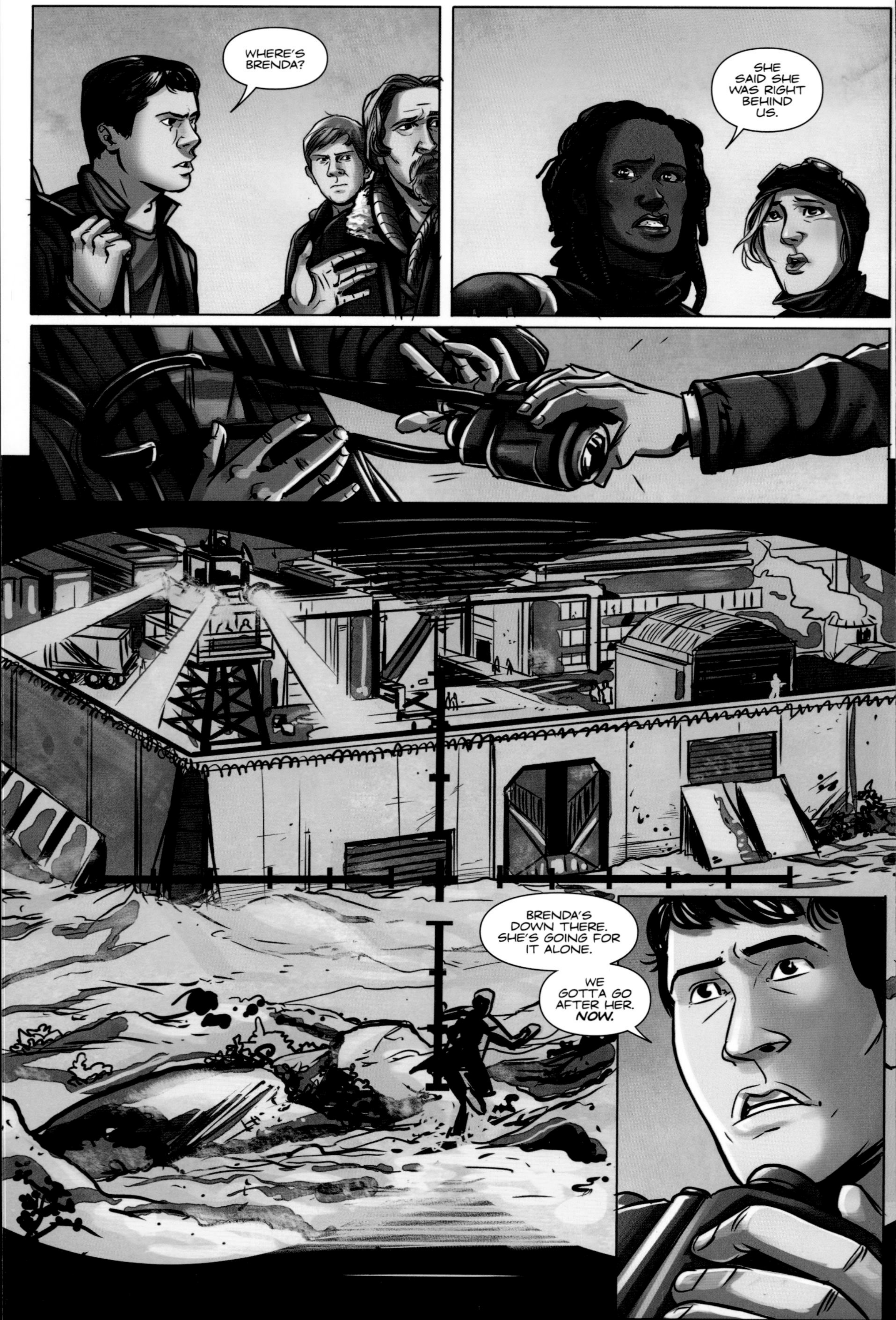

WHERE'S BRENDA?
SHE SAID SHE WAS RIGHT BEHIND US.
BRENDA'S DOWN THERE. SHE'S GOING FOR IT ALONE.
WE GOTTA GO AFTER HER. **NOW.**

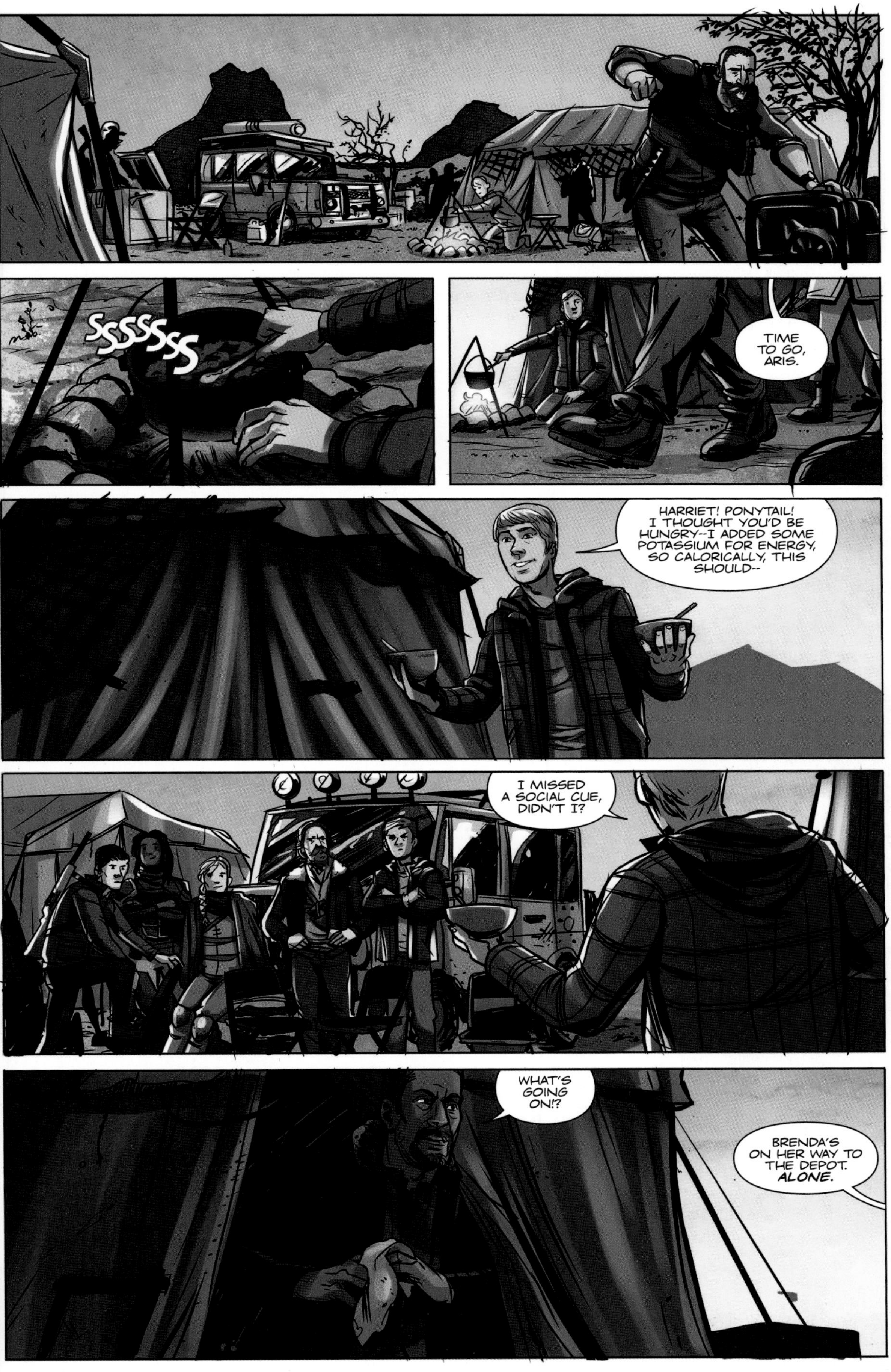
SSSSSSS
TIME TO GO, ARIS.
HARRIET! PONYTAIL! I THOUGHT YOU'D BE HUNGRY--I ADDED SOME POTASSIUM FOR ENERGY, SO CALORICALLY, THIS SHOULD--
I MISSED A SOCIAL CUE, DIDN'T I?
WHAT'S GOING ON!?
BRENDA'S ON HER WAY TO THE DEPOT. ALONE.

ALONE?!

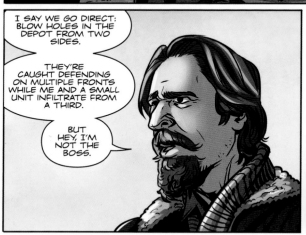

I SAY WE GO DIRECT: BLOW HOLES IN THE DEPOT FROM TWO SIDES.

THEY'RE CAUGHT DEFENDING ON MULTIPLE FRONTS WHILE ME AND A SMALL UNIT INFILTRATE FROM A THIRD.

BUT HEY, I'M NOT THE BOSS.

THOMAS?

I DON'T KNOW.

BUT YOU ALWAYS--

I DON'T KNOW!

WE CAN'T AFFORD TO PICK A FIGHT. WASTE OF AMMO, BIG RISK TO ANNOUNCE OURSELVES... I THINK WE GO STEALTH THE WHOLE WAY.

IF YOU THINK YOU CAN GET THROUGH THOSE WALLS WITHOUT A DIVERSION, YOU'RE A FOOL. THEY'LL BE WAITING.

WE DON'T KNOW WHERE BRENDA IS. MAYBE SHE'S FINE. OR MAYBE THEY CAUGHT HER. IF WE ATTACK THEM IN THE OPEN THEY COULD KILL HER.

THIS IS BIGGER THAN ONE PERSON, KID. YOU'RE GONNA GET US ALL KILLED.

YOU THINK I DON'T KNOW THAT? BUT WE'RE ALSO LOOKING FOR MINHO. AND EVERYONE ELSE THEY TOOK.

PEOPLE GET KILLED IN CROSSFIRE. MAYBE WE DO OUR BEST NOT TO CREATE IT. JORGE?

...

WE DO IT THOMAS'S WAY.

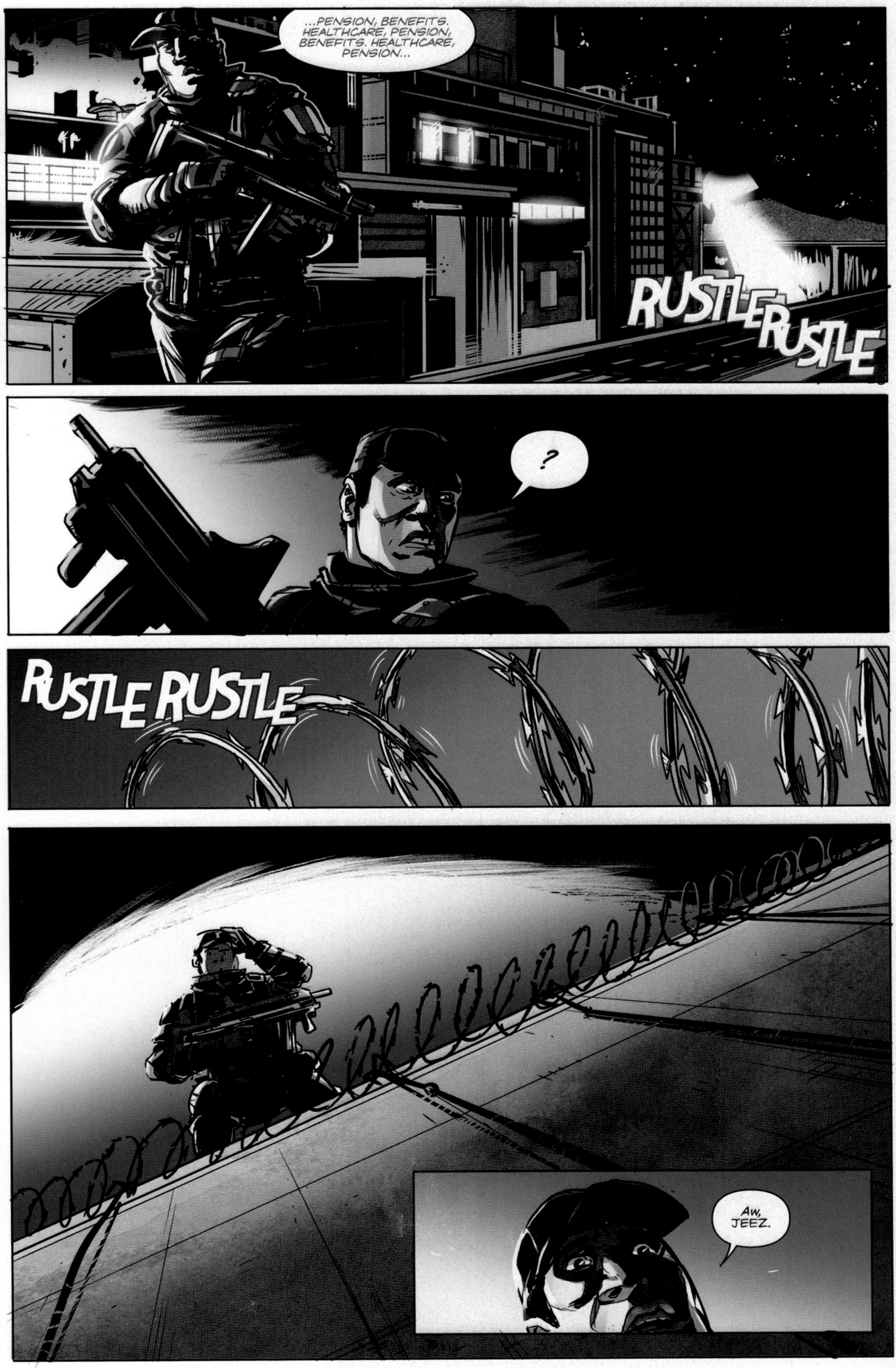
...PENSION, BENEFITS. HEALTHCARE, PENSION, BENEFITS. HEALTHCARE, PENSION...
RUSTLE RUSTLE
?
RUSTLE RUSTLE
AW, JEEZ.

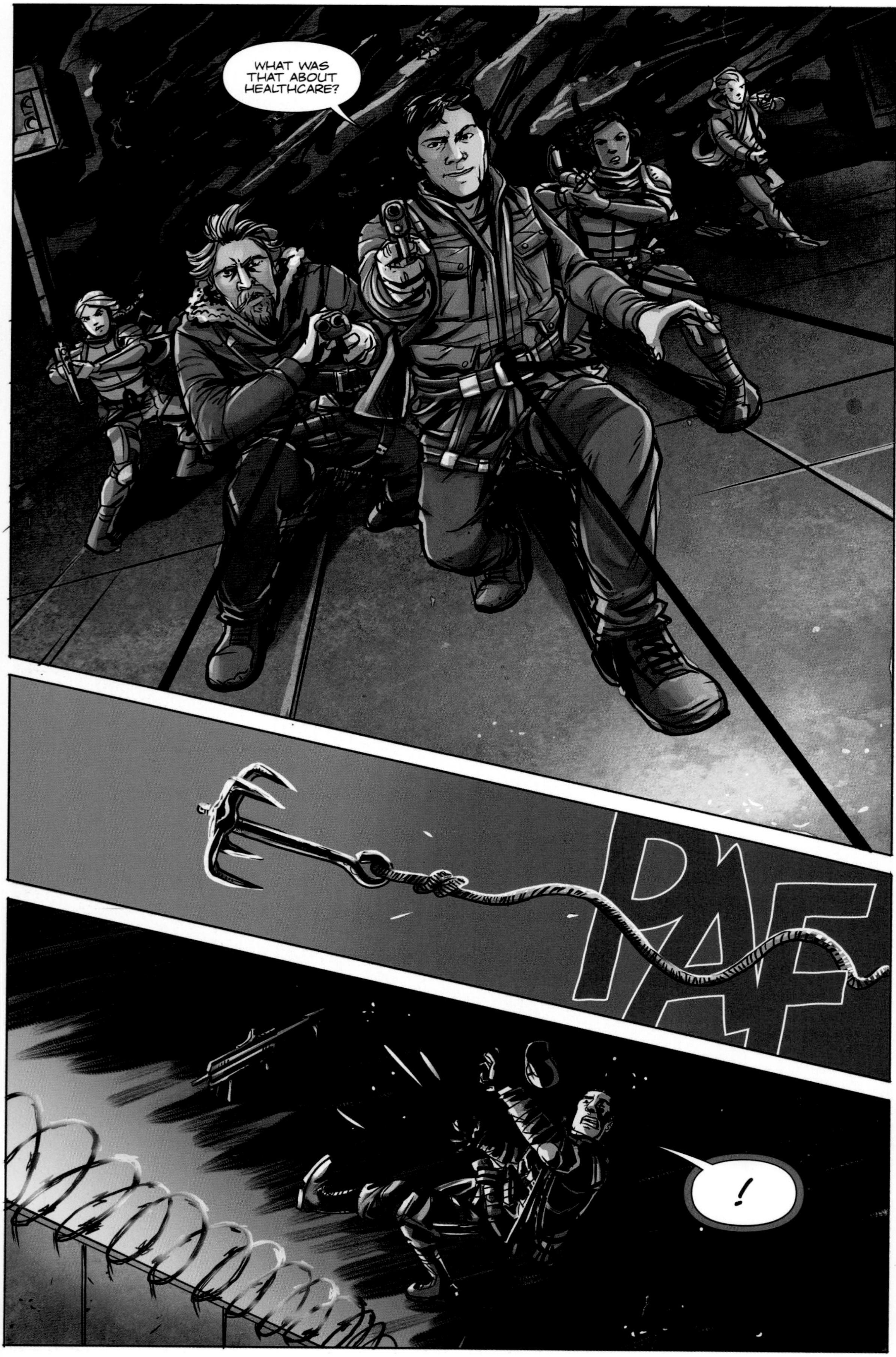
WHAT WAS THAT ABOUT HEALTHCARE?
PAF
!

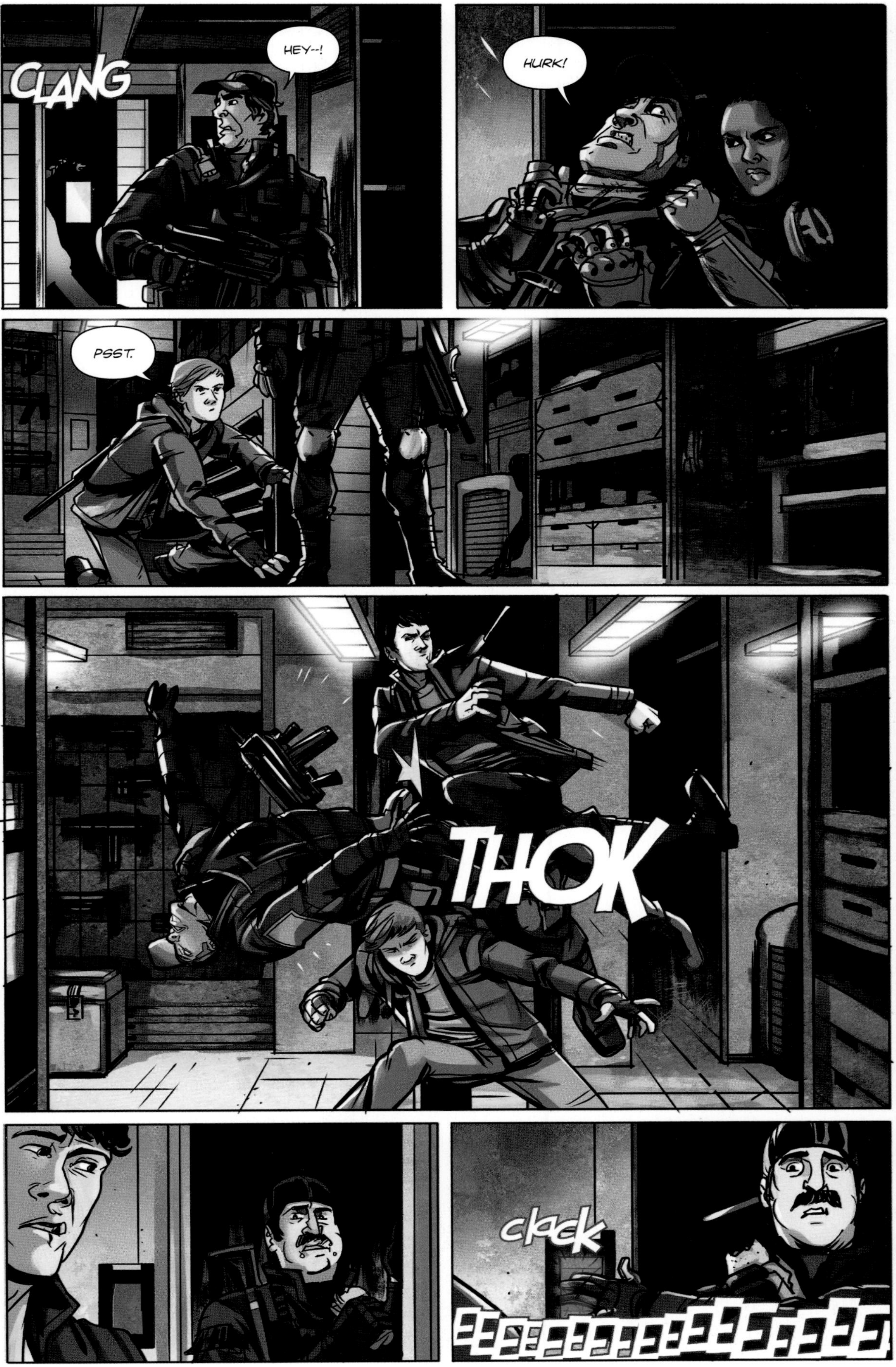
CLANG
HEY--!
HURK!
PSST.
THOK
clack
EEEEEEEEEEEEEEEEEEEEE

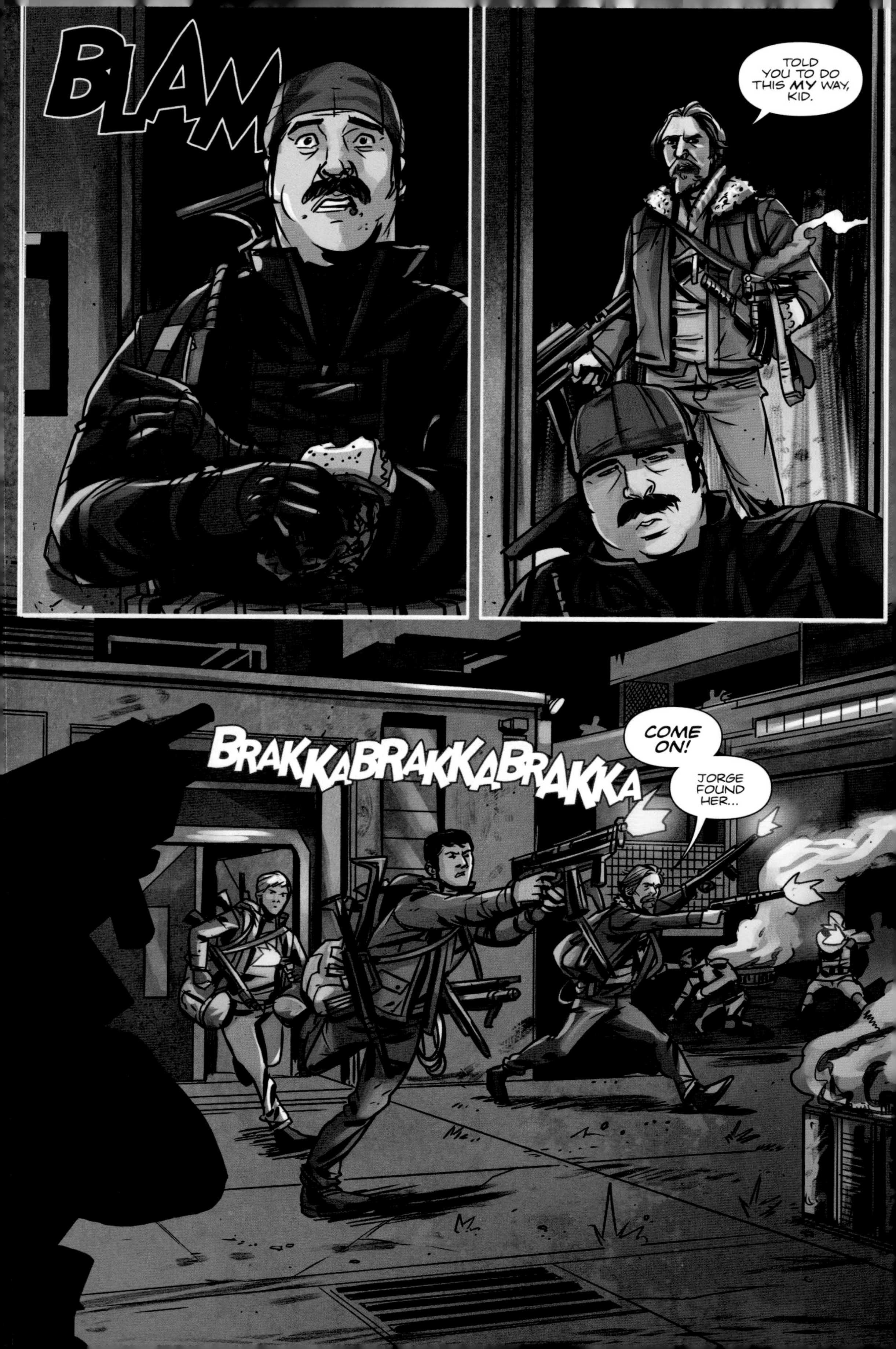
BLAM
TOLD YOU TO DO THIS MY WAY, KID.
BRAKKABRAKKABRAKKA
COME ON!
JORGE FOUND HER...

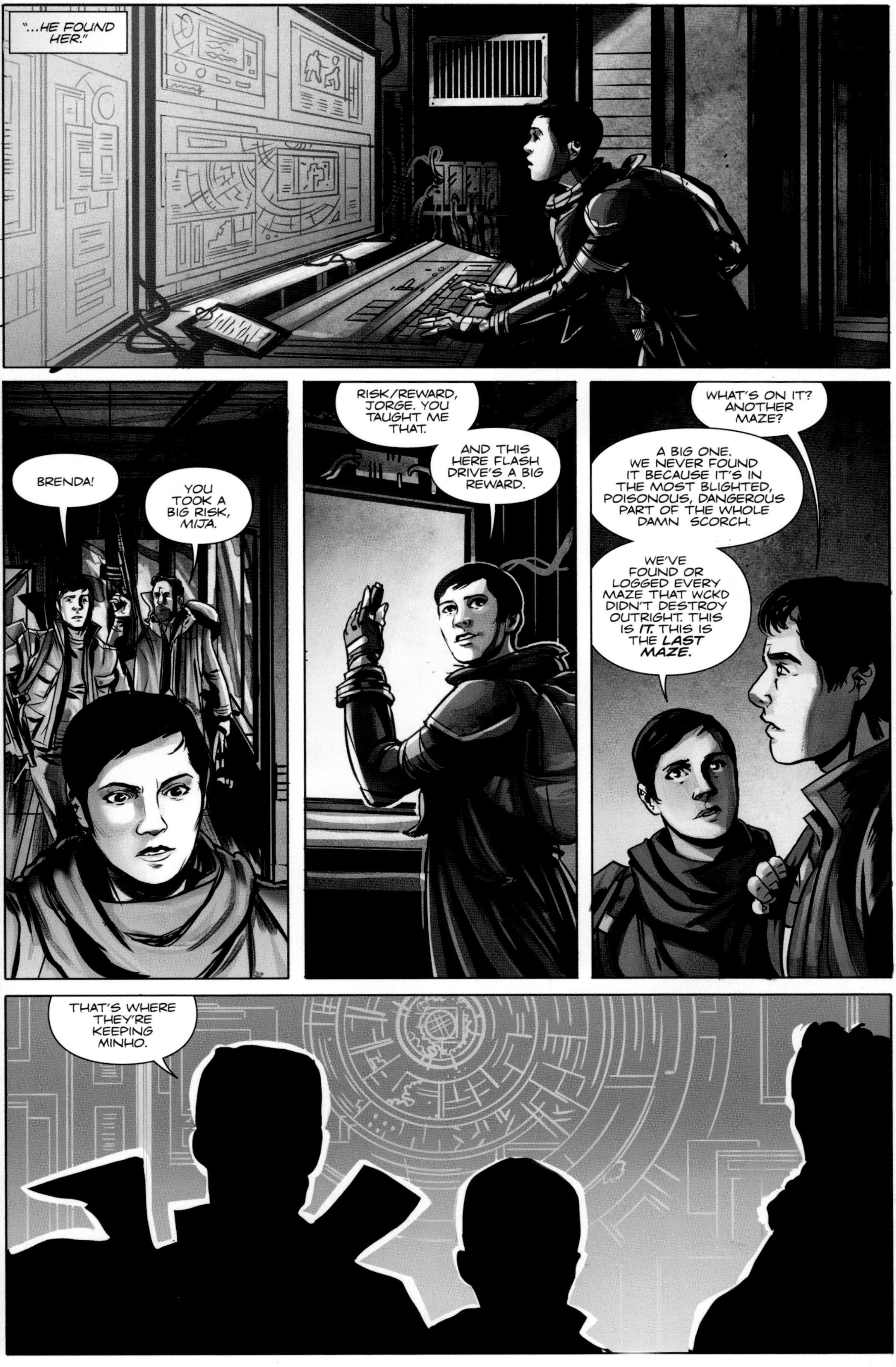
"...HE FOUND HER."
BRENDA!
YOU TOOK A BIG RISK, MIJA.
RISK/REWARD, JORGE. YOU TAUGHT ME THAT.
AND THIS HERE FLASH DRIVE'S A BIG REWARD.
WHAT'S ON IT? ANOTHER MAZE?
A BIG ONE. WE NEVER FOUND IT BECAUSE IT'S IN THE MOST BLIGHTED, POISONOUS, DANGEROUS PART OF THE WHOLE DAMN SCORCH.
WE'VE FOUND OR LOGGED EVERY MAZE THAT WCKD DIDN'T DESTROY OUTRIGHT. THIS IS IT. THIS IS THE LAST MAZE.
THAT'S WHERE THEY'RE KEEPING MINHO.

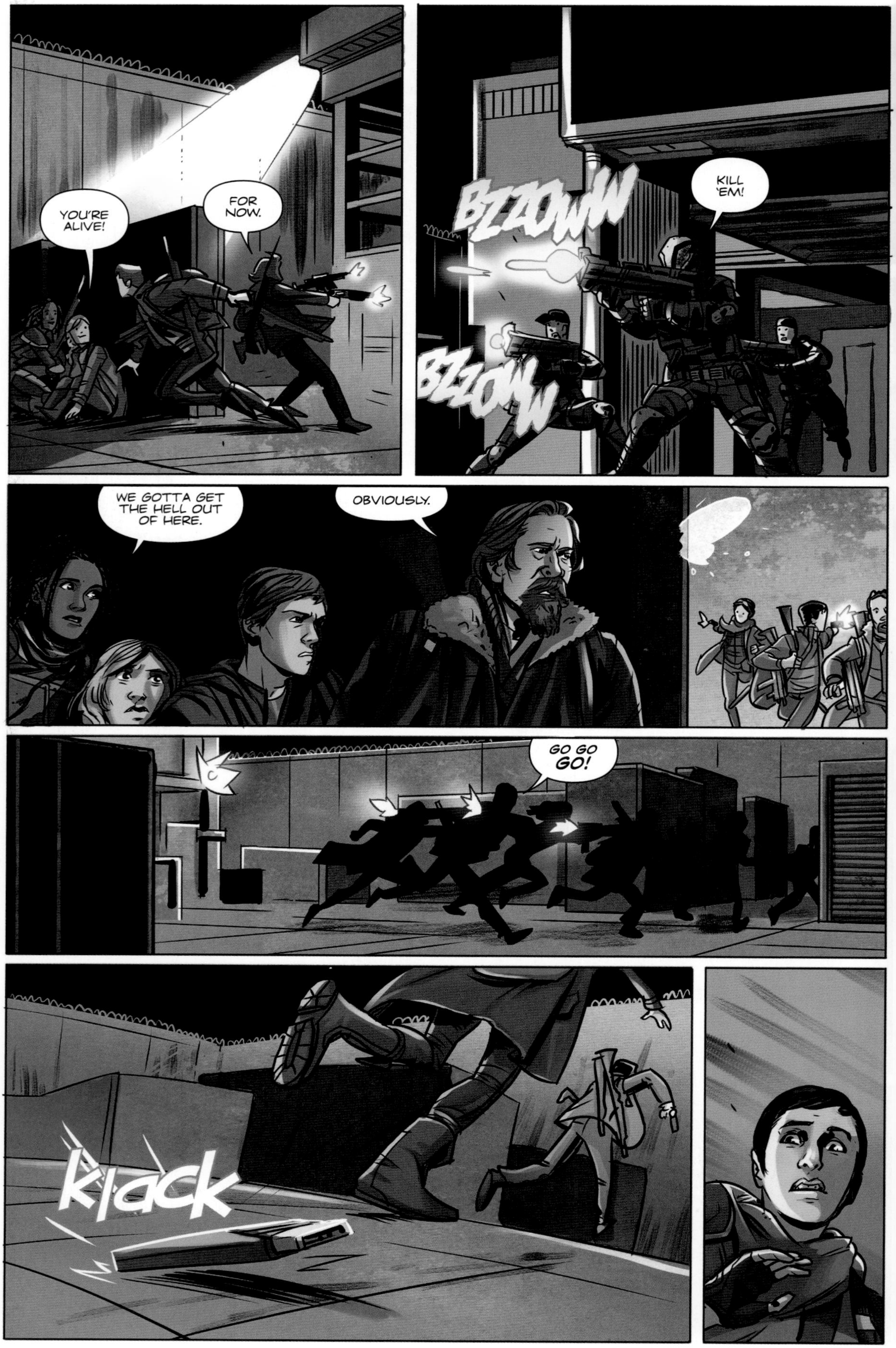
YOU'RE ALIVE!
FOR NOW.
BZZOWW
KILL 'EM!
BZZOWW
WE GOTTA GET THE HELL OUT OF HERE.
OBVIOUSLY.
GO GO GO!
KLACK

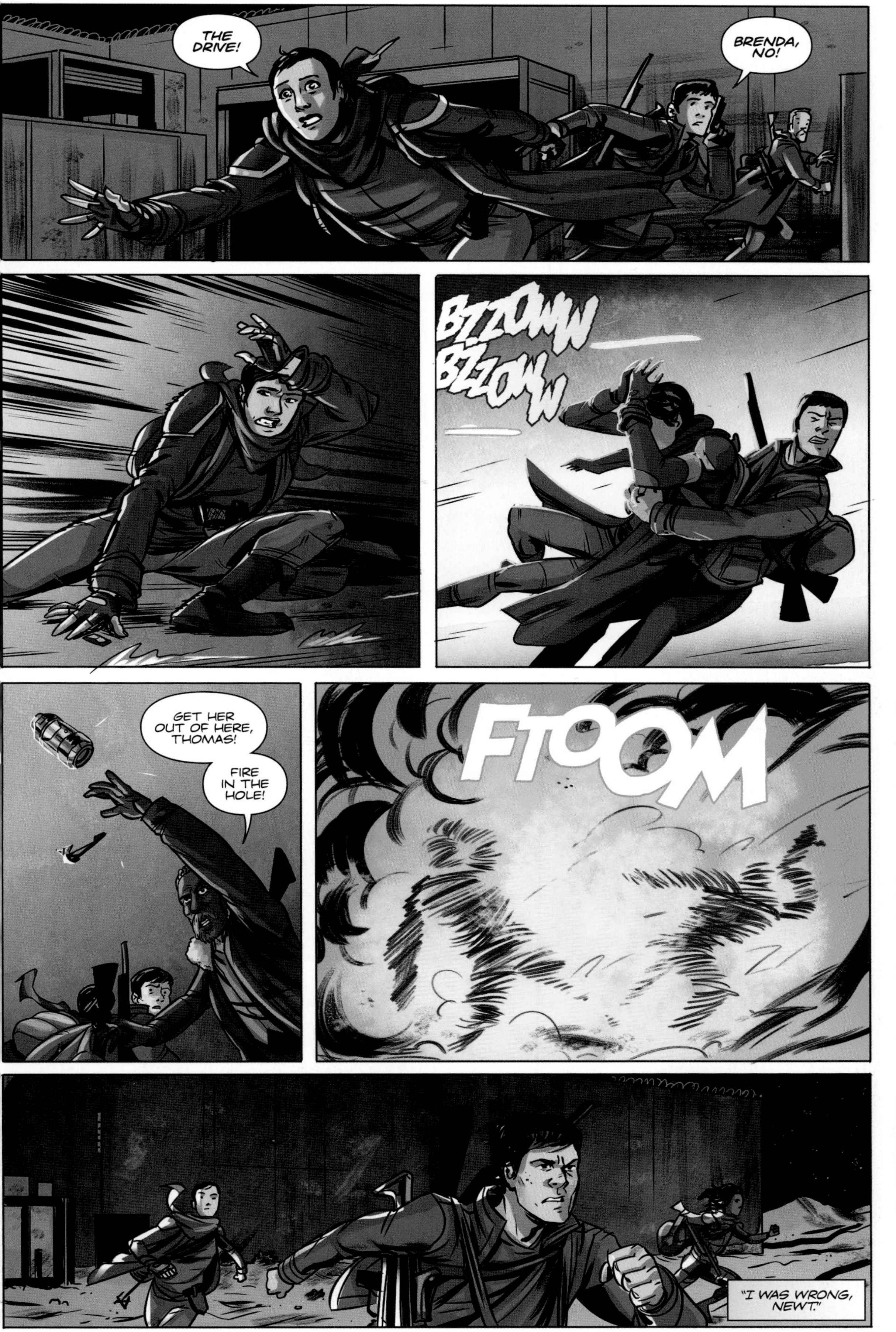
THE DRIVE!
BRENDA, NO!
BZZOWW
BZZOWW
GET HER OUT OF HERE, THOMAS!
FIRE IN THE HOLE!
FTOOM
"I WAS WRONG, NEWT."

Rebel base camp. Later.

I SHOULD HAVE LISTENED TO VINCE. I ALMOST GOT US KILLED.

YOU MEAN, "SOMEONE ALMOST KILLED US."

YOU DON'T THINK IT WAS MY FAULT?

NO, I JUST WANT YOU TO STOP USING PASSIVE VOICE. IT VERY MUCH YOUR FAULT.

JOKE.

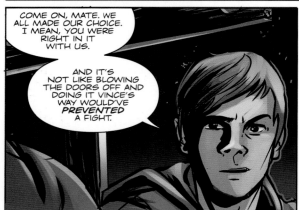

COME ON, MATE. WE ALL MADE OUR CHOICE. I MEAN, YOU WERE RIGHT IN IT WITH US.

AND IT'S NOT LIKE BLOWING THE DOORS OFF AND DOING IT VINCE'S WAY WOULD'VE *PREVENTED* A FIGHT.

I KNOW, I *KNOW*. I WAS JUST SO WORRIED ABOUT--

YOU GUYS IN THE MIDDLE OF SOMETHING?

NOPE! YOU'RE UP, BRENDA. HOPE YOU DO BETTER THAN ME.

SLAP

OW!

THERE. YOU HAVE BEEN SLAPPED FOR YOUR FAILURE. YOU CAN STOP BEING SO DOWN ON YOURSELF NOW.

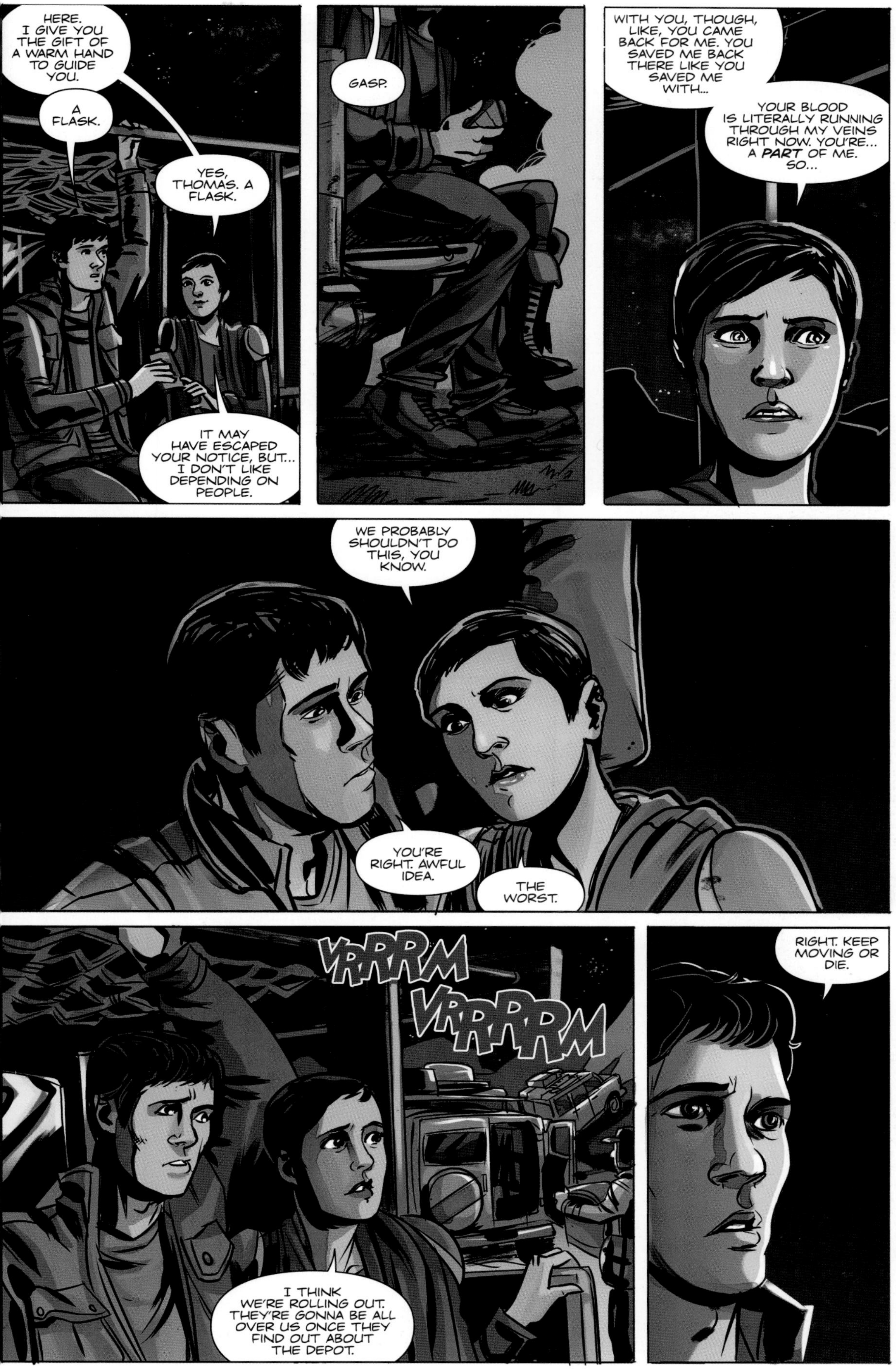
HERE. I GIVE YOU THE GIFT OF A WARM HAND TO GUIDE YOU.
A FLASK.
YES, THOMAS. A FLASK.
IT MAY HAVE ESCAPED YOUR NOTICE, BUT... I DON'T LIKE DEPENDING ON PEOPLE.
GASP.
WITH YOU, THOUGH, LIKE, YOU CAME BACK FOR ME. YOU SAVED ME BACK THERE LIKE YOU SAVED ME WITH...
YOUR BLOOD IS LITERALLY RUNNING THROUGH MY VEINS RIGHT NOW. YOU'RE... A *PART* OF ME. SO...
WE PROBABLY SHOULDN'T DO THIS, YOU KNOW.
YOU'RE RIGHT. AWFUL IDEA.
THE WORST.
VRRRM
VRRRRM
I THINK WE'RE ROLLING OUT. THEY'RE GONNA BE ALL OVER US ONCE THEY FIND OUT ABOUT THE DEPOT.
RIGHT. KEEP MOVING OR DIE.

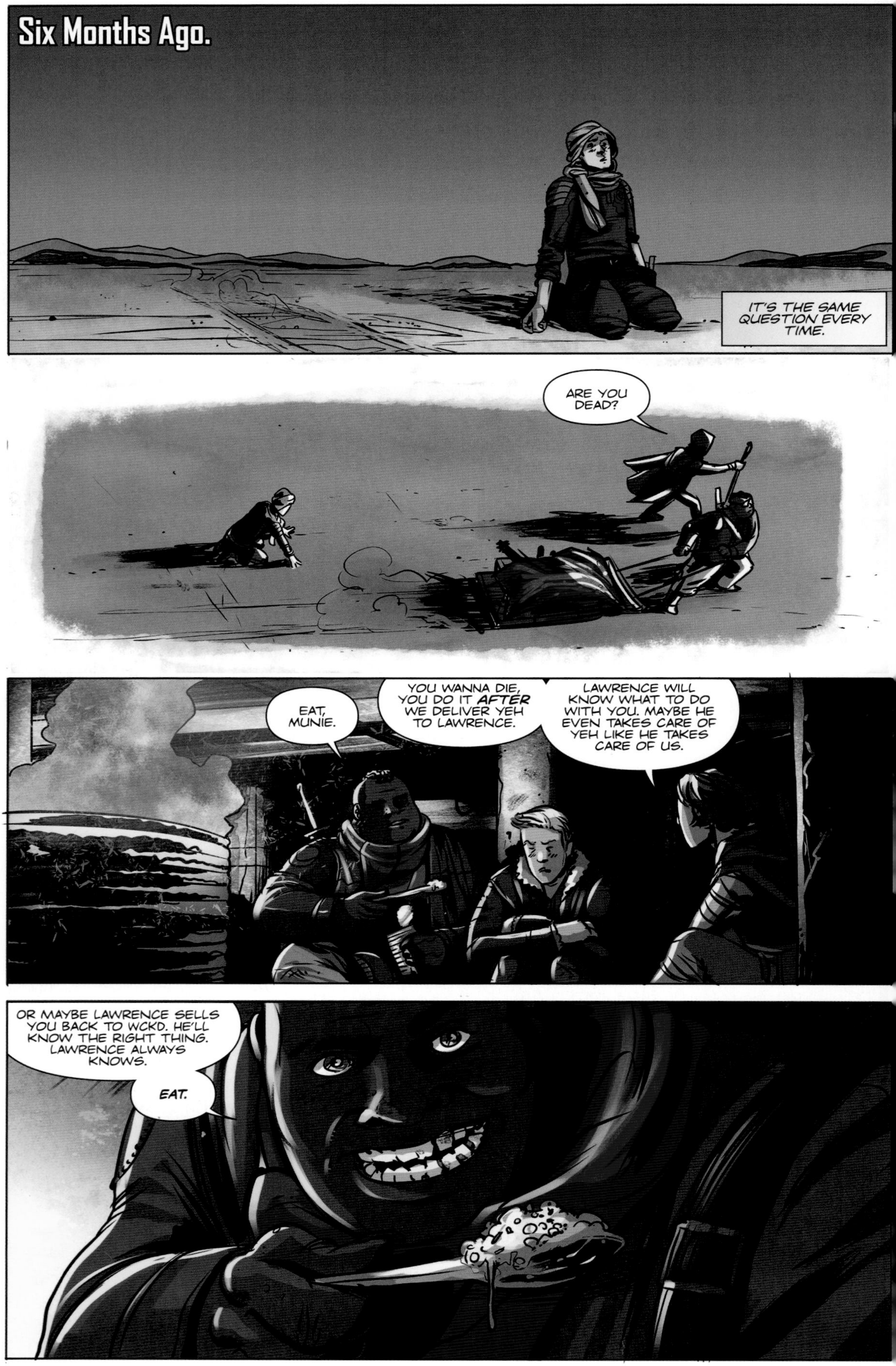
Six Months Ago.
IT'S THE SAME QUESTION EVERY TIME.
ARE YOU DEAD?
EAT, MUNIE.
YOU WANNA DIE, YOU DO IT *AFTER* WE DELIVER YEH TO LAWRENCE.
LAWRENCE WILL KNOW WHAT TO DO WITH YOU. MAYBE HE EVEN TAKES CARE OF YEH LIKE HE TAKES CARE OF US.
OR MAYBE LAWRENCE SELLS YOU BACK TO WCKD. HE'LL KNOW THE RIGHT THING. LAWRENCE ALWAYS KNOWS.
EAT.

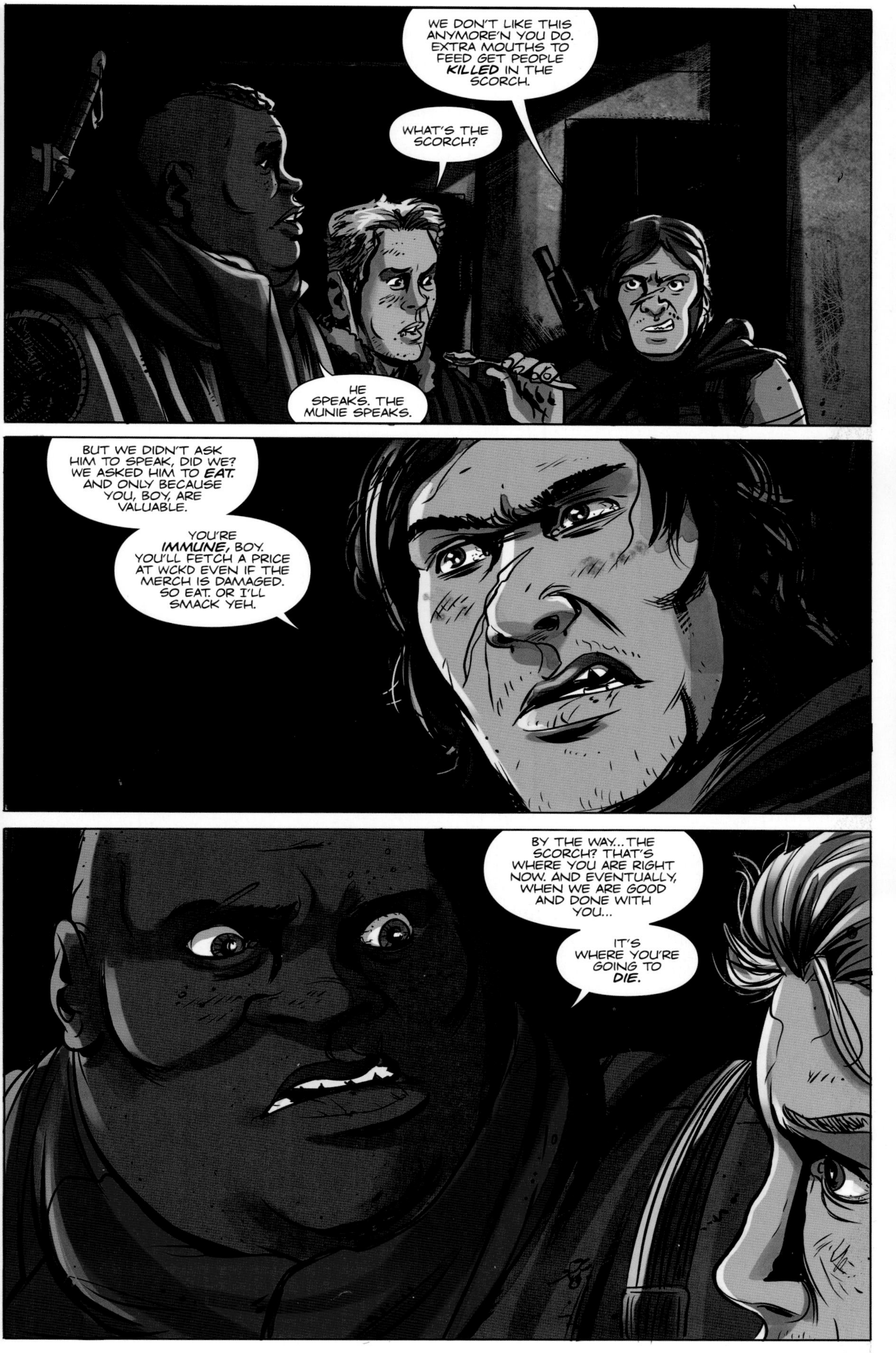
WE DON'T LIKE THIS ANYMORE'N YOU DO. EXTRA MOUTHS TO FEED GET PEOPLE **KILLED** IN THE SCORCH.
WHAT'S THE SCORCH?
HE SPEAKS. THE MUNIE SPEAKS.
BUT WE DIDN'T ASK HIM TO SPEAK, DID WE? WE ASKED HIM TO **EAT.** AND ONLY BECAUSE YOU, BOY, ARE VALUABLE.
YOU'RE **IMMUNE,** BOY. YOU'LL FETCH A PRICE AT WCKD EVEN IF THE MERCH IS DAMAGED. SO EAT. OR I'LL SMACK YEH.
BY THE WAY... THE SCORCH? THAT'S WHERE YOU ARE RIGHT NOW. AND EVENTUALLY, WHEN WE ARE GOOD AND DONE WITH YOU...
IT'S WHERE YOU'RE GOING TO **DIE.**

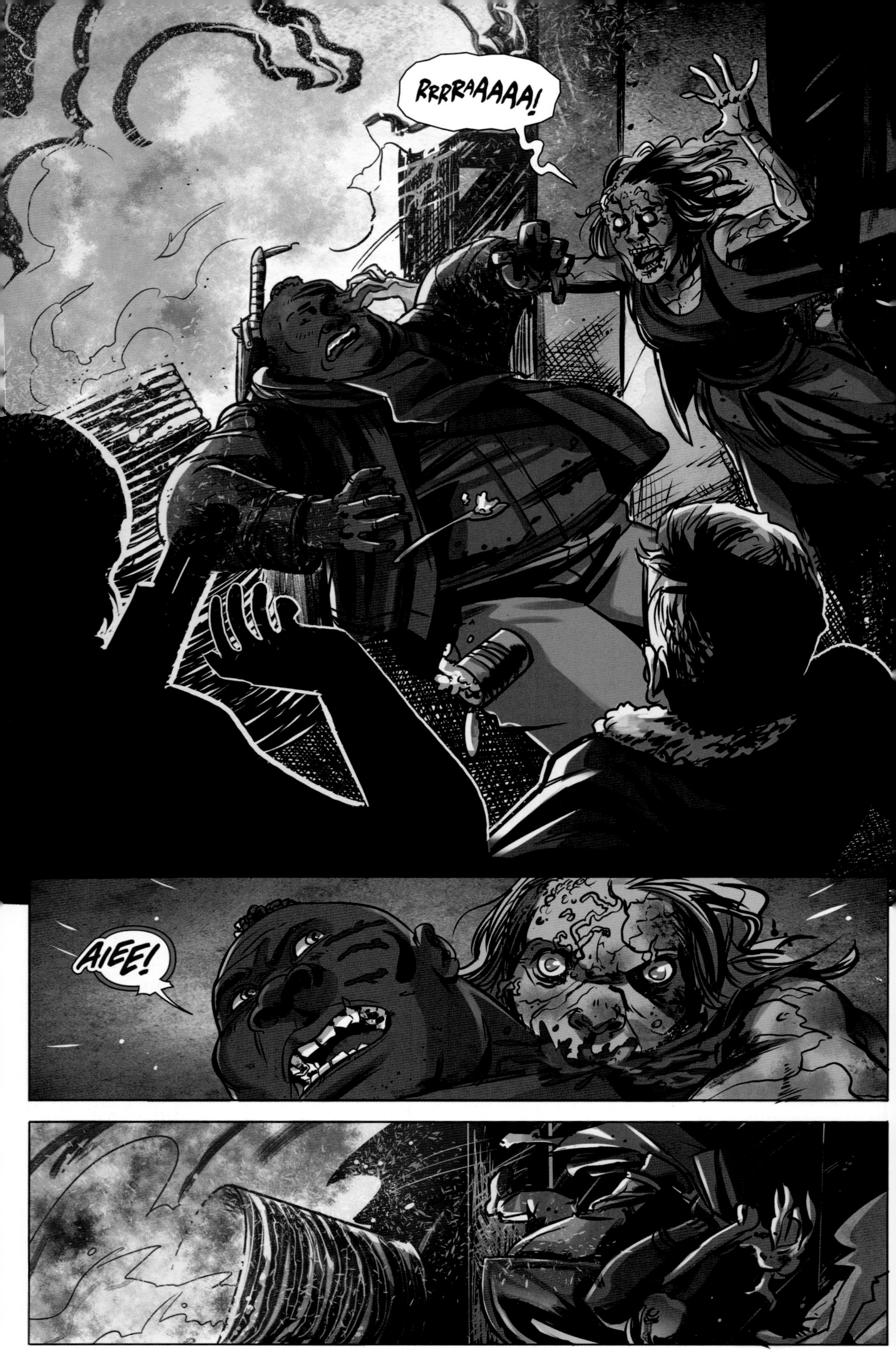
RRRRAAAAA!
AIEE!

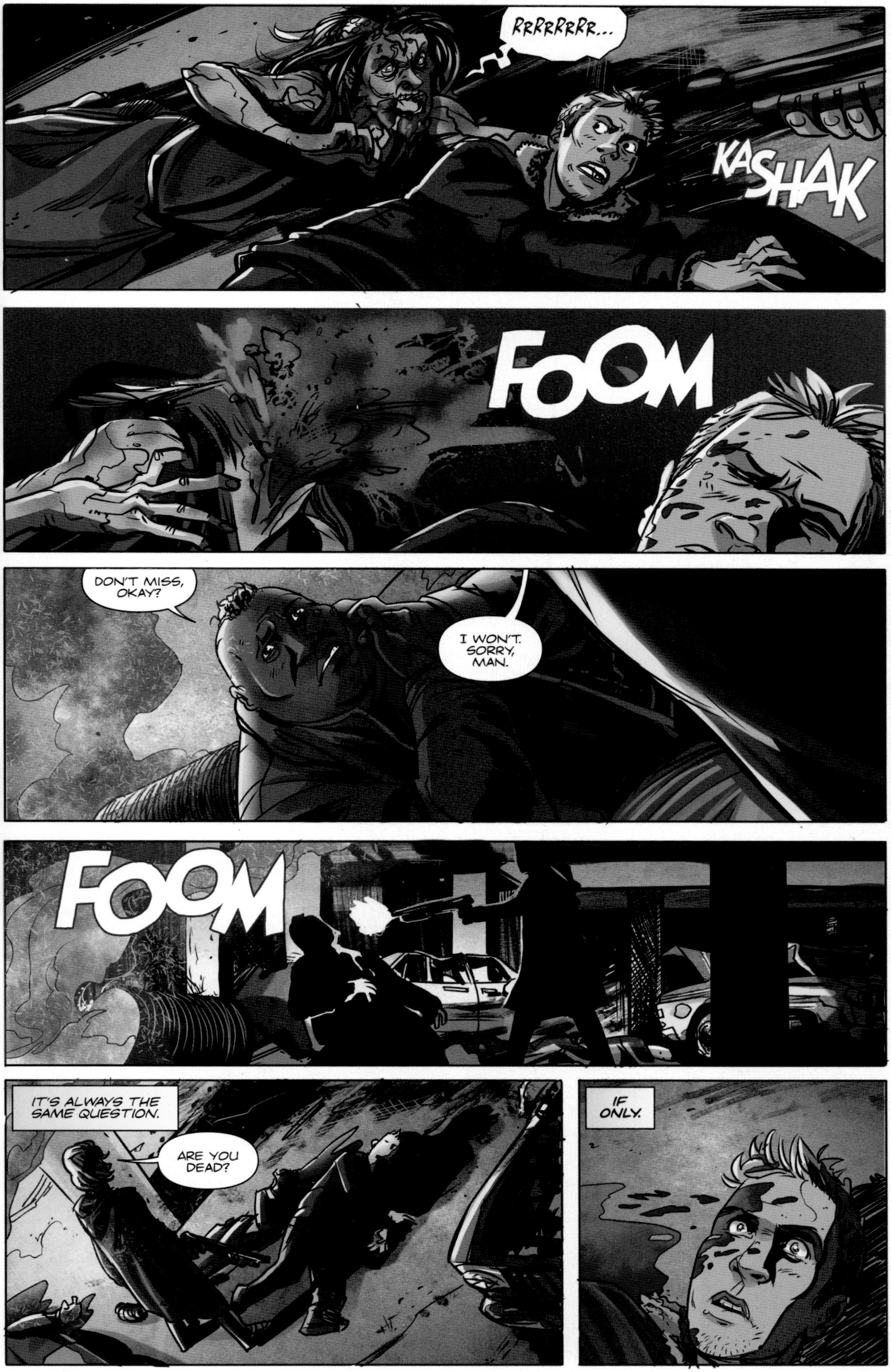
RRRRRRRR...
KASHAK
FOOM
DON'T MISS, OKAY?
I WON'T. SORRY, MAN.
FOOM
IT'S ALWAYS THE SAME QUESTION.
ARE YOU DEAD?
IF ONLY.

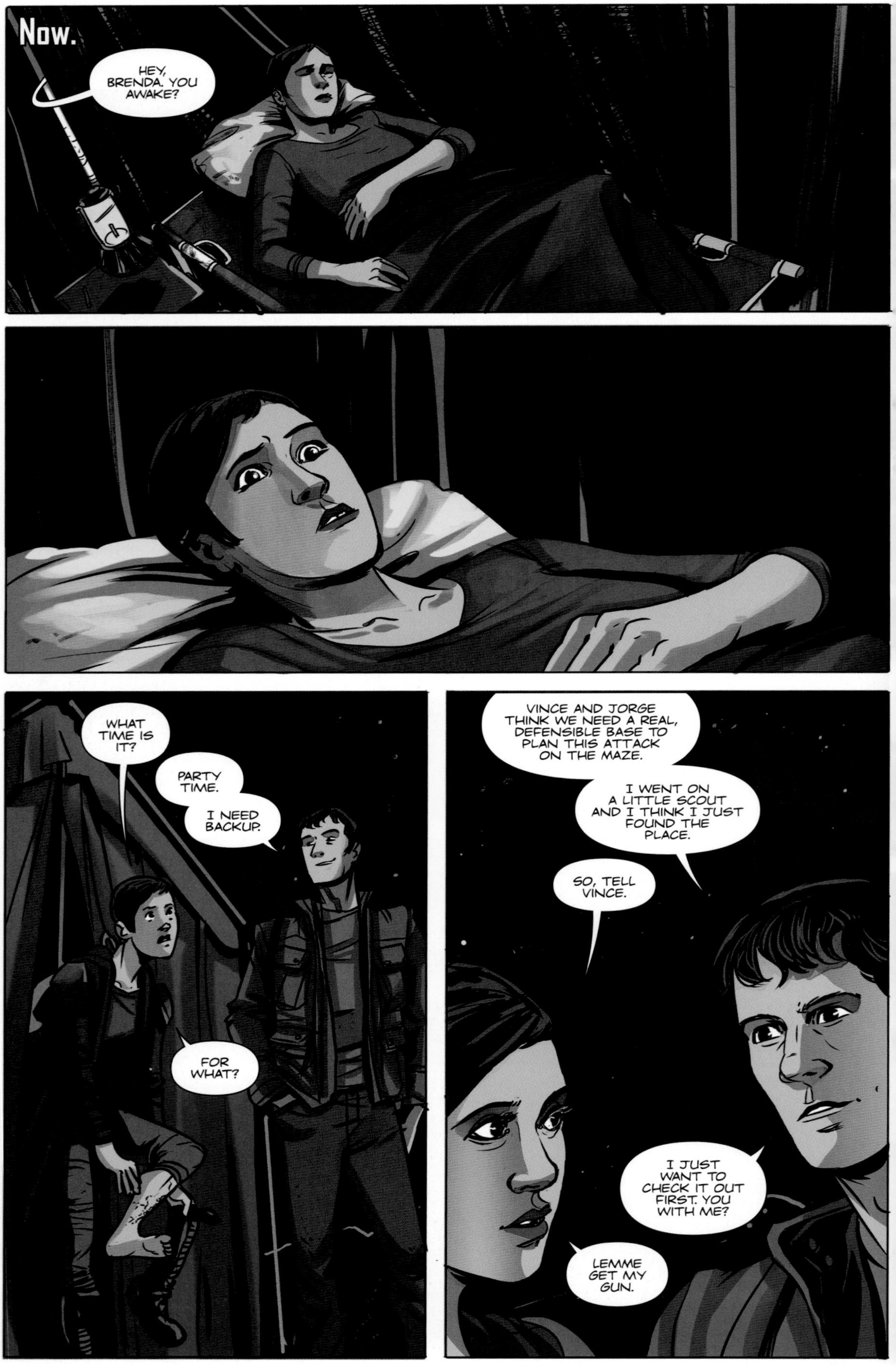
Now.
HEY, BRENDA. YOU AWAKE?
WHAT TIME IS IT?
PARTY TIME.
I NEED BACKUP.
FOR WHAT?
VINCE AND JORGE THINK WE NEED A REAL, DEFENSIBLE BASE TO PLAN THIS ATTACK ON THE MAZE.
I WENT ON A LITTLE SCOUT AND I THINK I JUST FOUND THE PLACE.
SO, TELL VINCE.
I JUST WANT TO CHECK IT OUT FIRST. YOU WITH ME?
LEMME GET MY GUN.

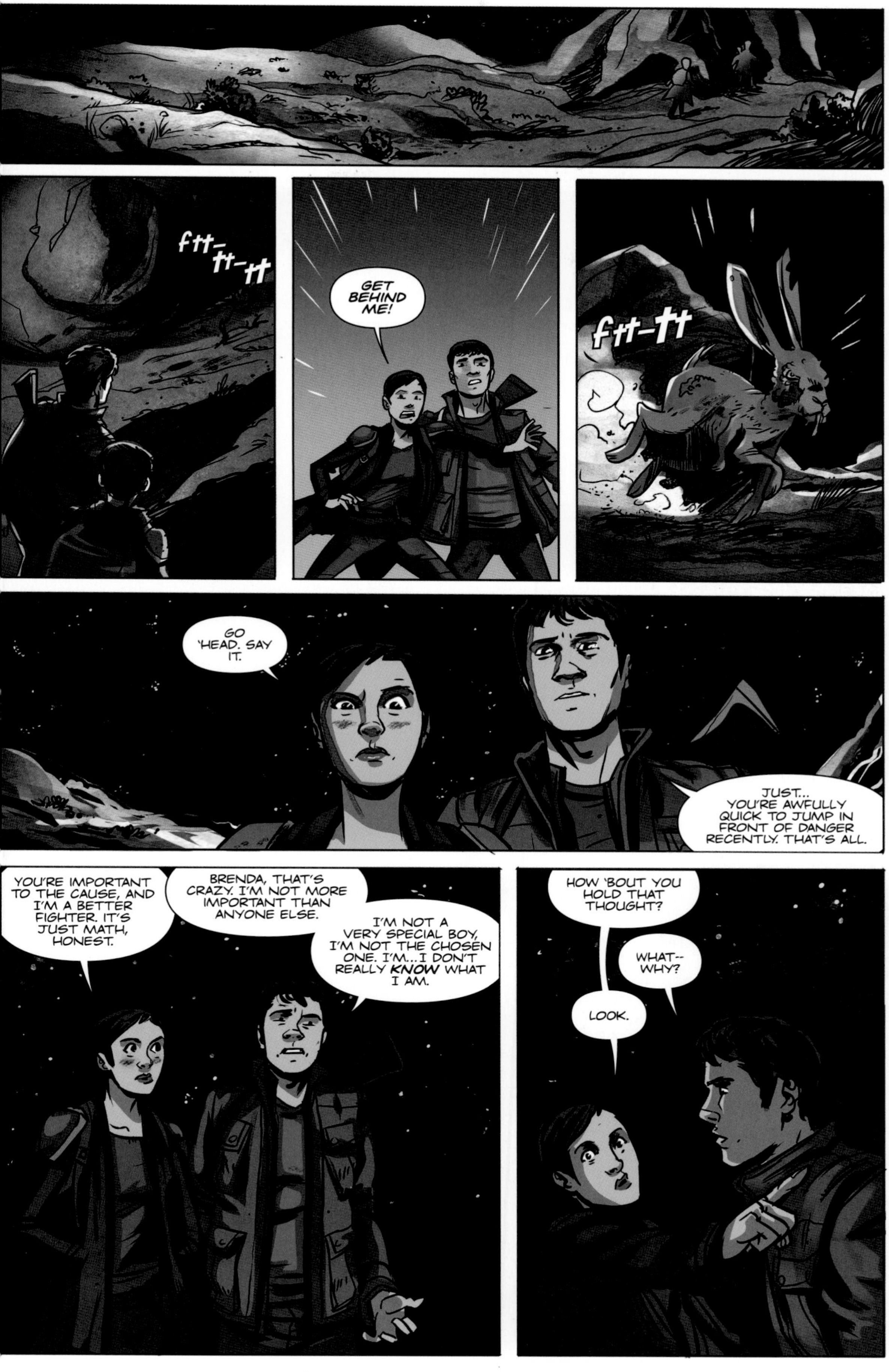

ftt-tt-tt
GET BEHIND ME!
ftt-tt
GO 'HEAD. SAY IT.
JUST... YOU'RE AWFULLY QUICK TO JUMP IN FRONT OF DANGER RECENTLY. THAT'S ALL.
YOU'RE IMPORTANT TO THE CAUSE, AND I'M A BETTER FIGHTER. IT'S JUST MATH, HONEST.
BRENDA, THAT'S CRAZY. I'M NOT MORE IMPORTANT THAN ANYONE ELSE.
I'M NOT A VERY SPECIAL BOY, I'M NOT THE CHOSEN ONE. I'M...I DON'T REALLY KNOW WHAT I AM.
HOW 'BOUT YOU HOLD THAT THOUGHT?
WHAT-- WHY?
LOOK.

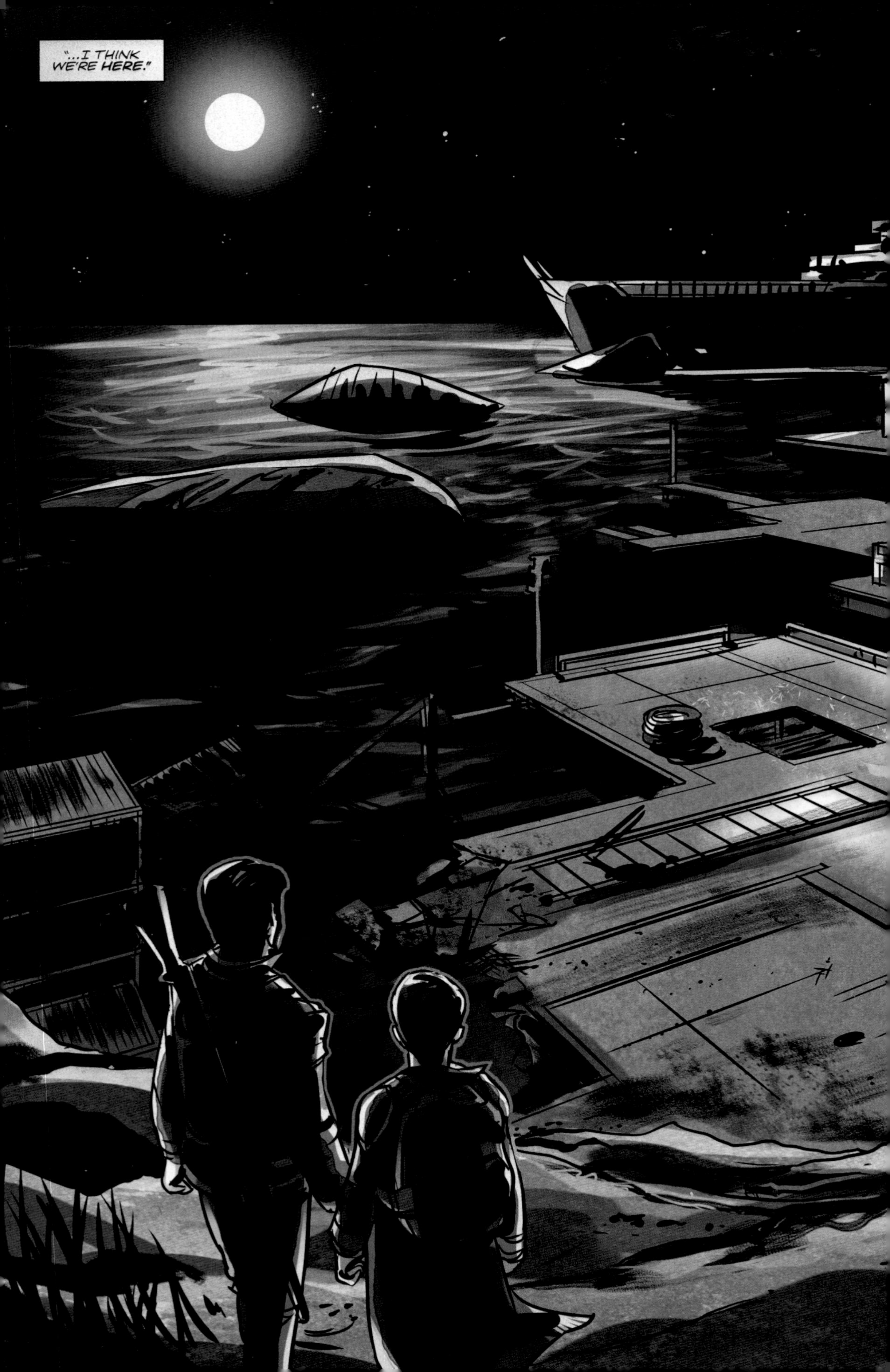
"...I THINK WE'RE HERE."

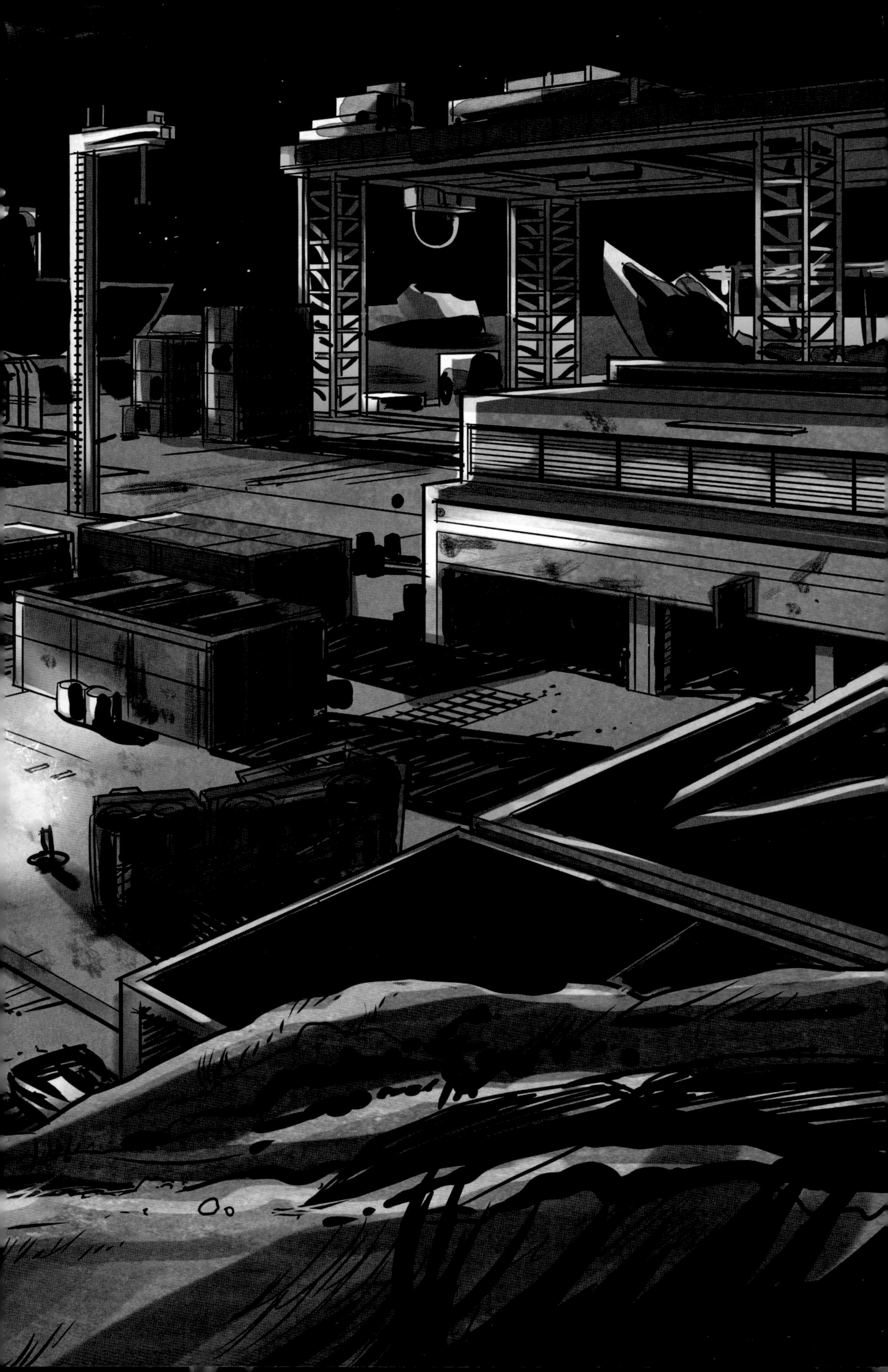

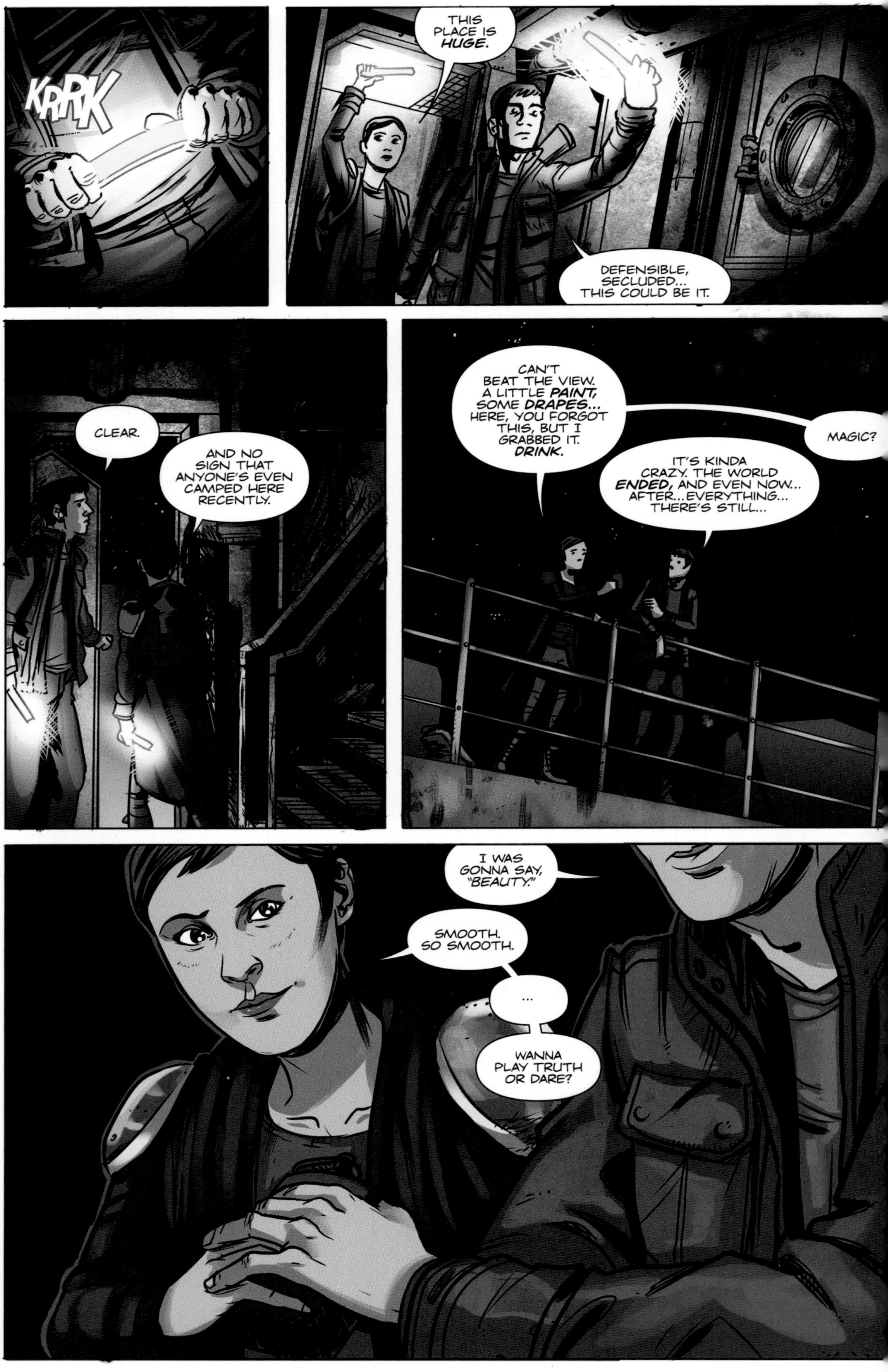
KRRK
THIS PLACE IS HUGE.
DEFENSIBLE, SECLUDED... THIS COULD BE IT.
CLEAR.
AND NO SIGN THAT ANYONE'S EVEN CAMPED HERE RECENTLY.
CAN'T BEAT THE VIEW. A LITTLE PAINT, SOME DRAPES... HERE, YOU FORGOT THIS, BUT I GRABBED IT. DRINK.
IT'S KINDA CRAZY. THE WORLD ENDED, AND EVEN NOW... AFTER...EVERYTHING... THERE'S STILL...
MAGIC?
I WAS GONNA SAY, "BEAUTY."
SMOOTH. SO SMOOTH.
...
WANNA PLAY TRUTH OR DARE?

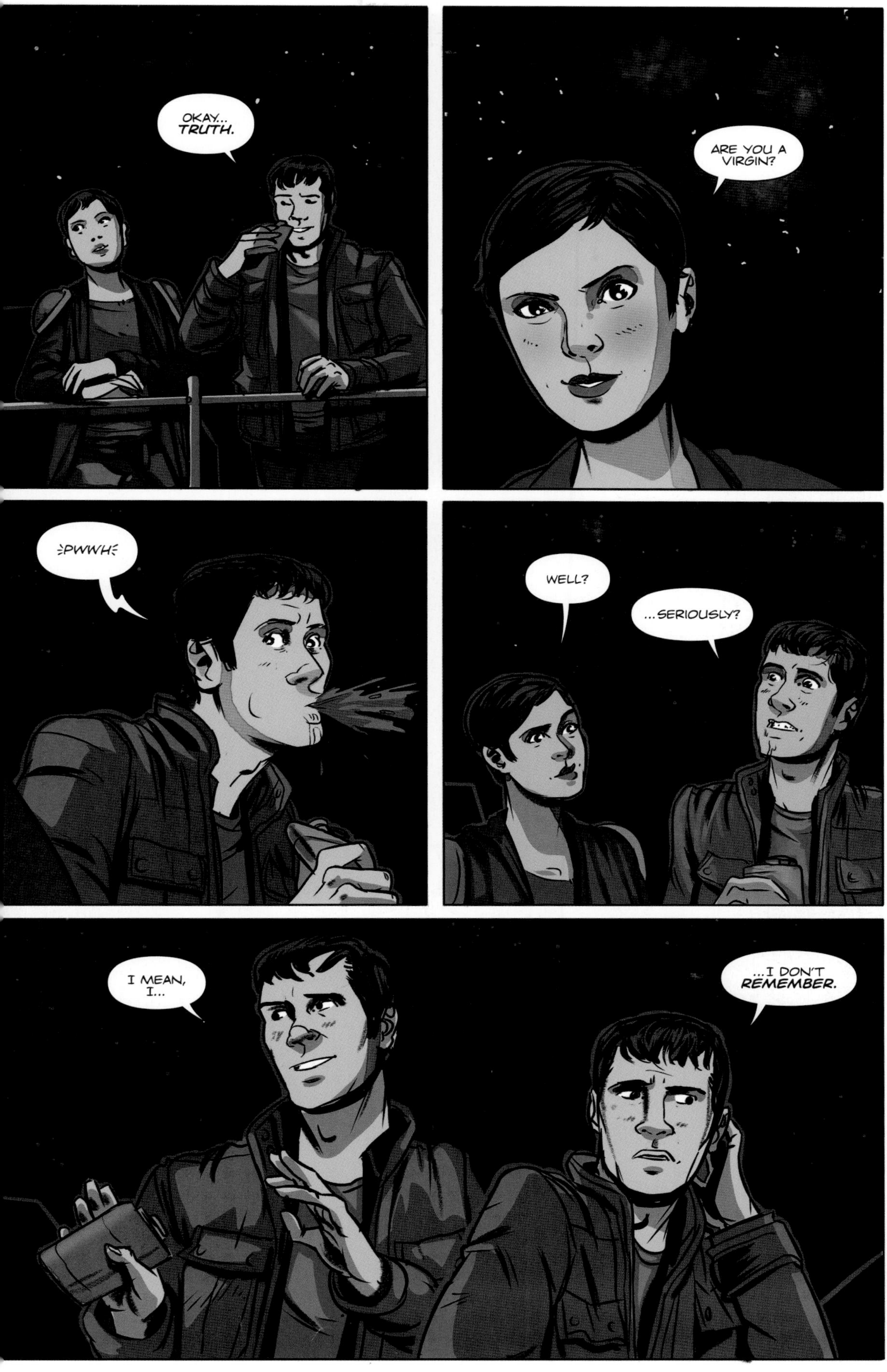
OKAY... TRUTH.
ARE YOU A VIRGIN?
PWWH
WELL?
...SERIOUSLY?
I MEAN, I...
...I DON'T REMEMBER.

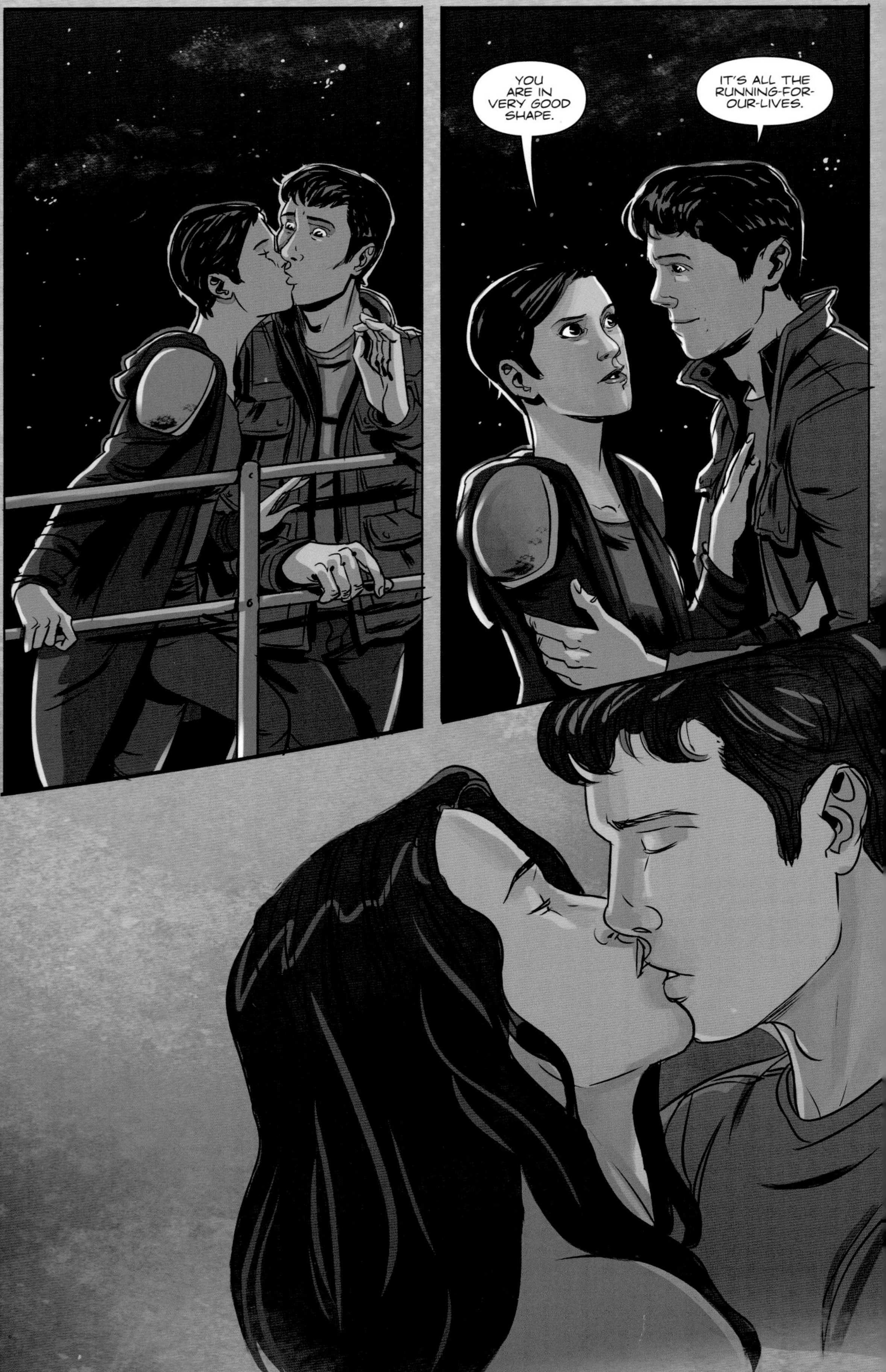
YOU ARE IN VERY GOOD SHAPE.
IT'S ALL THE RUNNING-FOR-OUR-LIVES.

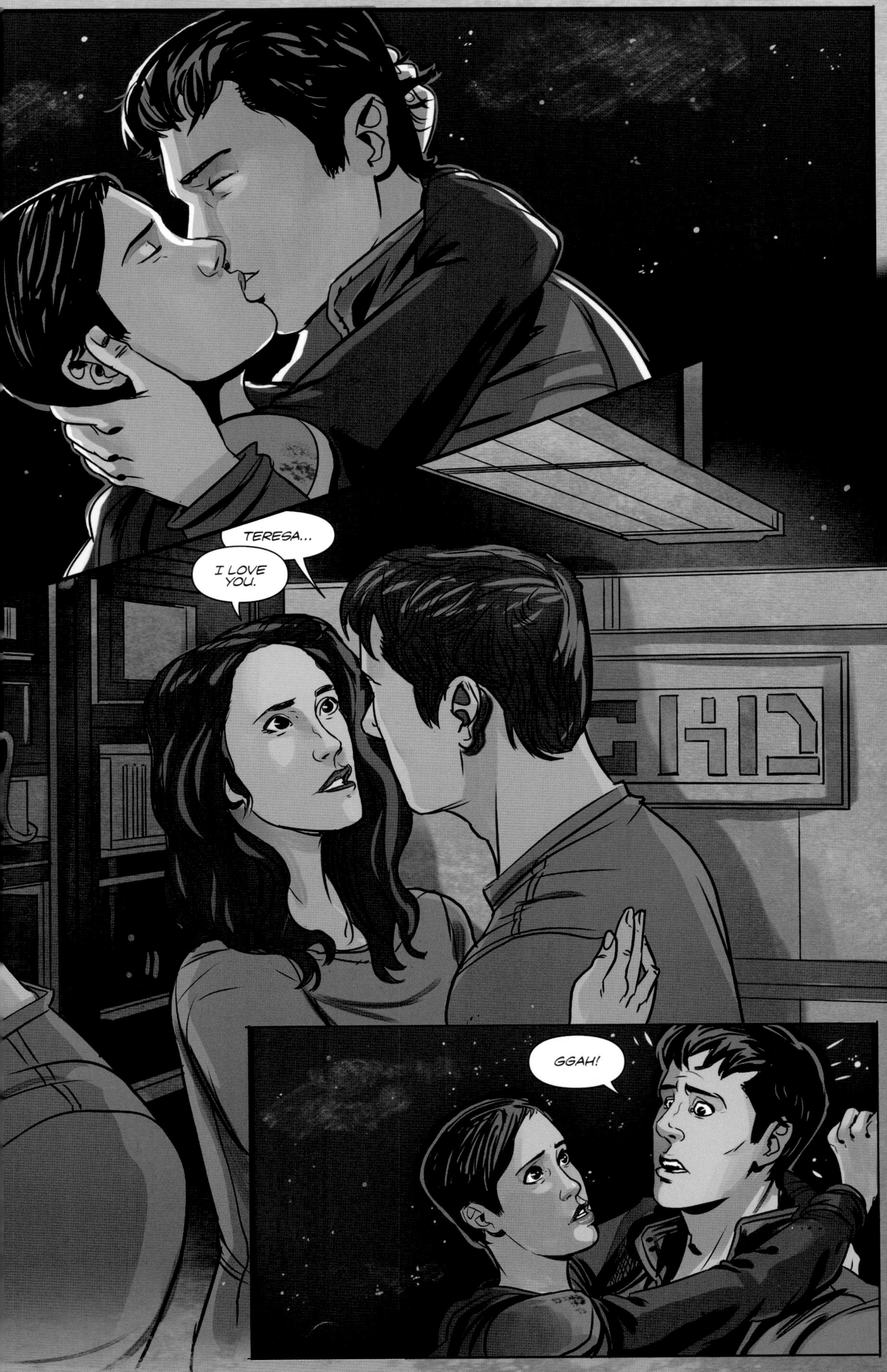

TERESA...
I LOVE YOU.
GGAH!

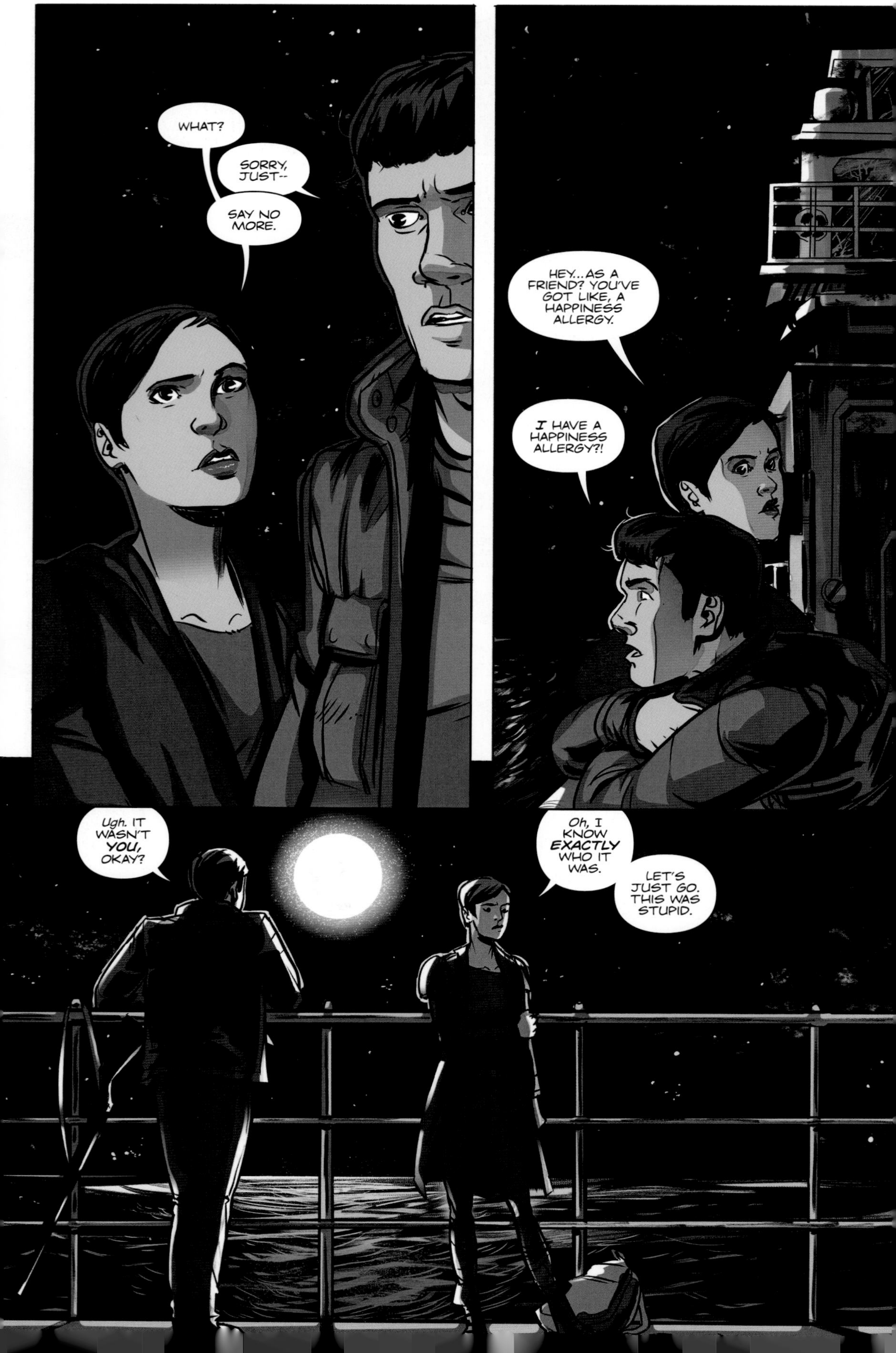
WHAT?
SORRY, JUST--
SAY NO MORE.
HEY...AS A FRIEND? YOU'VE GOT LIKE, A HAPPINESS ALLERGY.
I HAVE A HAPPINESS ALLERGY?!
Ugh. IT WASN'T **YOU,** OKAY?
Oh, I KNOW **EXACTLY** WHO IT WAS.
LET'S JUST GO. THIS WAS STUPID.

I CAN'T SEE.

WHERE ARE YOU GOING?

'SOKAY. I BEEN DOWN HERE BEFORE.

I DON'T KNOW WHY I KEEP WALKING. IT ALL FEELS POINTLESS. HALF THE TIME THE ONLY PERSON KEEPING ME ALIVE--THE ONLY PERSON WHO HAS MY BACK...

...IS MY KIDNAPPER.

THIS IS LIKE A DREAM AMBUSH SPOT. THERE COULD BE CRANKS--THERE COULD BE--

WELL, I NEVER SEEN ONE DOWN HERE, HAVE I?

I DON'T KNOW, HAVE YOU?

THAT WAS WHAT WE CALL A RHETORICAL QUESTION. DON'T BE AN ASS.

HE'S THE CLOSEST THING I HAVE TO A FRIEND.

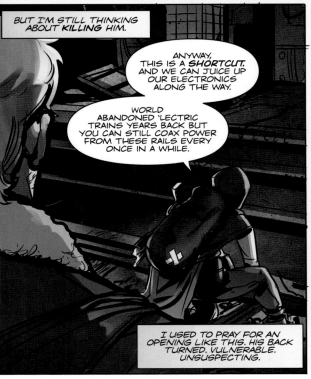

BUT I'M STILL THINKING ABOUT KILLING HIM.

ANYWAY, THIS IS A SHORTCUT. AND WE CAN JUICE UP OUR ELECTRONICS ALONG THE WAY.

WORLD ABANDONED 'LECTRIC TRAINS YEARS BACK BUT YOU CAN STILL COAX POWER FROM THESE RAILS EVERY ONCE IN A WHILE.

I USED TO PRAY FOR AN OPENING LIKE THIS. HIS BACK TURNED. VULNERABLE. UNSUSPECTING.

BUT THE THING I'VE REALIZED OUT HERE IN THE SCORCH? LIFE DOESN'T CARE ABOUT YOU OR YOUR PLANS. IT DOESN'T EVEN LAUGH AT YOU.

IT DOESN'T CARE ENOUGH TO LAUGH. AND ALL IT TAKES IS A SLIP.

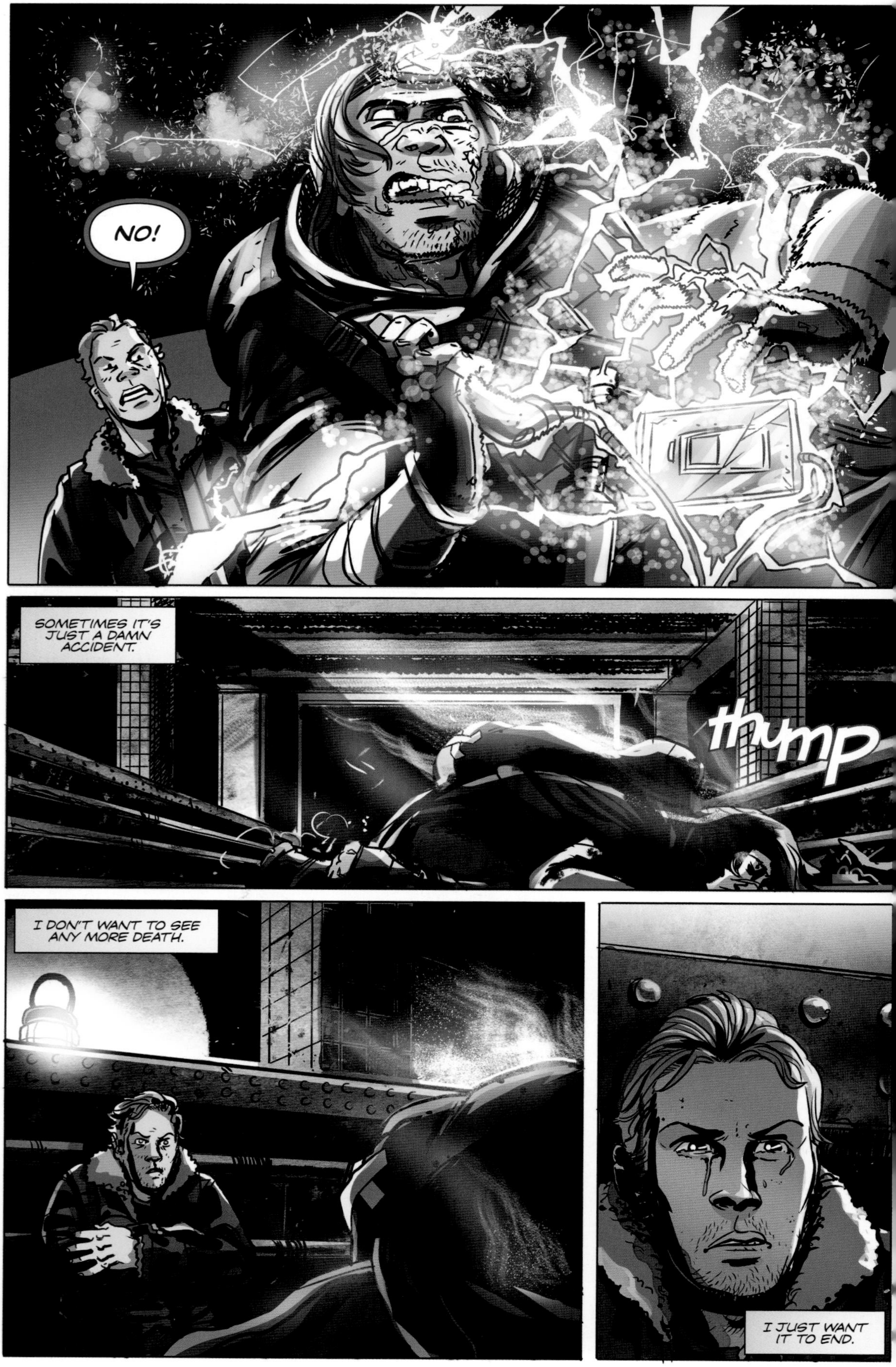
NO!
SOMETIMES IT'S JUST A DAMN ACCIDENT.
thump
I DON'T WANT TO SEE ANY MORE DEATH.
I JUST WANT IT TO END.

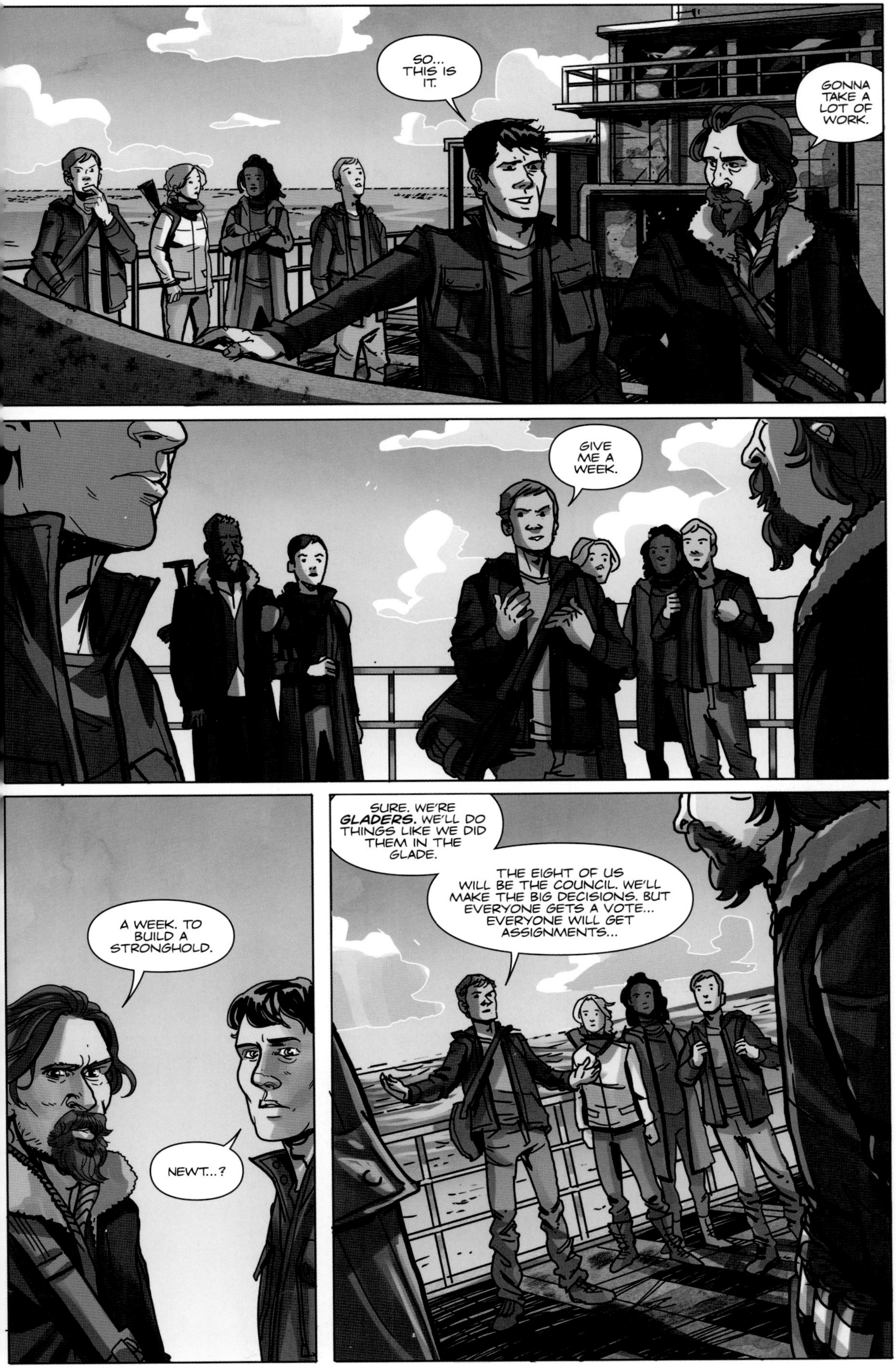
SO... THIS IS IT.
GONNA TAKE A LOT OF WORK.
GIVE ME A WEEK.
A WEEK. TO BUILD A STRONGHOLD.
NEWT...?
SURE. WE'RE **GLADERS.** WE'LL DO THINGS LIKE WE DID THEM IN THE GLADE.
THE EIGHT OF US WILL BE THE COUNCIL. WE'LL MAKE THE BIG DECISIONS. BUT EVERYONE GETS A VOTE... EVERYONE WILL GET ASSIGNMENTS...

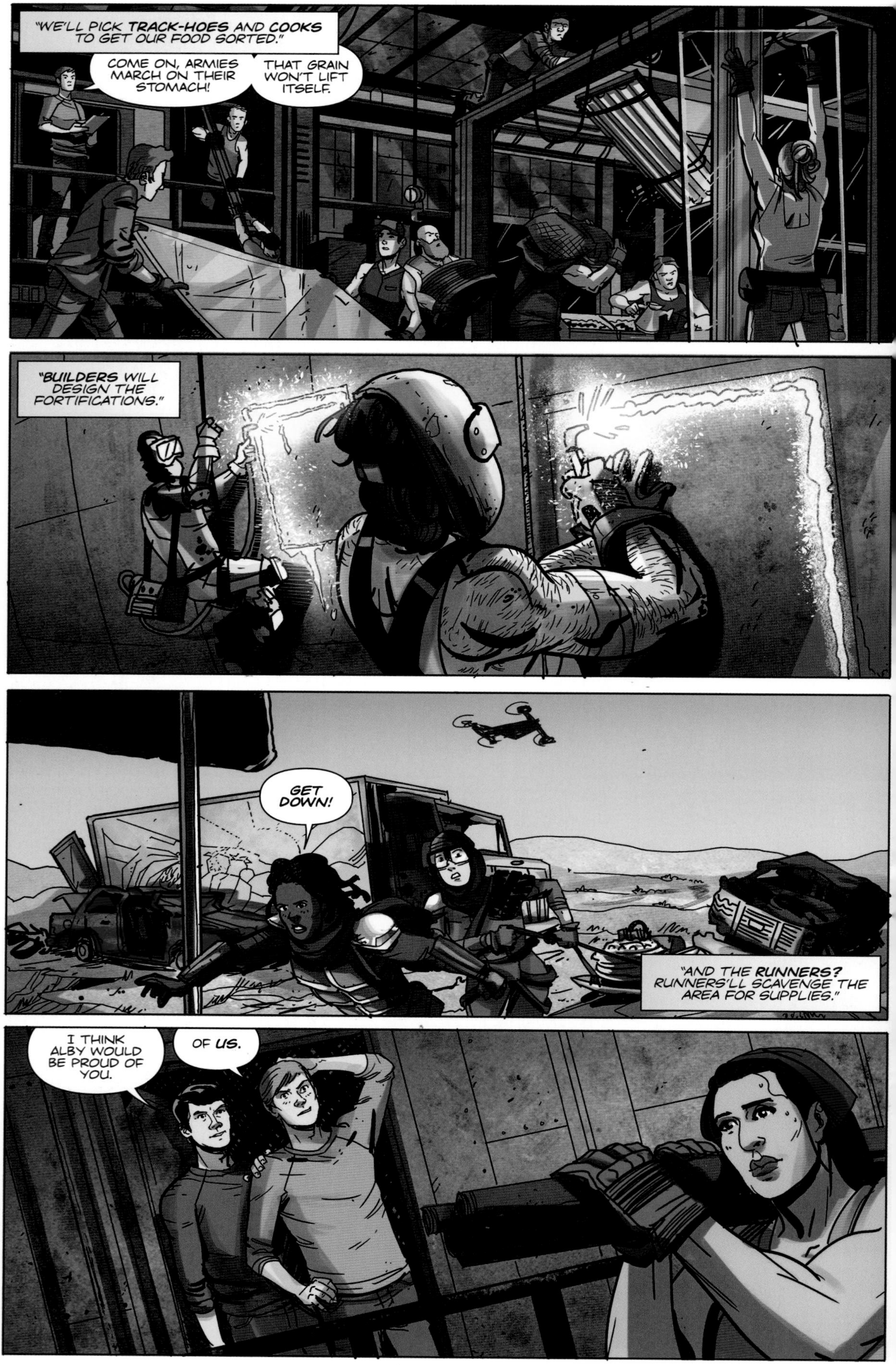
"WE'LL PICK **TRACK-HOES** AND **COOKS** TO GET OUR FOOD SORTED."
COME ON, ARMIES MARCH ON THEIR STOMACH!
THAT GRAIN WON'T LIFT ITSELF.
"**BUILDERS** WILL DESIGN THE FORTIFICATIONS."
GET DOWN!
"AND THE **RUNNERS?** RUNNERS'LL SCAVENGE THE AREA FOR SUPPLIES."
I THINK ALBY WOULD BE PROUD OF YOU.
OF ***US.***

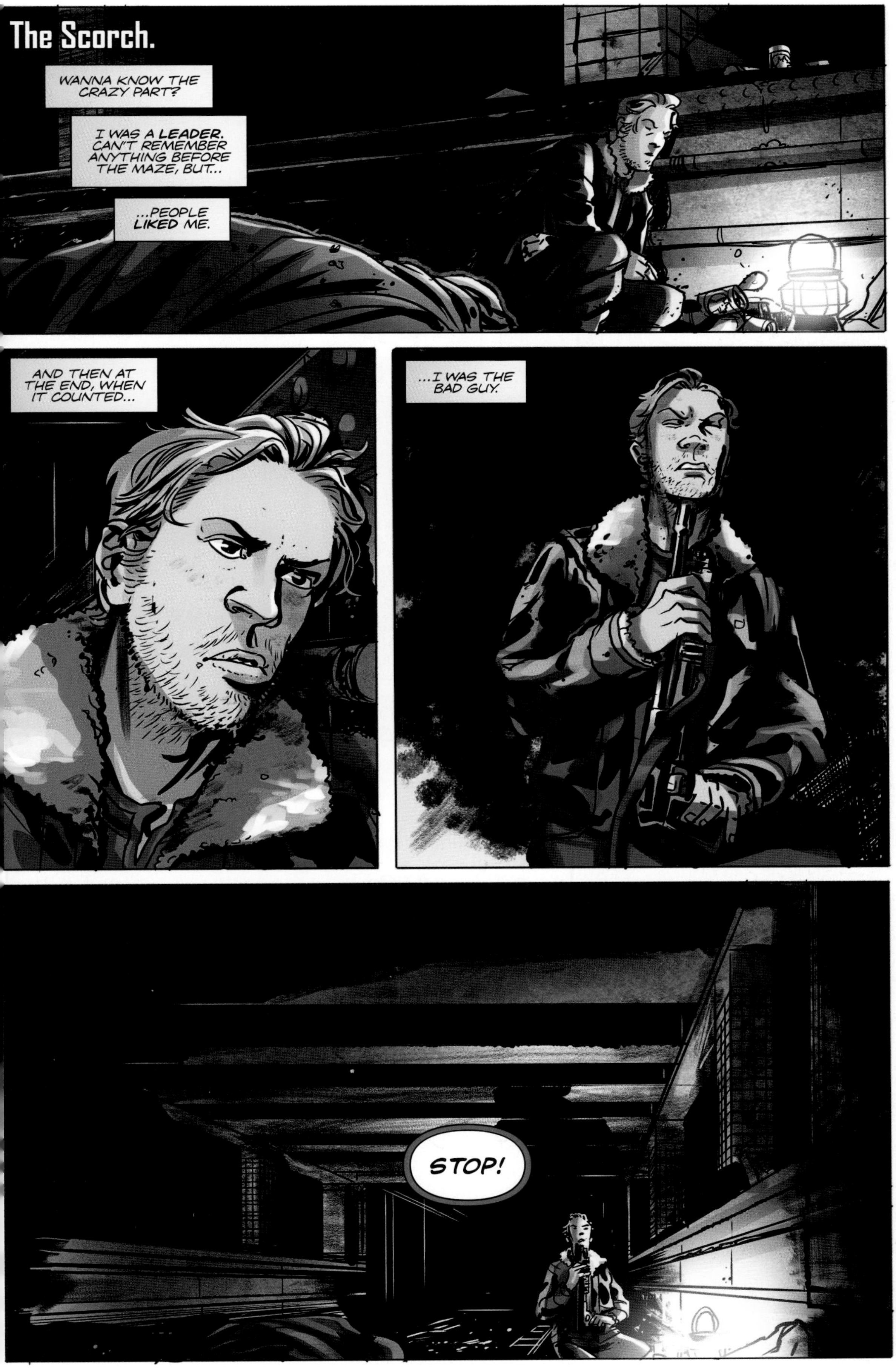
The Scorch.
WANNA KNOW THE CRAZY PART?
I WAS A LEADER. CAN'T REMEMBER ANYTHING BEFORE THE MAZE, BUT...
...PEOPLE LIKED ME.
AND THEN AT THE END, WHEN IT COUNTED...
...I WAS THE BAD GUY.
STOP!

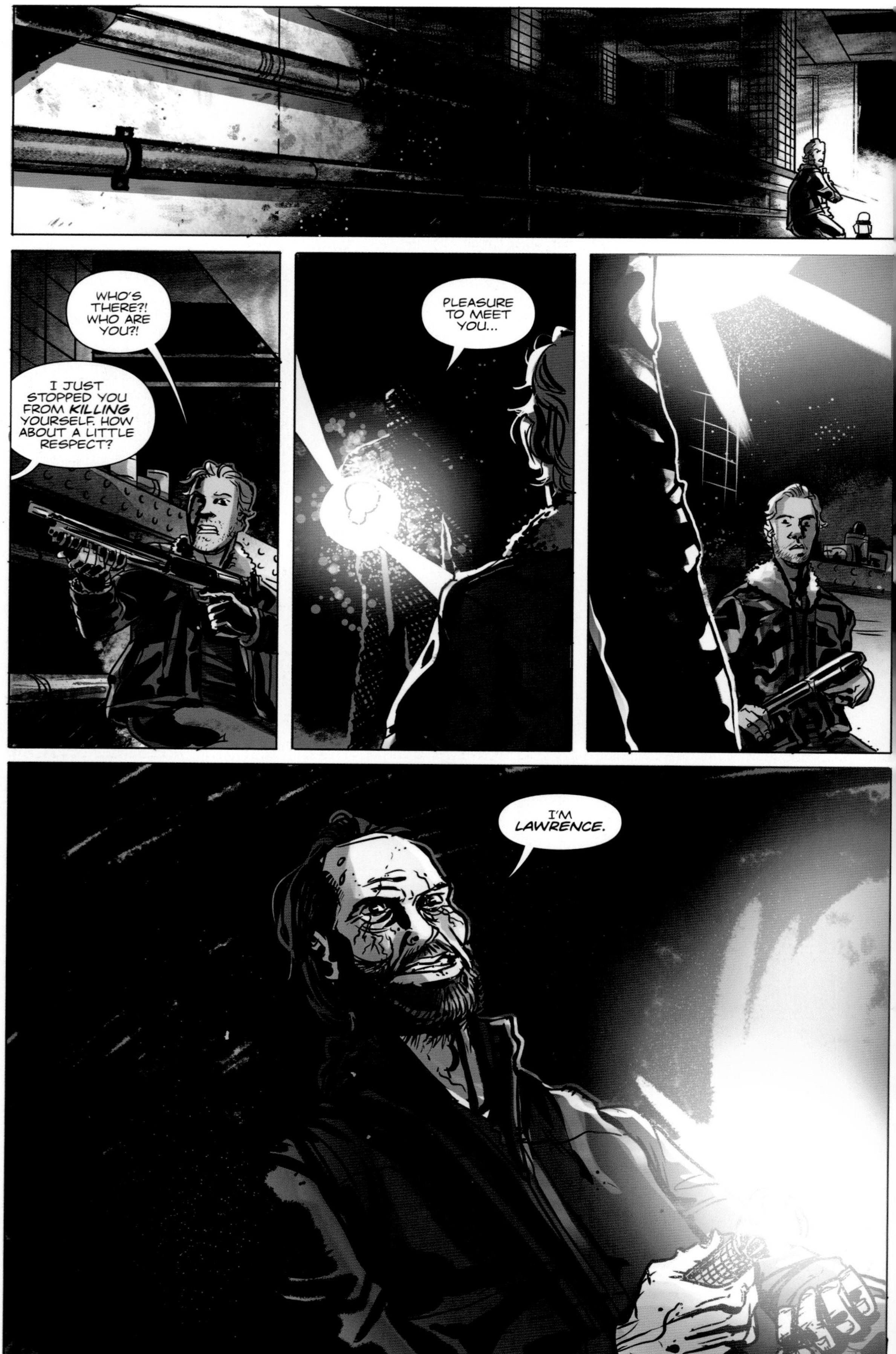
WHO'S THERE?! WHO ARE YOU?!
I JUST STOPPED YOU FROM KILLING YOURSELF. HOW ABOUT A LITTLE RESPECT?
PLEASURE TO MEET YOU...
I'M LAWRENCE.

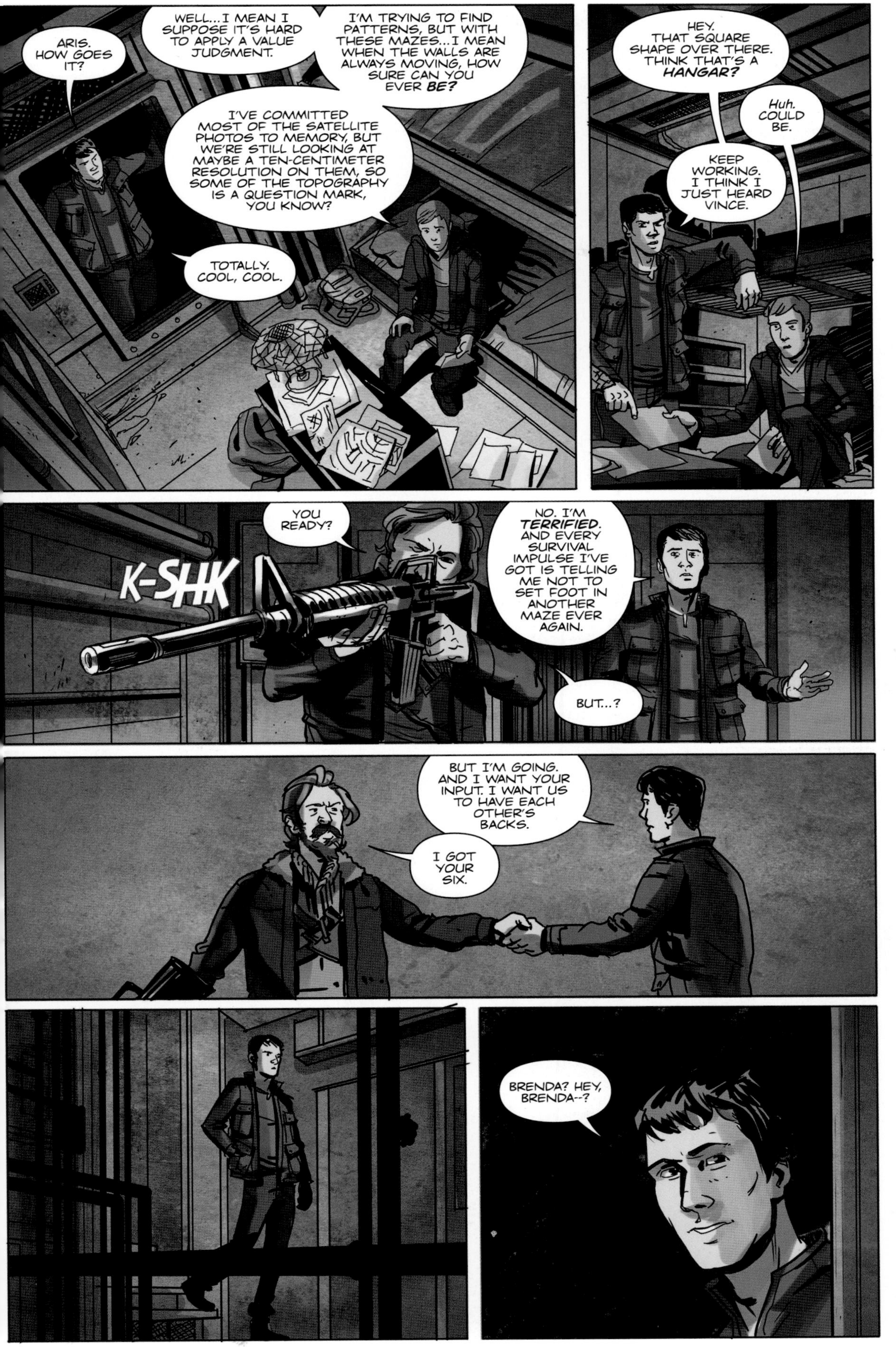

ARIS. HOW GOES IT?
WELL...I MEAN I SUPPOSE IT'S HARD TO APPLY A VALUE JUDGMENT.
I'M TRYING TO FIND PATTERNS, BUT WITH THESE MAZES...I MEAN WHEN THE WALLS ARE ALWAYS MOVING, HOW SURE CAN YOU EVER *BE?*
I'VE COMMITTED MOST OF THE SATELLITE PHOTOS TO MEMORY, BUT WE'RE STILL LOOKING AT MAYBE A TEN-CENTIMETER RESOLUTION ON THEM, SO SOME OF THE TOPOGRAPHY IS A QUESTION MARK, YOU KNOW?
TOTALLY. COOL, COOL.
HEY. THAT SQUARE SHAPE OVER THERE. THINK THAT'S A *HANGAR?*
Huh. COULD BE.
KEEP WORKING. I THINK I JUST HEARD VINCE.
YOU READY?
K-SHK
NO. I'M *TERRIFIED*. AND EVERY SURVIVAL IMPULSE I'VE GOT IS TELLING ME NOT TO SET FOOT IN ANOTHER MAZE EVER AGAIN.
BUT...?
BUT I'M GOING. AND I WANT YOUR INPUT. I WANT US TO HAVE EACH OTHER'S BACKS.
I GOT YOUR SIX.
BRENDA? HEY, BRENDA--?

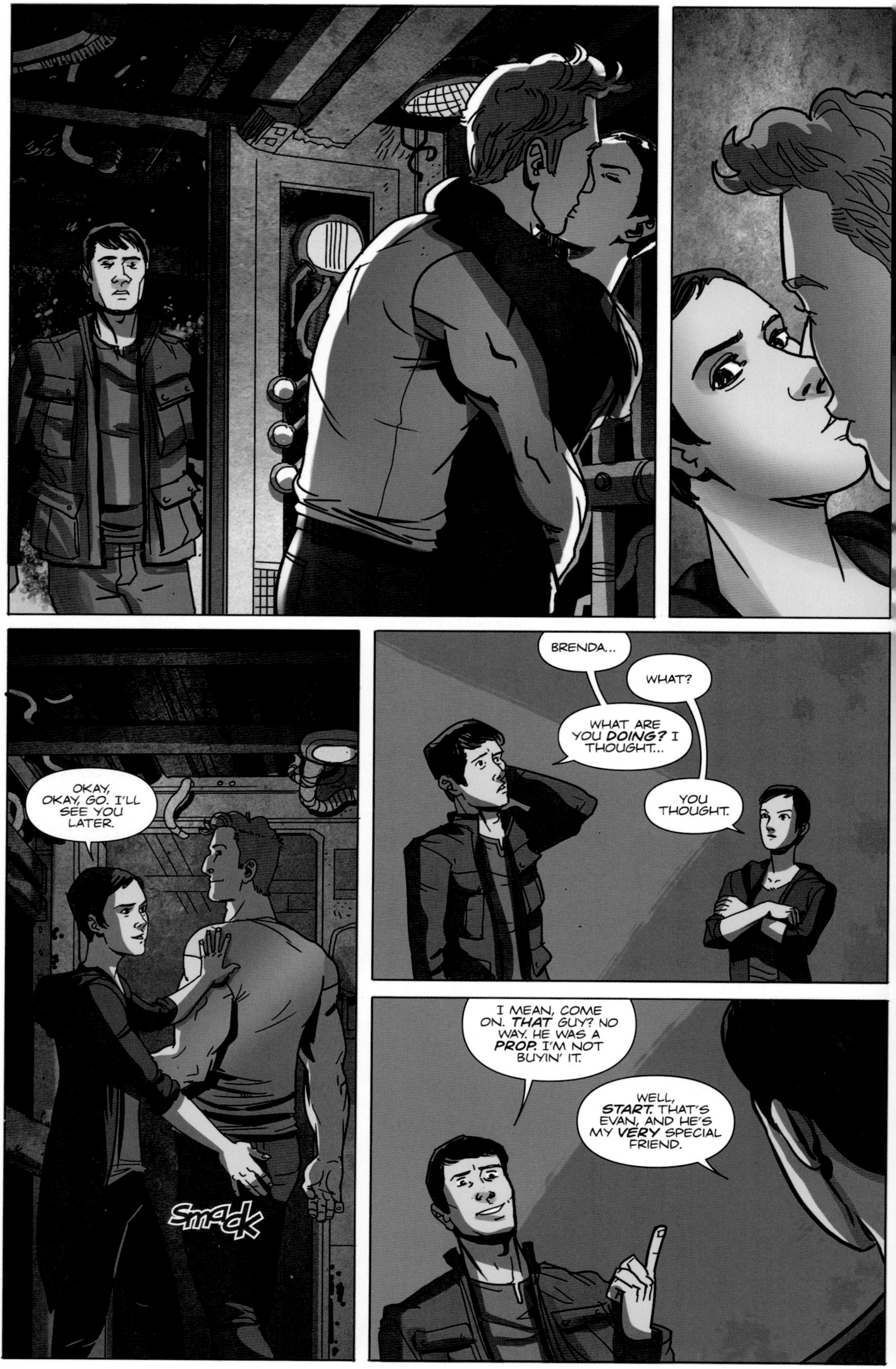
OKAY, OKAY, GO. I'LL SEE YOU LATER.
SMACK
BRENDA...
WHAT?
WHAT ARE YOU **DOING?** I THOUGHT...
YOU THOUGHT.
I MEAN, COME ON. **THAT** GUY? NO WAY. HE WAS A **PROP.** I'M NOT BUYIN' IT.
WELL, **START.** THAT'S EVAN, AND HE'S MY **VERY** SPECIAL FRIEND.

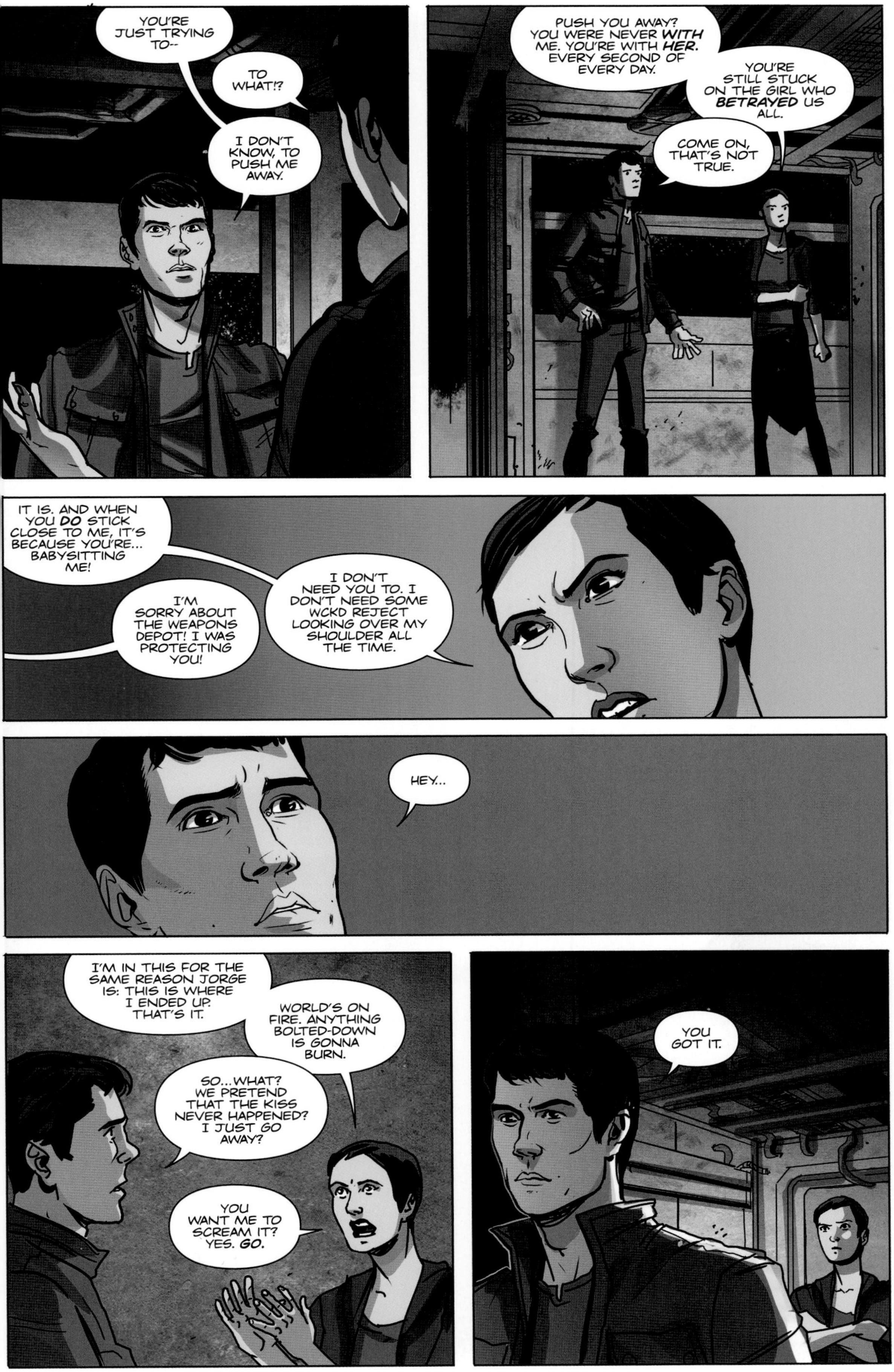
YOU'RE JUST TRYING TO--
TO WHAT!?
I DON'T KNOW, TO PUSH ME AWAY.
PUSH YOU AWAY? YOU WERE NEVER **WITH** ME. YOU'RE WITH **HER.** EVERY SECOND OF EVERY DAY.
YOU'RE STILL STUCK ON THE GIRL WHO **BETRAYED** US ALL.
COME ON, THAT'S NOT TRUE.
IT IS. AND WHEN YOU **DO** STICK CLOSE TO ME, IT'S BECAUSE YOU'RE... BABYSITTING ME!
I'M SORRY ABOUT THE WEAPONS DEPOT! I WAS PROTECTING YOU!
I DON'T NEED YOU TO. I DON'T NEED SOME WCKD REJECT LOOKING OVER MY SHOULDER ALL THE TIME.
HEY...
I'M IN THIS FOR THE SAME REASON JORGE IS: THIS IS WHERE I ENDED UP. THAT'S IT.
WORLD'S ON FIRE. ANYTHING BOLTED-DOWN IS GONNA BURN.
SO...WHAT? WE PRETEND THAT THE KISS NEVER HAPPENED? I JUST GO AWAY?
YOU WANT ME TO SCREAM IT? YES. **GO.**
YOU GOT IT.

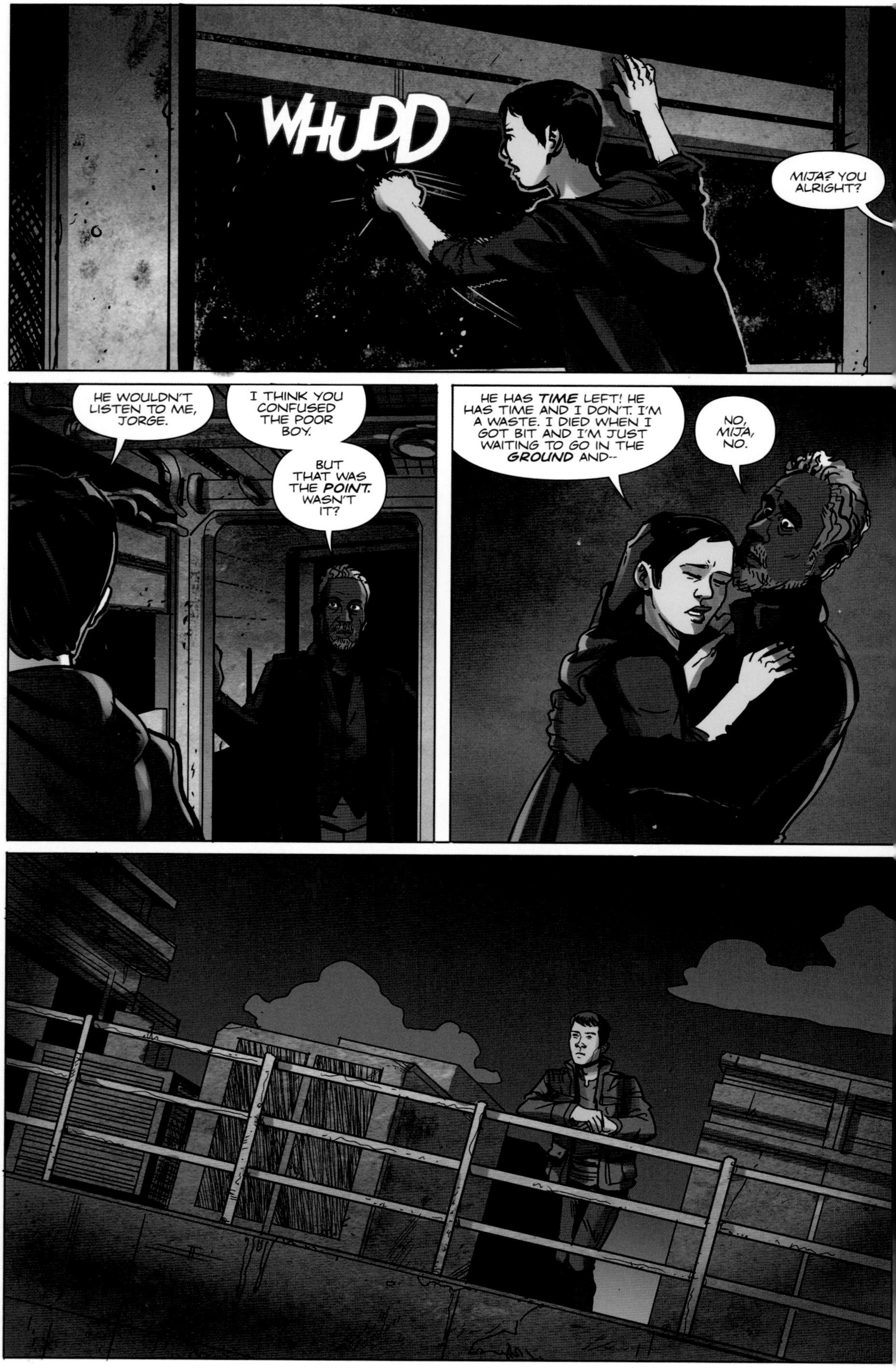
WHUDD
MIJA? YOU ALRIGHT?
HE WOULDN'T LISTEN TO ME, JORGE.
I THINK YOU CONFUSED THE POOR BOY.
BUT THAT WAS THE POINT. WASN'T IT?
HE HAS TIME LEFT! HE HAS TIME AND I DON'T. I'M A WASTE. I DIED WHEN I GOT BIT AND I'M JUST WAITING TO GO IN THE GROUND AND--
NO, MIJA, NO.

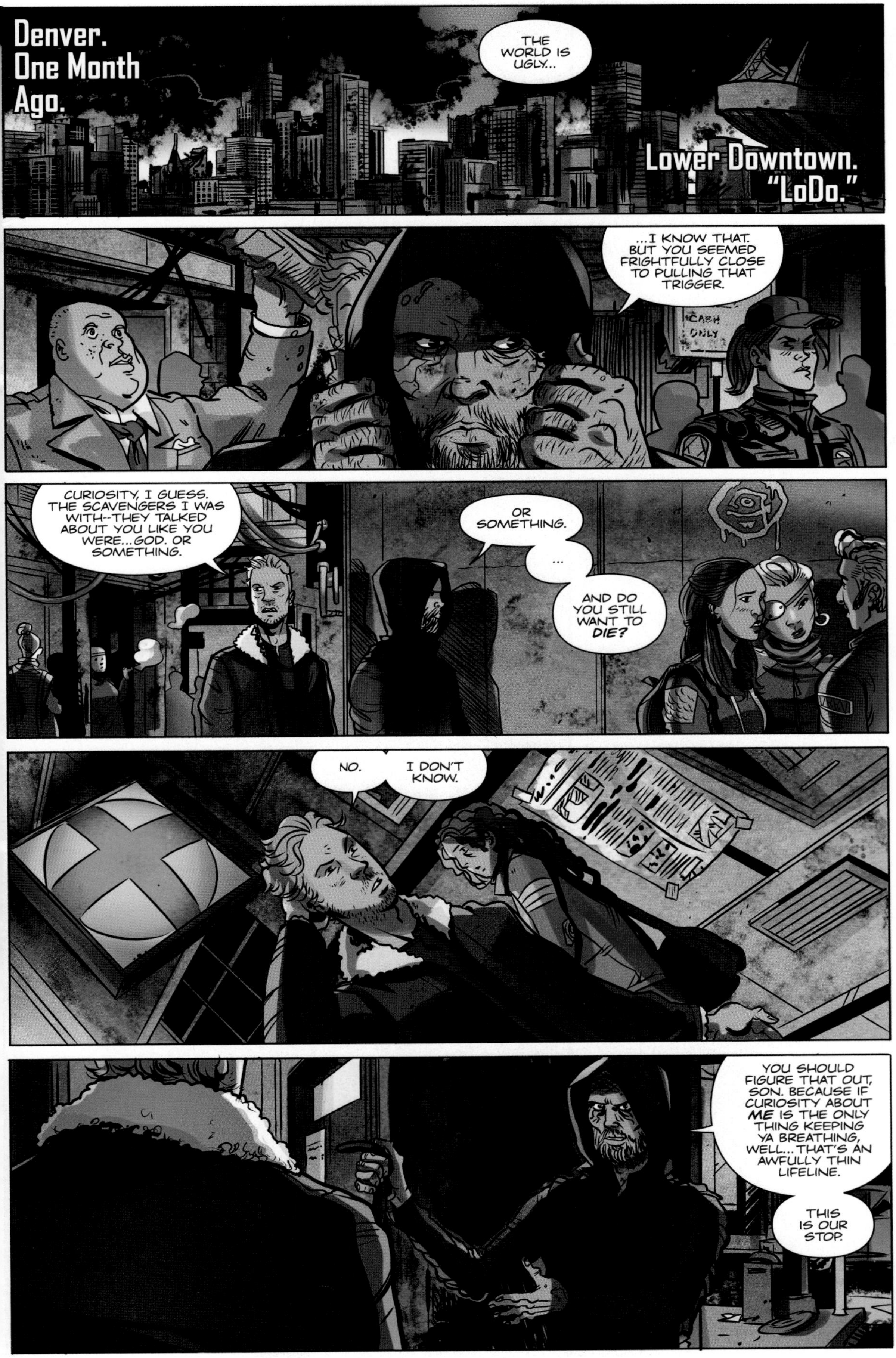
Denver. One Month Ago.
THE WORLD IS UGLY...
Lower Downtown. "LoDo."
...I KNOW THAT. BUT YOU SEEMED FRIGHTFULLY CLOSE TO PULLING THAT TRIGGER.
CASH ONLY
CURIOSITY, I GUESS. THE SCAVENGERS I WAS WITH--THEY TALKED ABOUT YOU LIKE YOU WERE...GOD. OR SOMETHING.
OR SOMETHING.
...
AND DO YOU STILL WANT TO DIE?
NO.
I DON'T KNOW.
YOU SHOULD FIGURE THAT OUT, SON. BECAUSE IF CURIOSITY ABOUT ME IS THE ONLY THING KEEPING YA BREATHING, WELL...THAT'S AN AWFULLY THIN LIFELINE.
THIS IS OUR STOP.

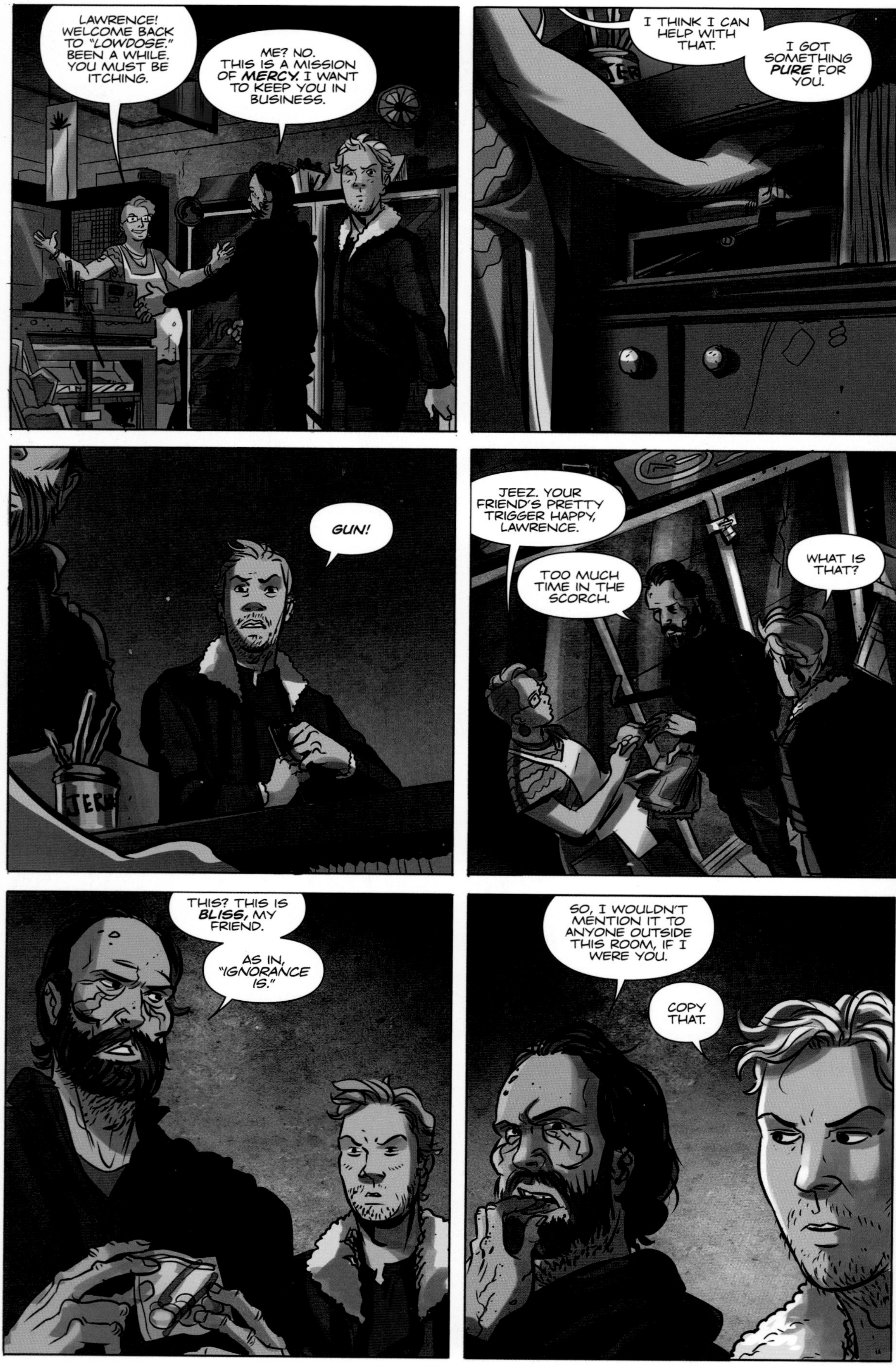
LAWRENCE! WELCOME BACK TO "LOWDOSE." BEEN A WHILE. YOU MUST BE ITCHING.
ME? NO. THIS IS A MISSION OF MERCY. I WANT TO KEEP YOU IN BUSINESS.
I THINK I CAN HELP WITH THAT.
I GOT SOMETHING PURE FOR YOU.
GUN!
JEEZ. YOUR FRIEND'S PRETTY TRIGGER HAPPY, LAWRENCE.
TOO MUCH TIME IN THE SCORCH.
WHAT IS THAT?
THIS? THIS IS BLISS, MY FRIEND.
AS IN, "IGNORANCE IS."
SO, I WOULDN'T MENTION IT TO ANYONE OUTSIDE THIS ROOM, IF I WERE YOU.
COPY THAT.

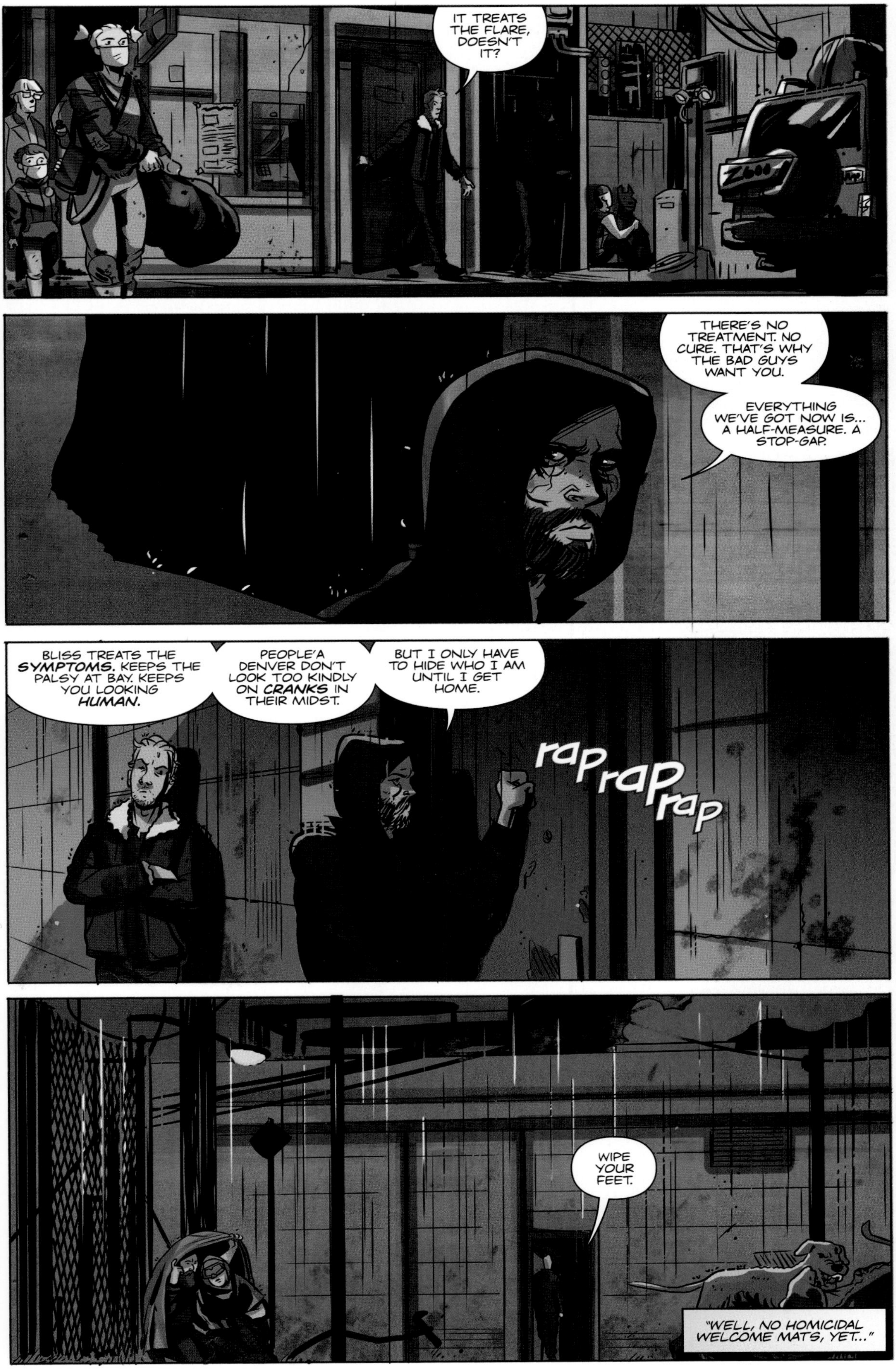
IT TREATS THE FLARE, DOESN'T IT?
THERE'S NO TREATMENT. NO CURE. THAT'S WHY THE BAD GUYS WANT YOU.
EVERYTHING WE'VE GOT NOW IS... A HALF-MEASURE. A STOP-GAP.
BLISS TREATS THE SYMPTOMS. KEEPS THE PALSY AT BAY. KEEPS YOU LOOKING HUMAN.
PEOPLE'A DENVER DON'T LOOK TOO KINDLY ON CRANKS IN THEIR MIDST.
BUT I ONLY HAVE TO HIDE WHO I AM UNTIL I GET HOME.
rap rap rap
WIPE YOUR FEET.
"WELL, NO HOMICIDAL WELCOME MATS, YET..."

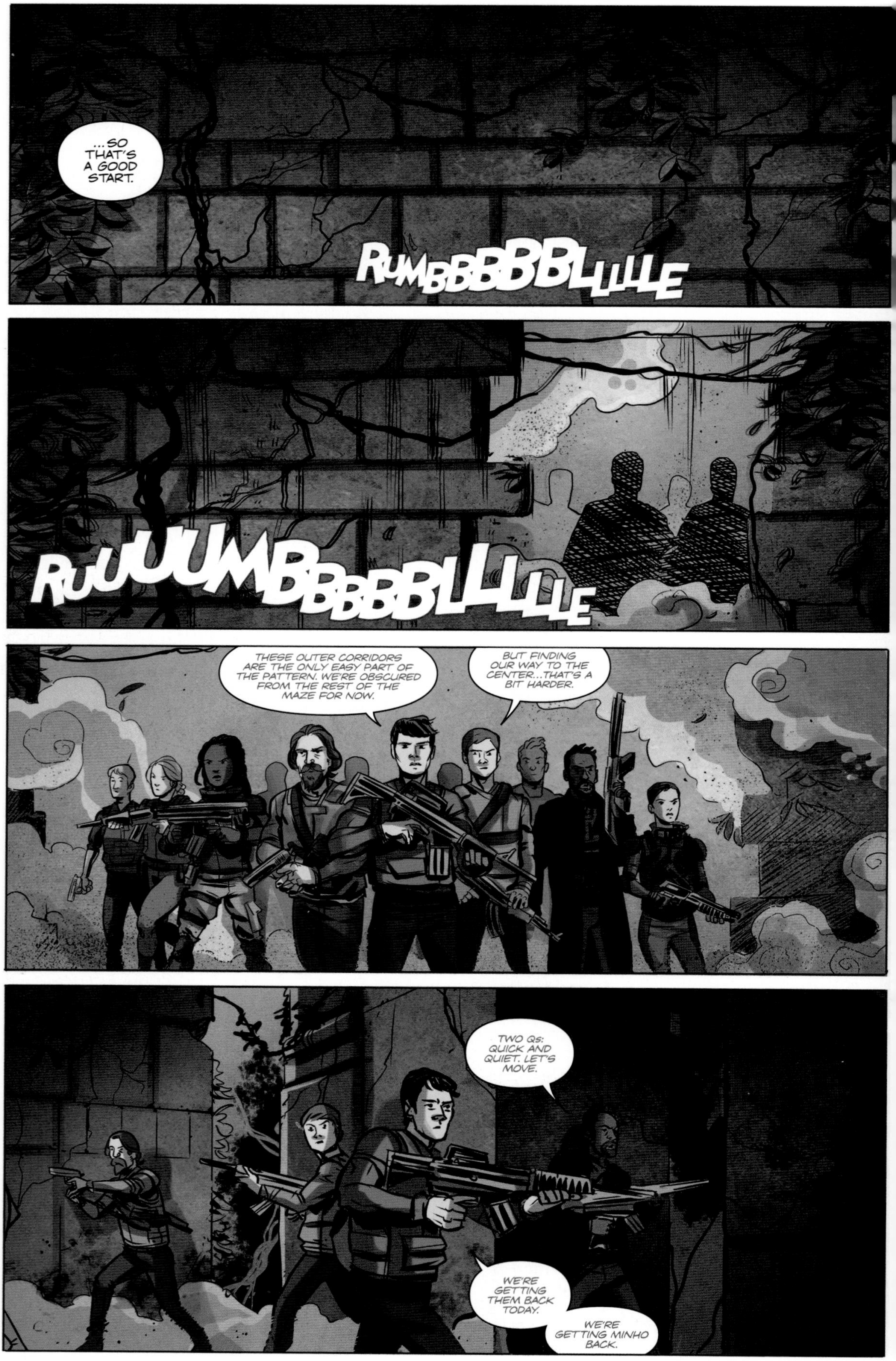
...SO THAT'S A GOOD START.
RUMBBBBBLLLLLE
RUUUUMBBBBBBLLLLLLE
THESE OUTER CORRIDORS ARE THE ONLY EASY PART OF THE PATTERN. WE'RE OBSCURED FROM THE REST OF THE MAZE FOR NOW.
BUT FINDING OUR WAY TO THE CENTER...THAT'S A BIT HARDER.
TWO Qs: QUICK AND QUIET. LET'S MOVE.
WE'RE GETTING THEM BACK TODAY.
WE'RE GETTING MINHO BACK.

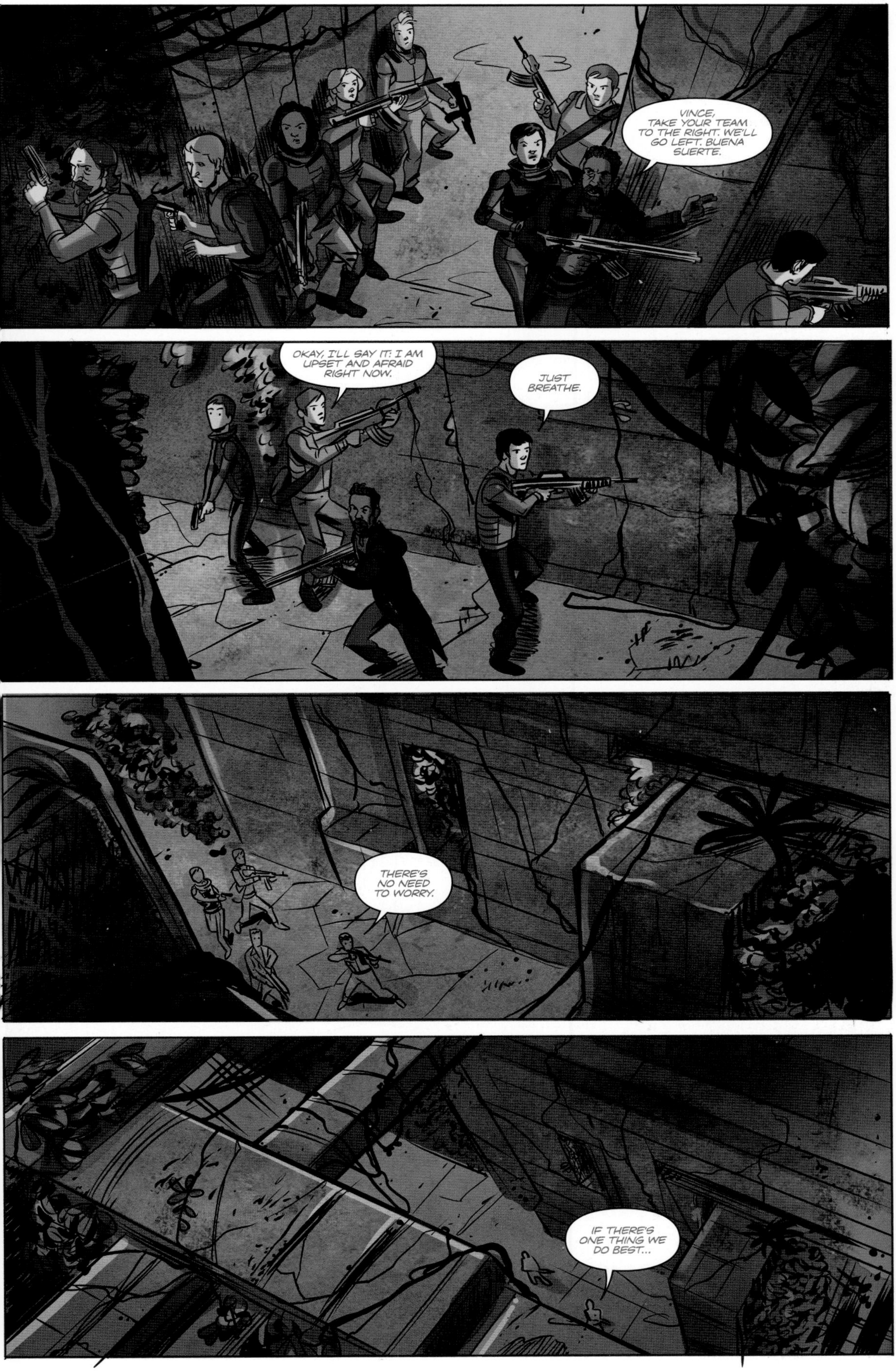
VINCE, TAKE YOUR TEAM TO THE RIGHT. WE'LL GO LEFT. BUENA SUERTE.
OKAY, I'LL SAY IT: I AM UPSET AND AFRAID RIGHT NOW.
JUST BREATHE.
THERE'S NO NEED TO WORRY.
IF THERE'S ONE THING WE DO BEST...

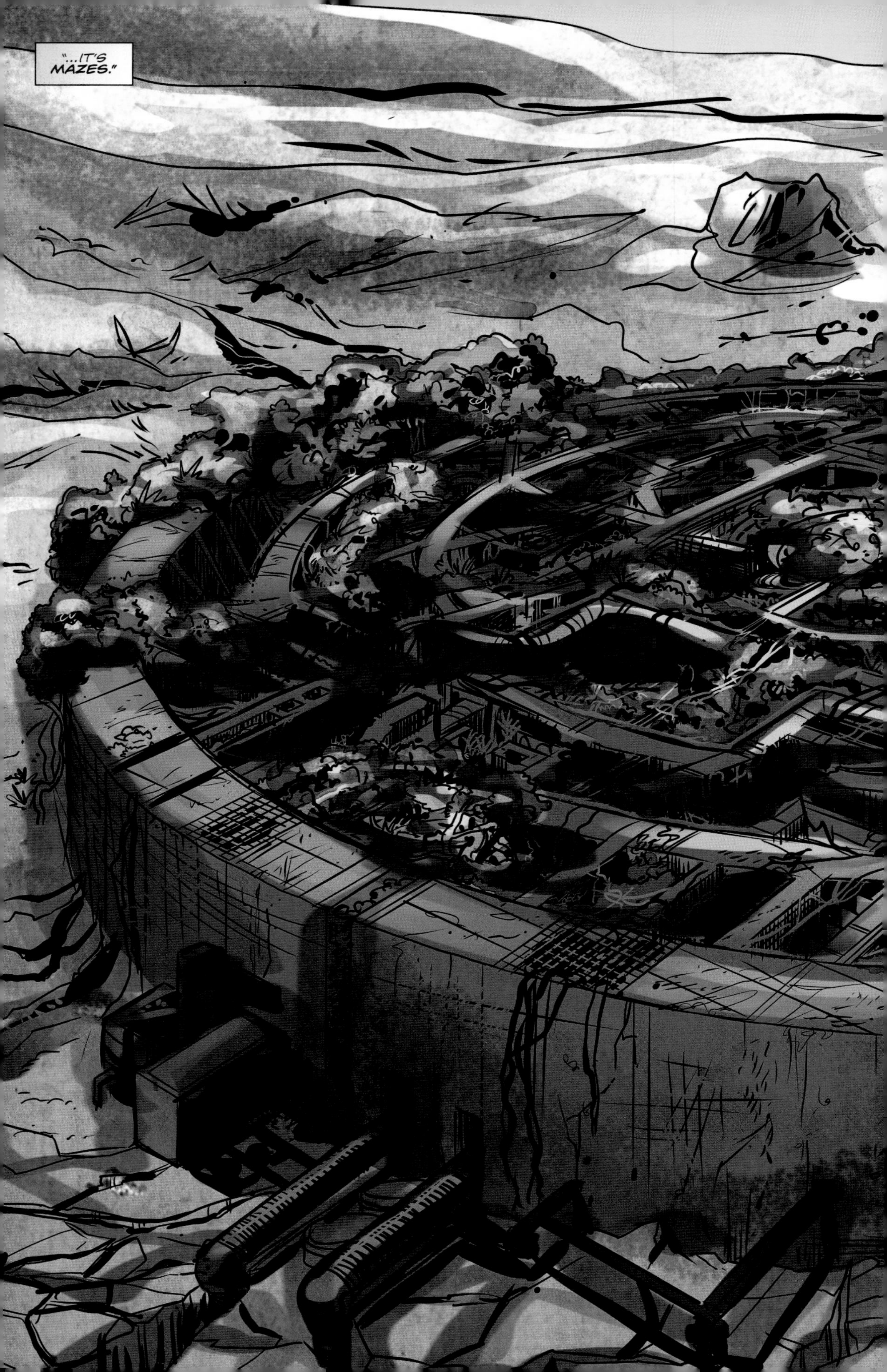
"...IT'S MAZES."

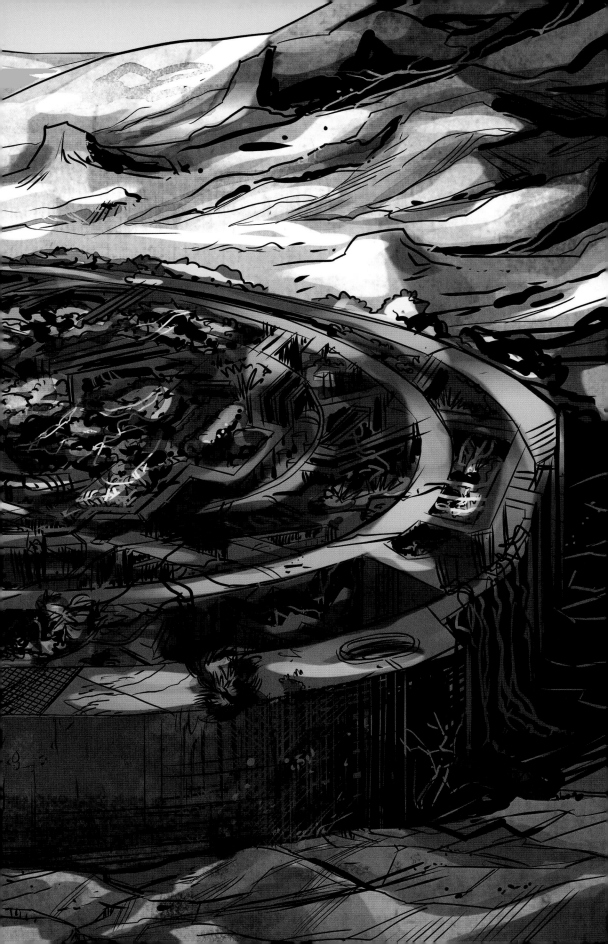

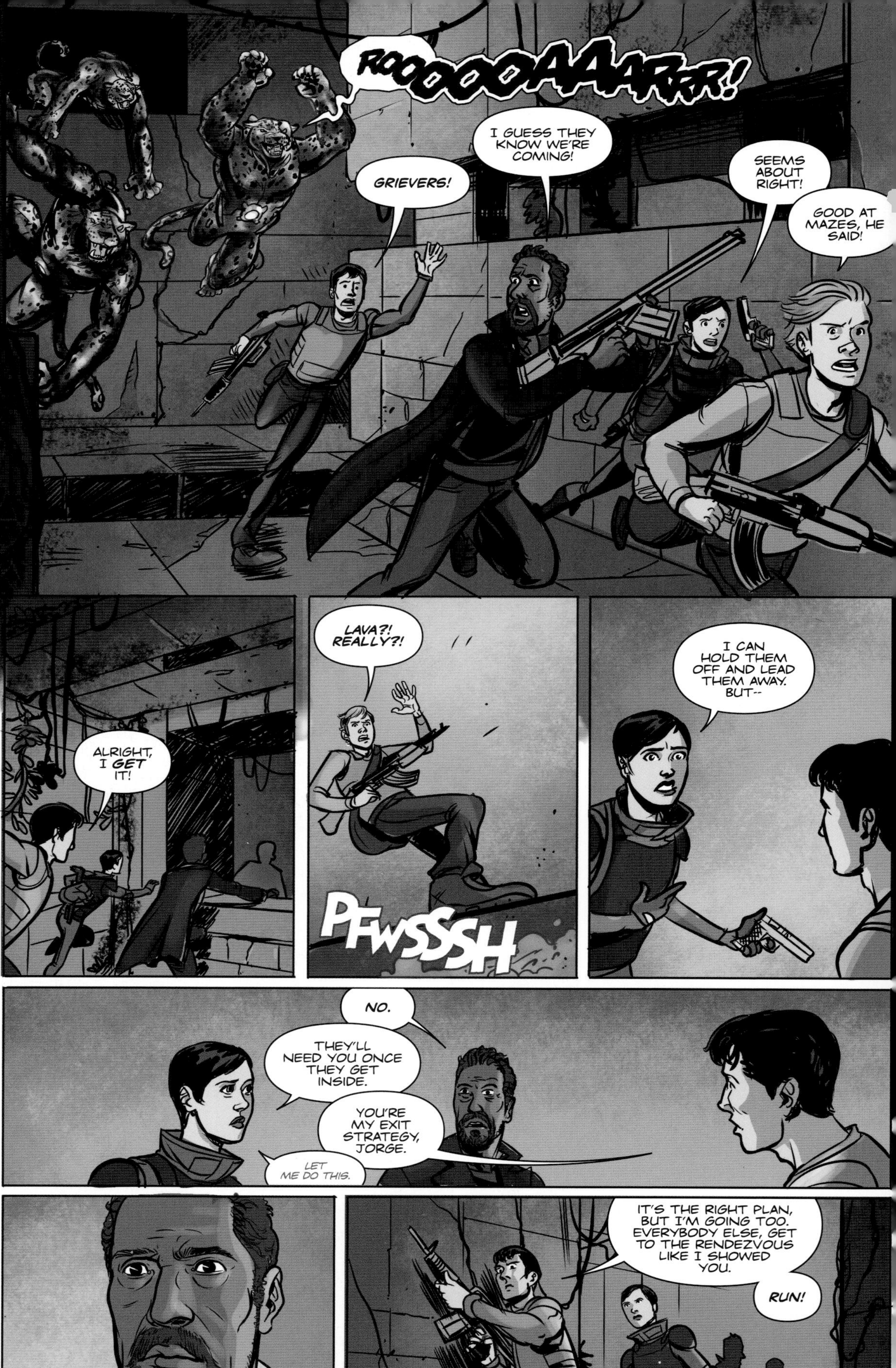
ROOOOOOAAARRR!
GRIEVERS!
I GUESS THEY KNOW WE'RE COMING!
SEEMS ABOUT RIGHT!
GOOD AT MAZES, HE SAID!
ALRIGHT, I GET IT!
LAVA?! REALLY?!
PFWSSSH
I CAN HOLD THEM OFF AND LEAD THEM AWAY. BUT--
NO.
THEY'LL NEED YOU ONCE THEY GET INSIDE.
YOU'RE MY EXIT STRATEGY, JORGE.
LET ME DO THIS.
IT'S THE RIGHT PLAN, BUT I'M GOING TOO. EVERYBODY ELSE, GET TO THE RENDEZVOUS LIKE I SHOWED YOU.
RUN!

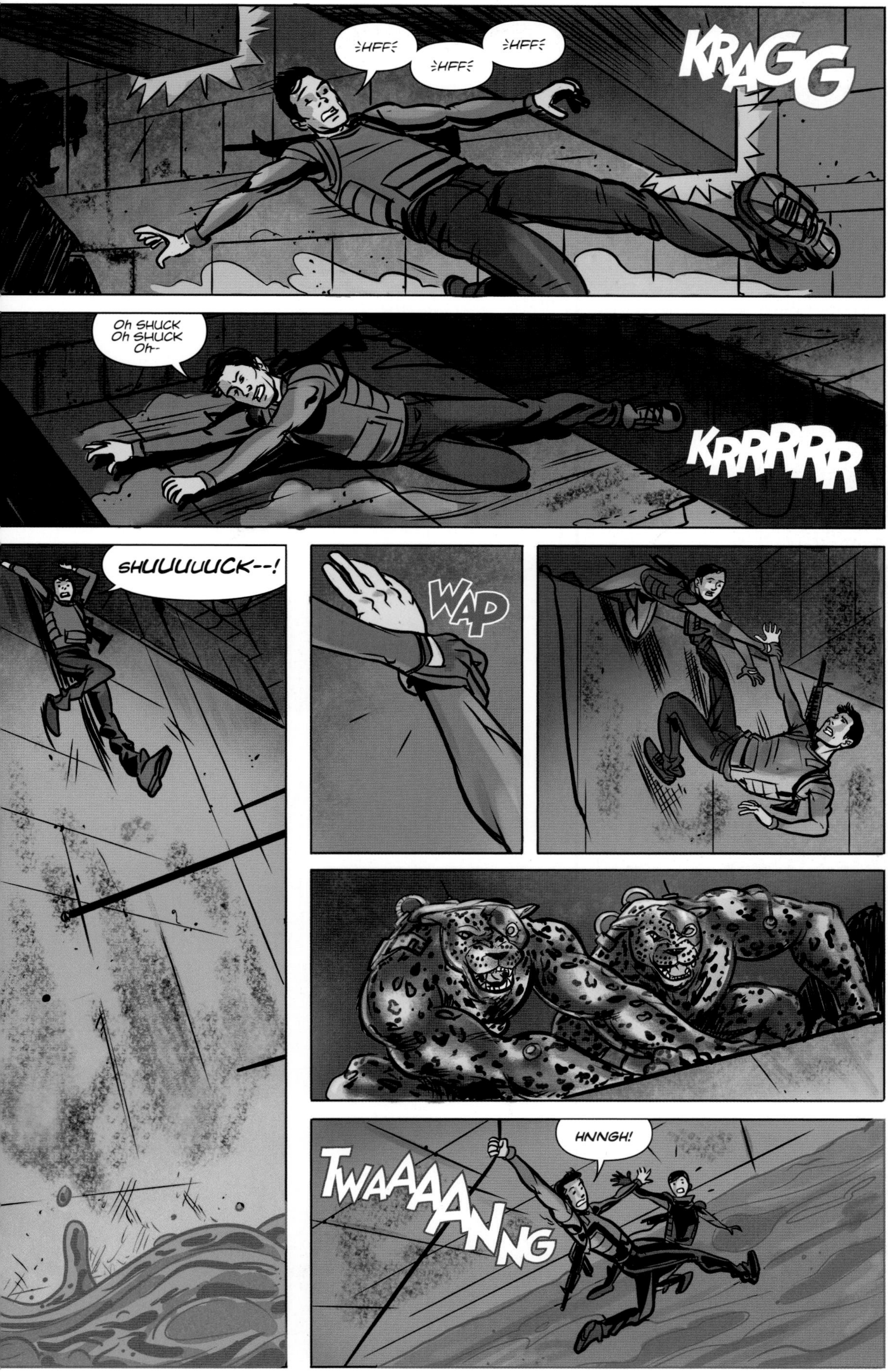
HFF
HFF
HFF
KRAGG
Oh SHUCK
Oh SHUCK
Oh--
KRRRRR
SHUUUUUCK--!
WAP
HNNGH!
TWAAAANNG

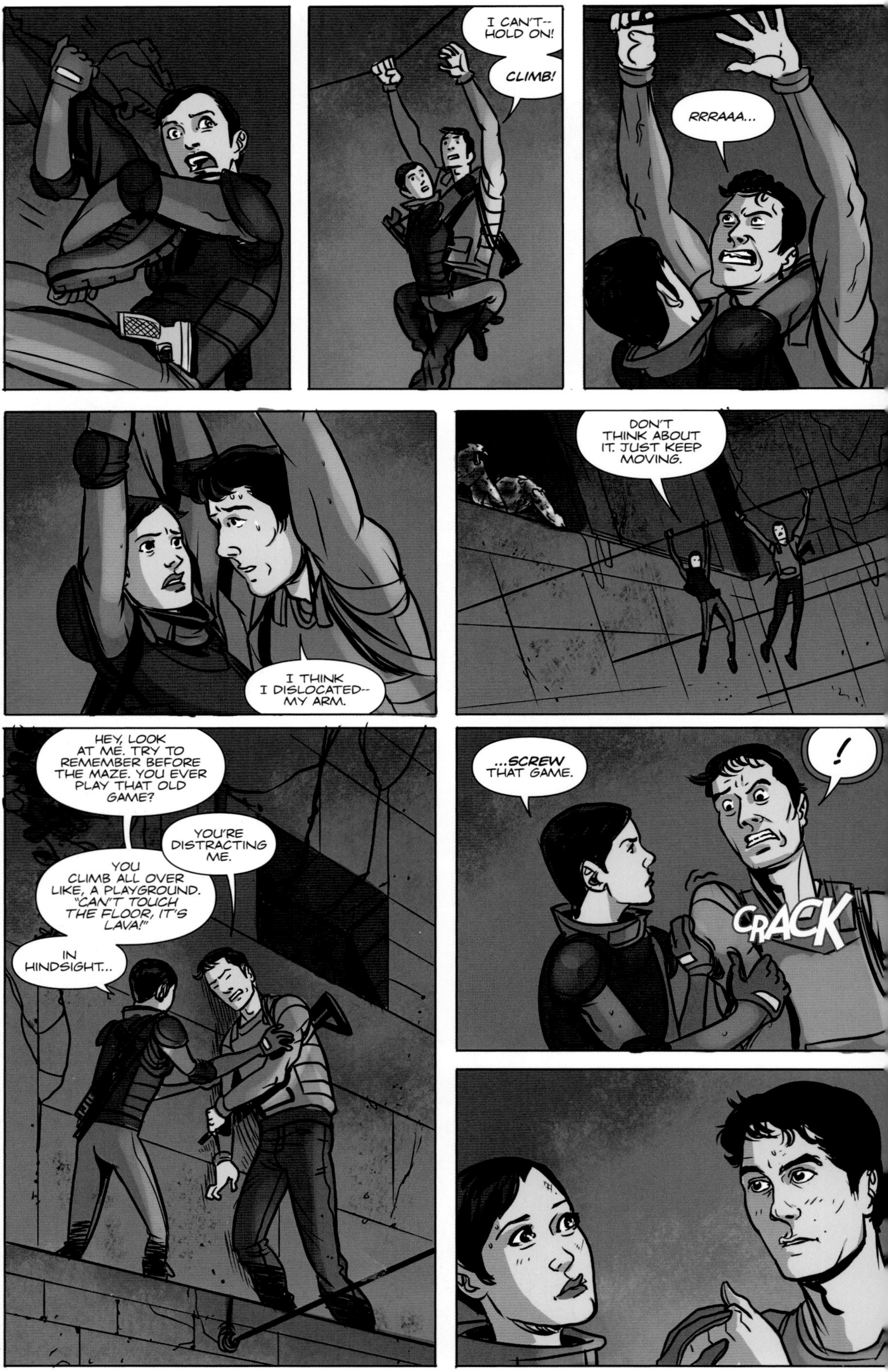
I CAN'T-- HOLD ON!
CLIMB!
RRRAAA...
I THINK I DISLOCATED-- MY ARM.
DON'T THINK ABOUT IT. JUST KEEP MOVING.
HEY, LOOK AT ME. TRY TO REMEMBER BEFORE THE MAZE. YOU EVER PLAY THAT OLD GAME?
YOU'RE DISTRACTING ME.
YOU CLIMB ALL OVER LIKE, A PLAYGROUND. "CAN'T TOUCH THE FLOOR, IT'S LAVA!"
IN HINDSIGHT...
...SCREW THAT GAME.
!
CRACK

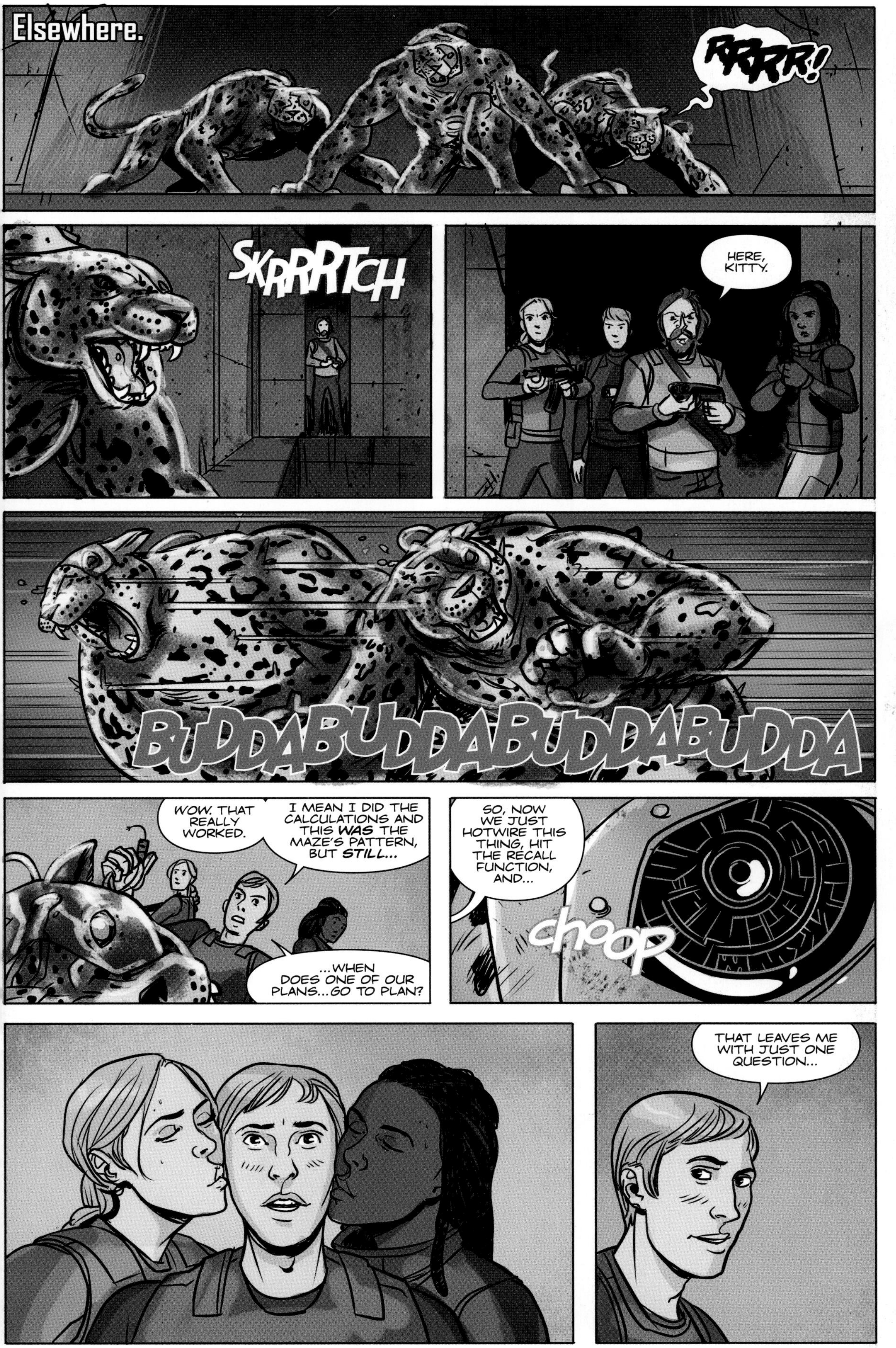
Elsewhere.
RRRRR!
SKRRRTCH
HERE, KITTY.
BUDDABUDDABUDDABUDDA
WOW. THAT REALLY WORKED.
I MEAN I DID THE CALCULATIONS AND THIS WAS THE MAZE'S PATTERN, BUT STILL...
...WHEN DOES ONE OF OUR PLANS...GO TO PLAN?
SO, NOW WE JUST HOTWIRE THIS THING, HIT THE RECALL FUNCTION, AND...
choop
THAT LEAVES ME WITH JUST ONE QUESTION...

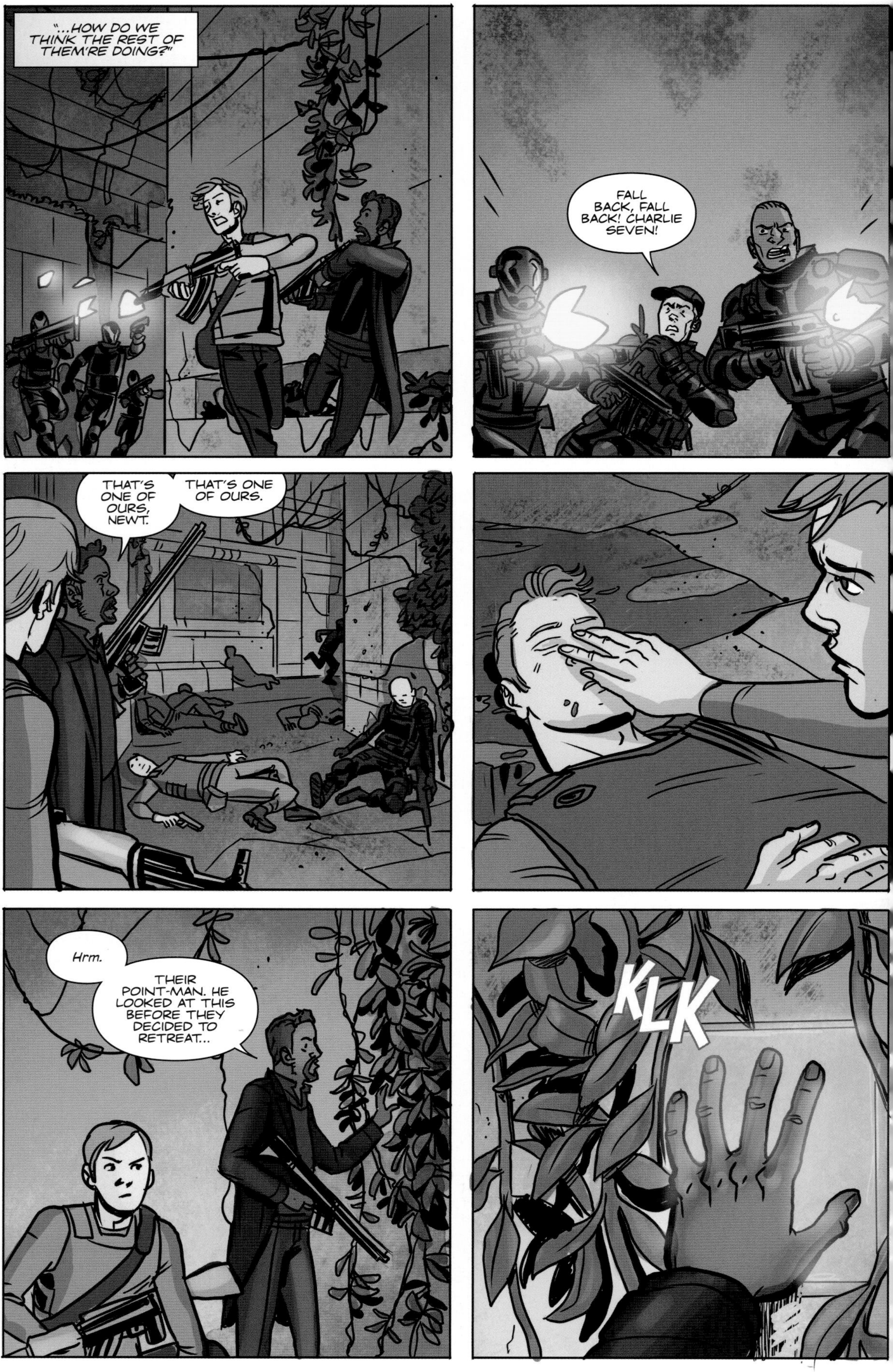
"...HOW DO WE THINK THE REST OF THEM'RE DOING?"
FALL BACK, FALL BACK! CHARLIE SEVEN!
THAT'S ONE OF OURS, NEWT.
THAT'S ONE OF OURS.
Hrm.
THEIR POINT-MAN. HE LOOKED AT THIS BEFORE THEY DECIDED TO RETREAT...
KLK

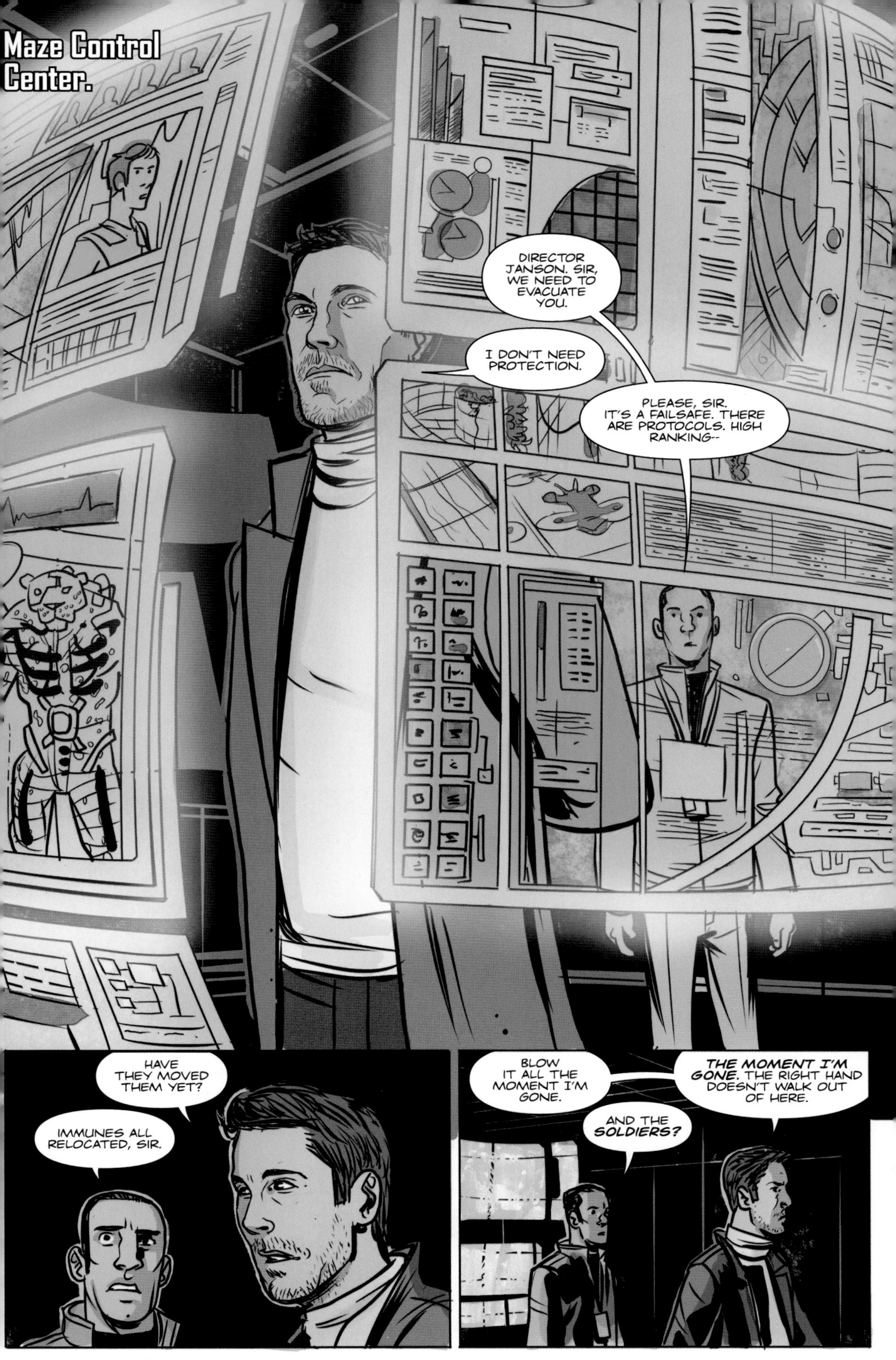
Maze Control Center.
DIRECTOR JANSON. SIR, WE NEED TO EVACUATE YOU.
I DON'T NEED PROTECTION.
PLEASE, SIR. IT'S A FAILSAFE. THERE ARE PROTOCOLS. HIGH RANKING--
HAVE THEY MOVED THEM YET?
IMMUNES ALL RELOCATED, SIR.
BLOW IT ALL THE MOMENT I'M GONE.
AND THE SOLDIERS?
THE MOMENT I'M GONE. THE RIGHT HAND DOESN'T WALK OUT OF HERE.

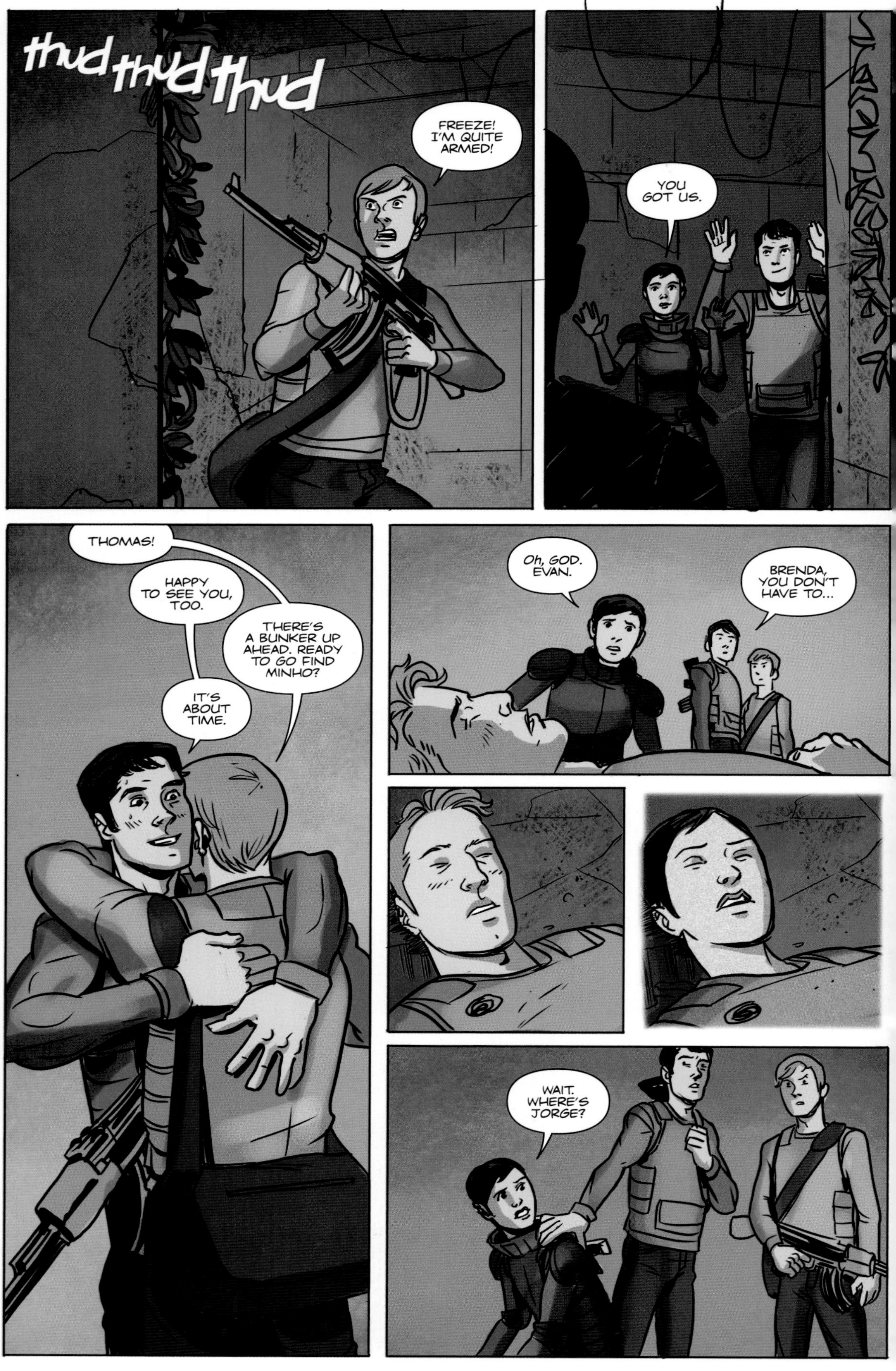
thud thud thud
FREEZE! I'M QUITE ARMED!
YOU GOT US.
THOMAS!
HAPPY TO SEE YOU, TOO.
THERE'S A BUNKER UP AHEAD. READY TO GO FIND MINHO?
IT'S ABOUT TIME.
Oh, GOD. EVAN.
BRENDA, YOU DON'T HAVE TO...
WAIT. WHERE'S JORGE?

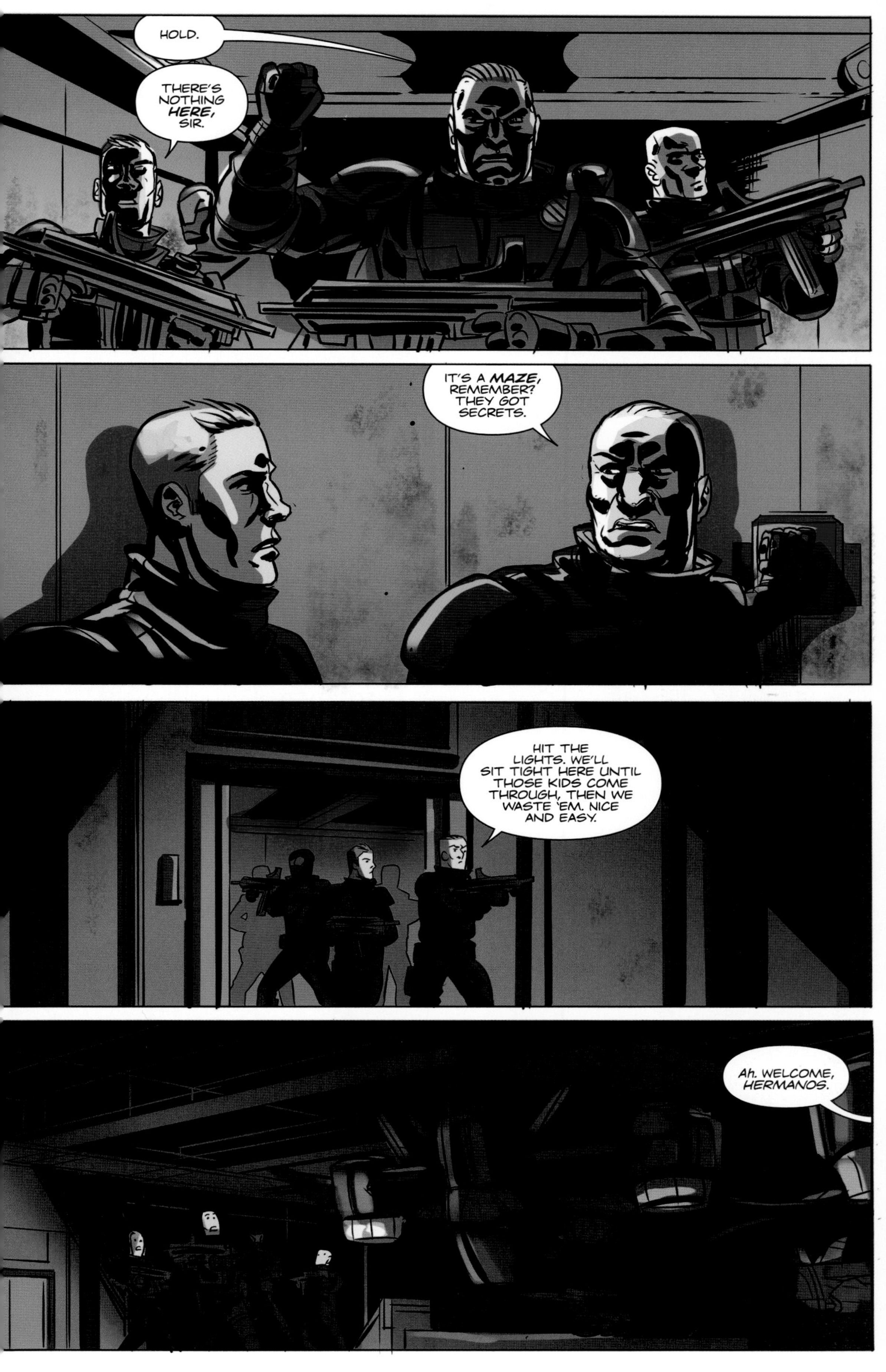
HOLD.
THERE'S NOTHING *HERE,* SIR.
IT'S A *MAZE,* REMEMBER? THEY GOT SECRETS.
HIT THE LIGHTS. WE'LL SIT TIGHT HERE UNTIL THOSE KIDS COME THROUGH, THEN WE WASTE 'EM. NICE AND EASY.
Ah. WELCOME, *HERMANOS.*

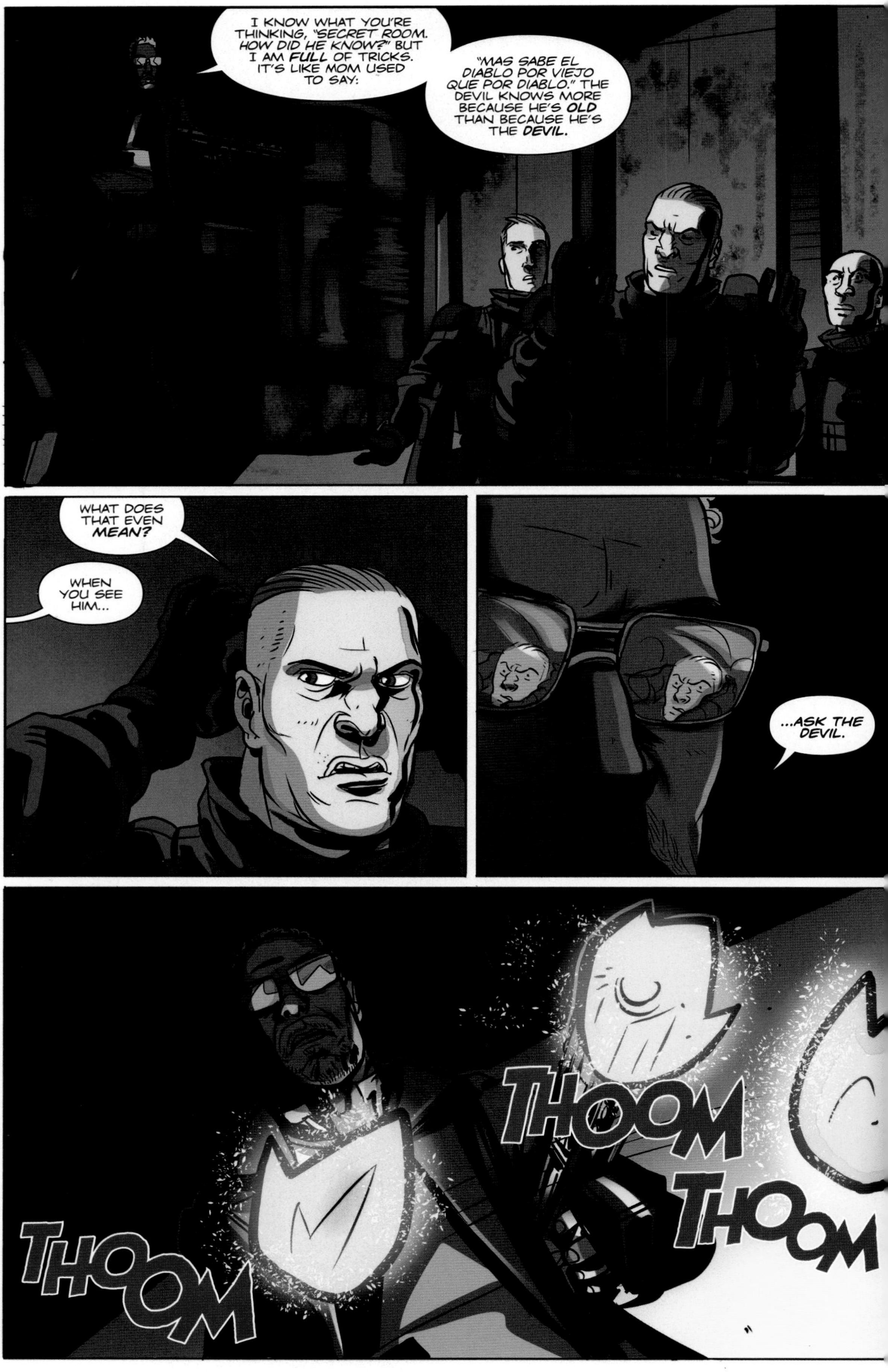
I KNOW WHAT YOU'RE THINKING, "SECRET ROOM. HOW DID HE KNOW?" BUT I AM FULL OF TRICKS. IT'S LIKE MOM USED TO SAY:
"MAS SABE EL DIABLO POR VIEJO QUE POR DIABLO." THE DEVIL KNOWS MORE BECAUSE HE'S OLD THAN BECAUSE HE'S THE DEVIL.
WHAT DOES THAT EVEN MEAN?
WHEN YOU SEE HIM...
...ASK THE DEVIL.
THOOM
THOOM
THOOM

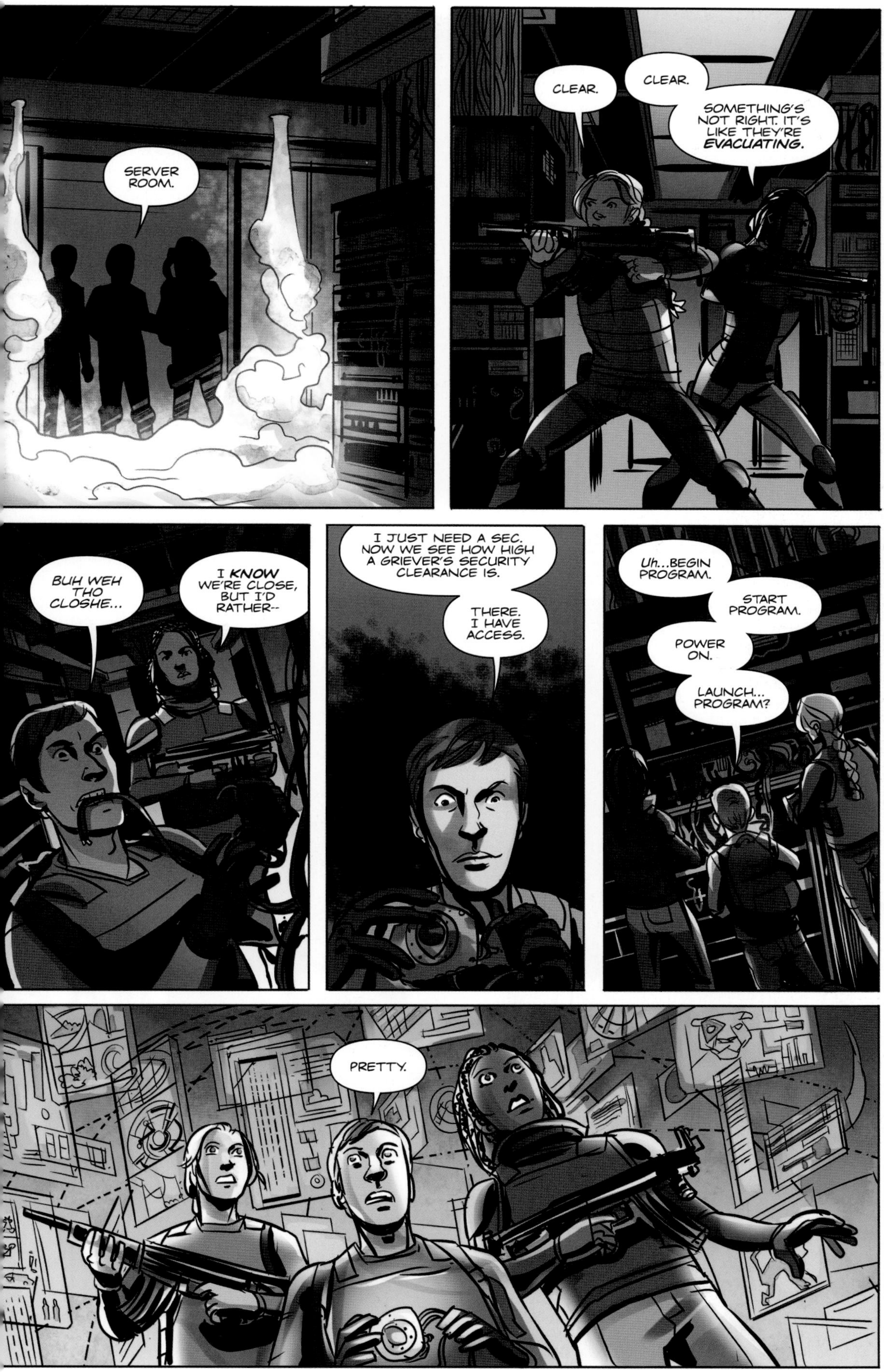
SERVER ROOM.
CLEAR.
CLEAR.
SOMETHING'S NOT RIGHT. IT'S LIKE THEY'RE *EVACUATING.*
BUH WEH THO CLOSHE...
I *KNOW* WE'RE CLOSE, BUT I'D RATHER--
I JUST NEED A SEC. NOW WE SEE HOW HIGH A GRIEVER'S SECURITY CLEARANCE IS.
THERE. I HAVE ACCESS.
Uh...BEGIN PROGRAM.
START PROGRAM.
POWER ON.
LAUNCH... PROGRAM?
PRETTY.

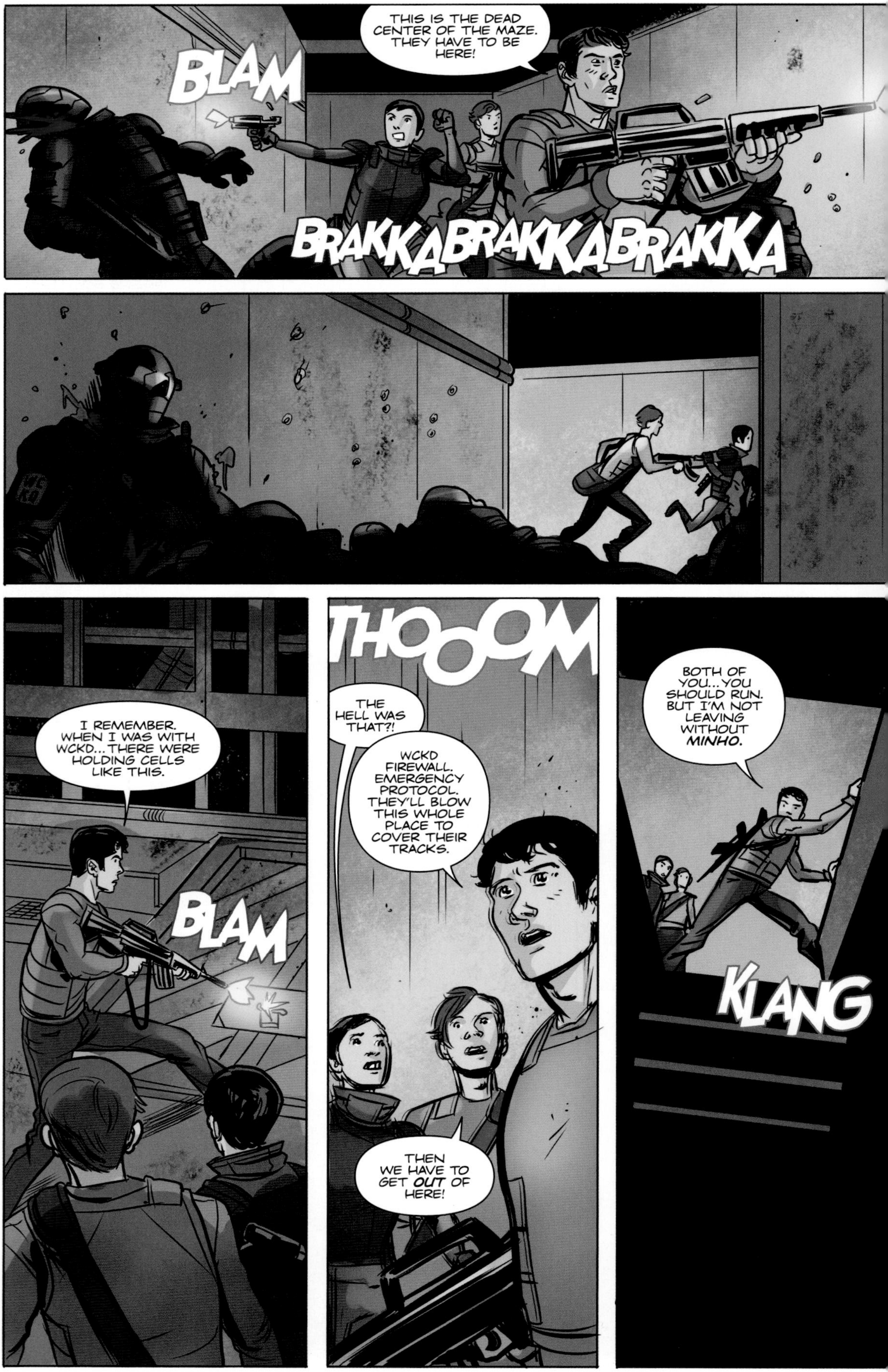

THIS IS THE DEAD CENTER OF THE MAZE. THEY HAVE TO BE HERE!
BLAM
BRAKKABRAKKABRAKKA
I REMEMBER. WHEN I WAS WITH WCKD... THERE WERE HOLDING CELLS LIKE THIS.
BLAM
THOOOOM
THE HELL WAS THAT?!
WCKD FIREWALL. EMERGENCY PROTOCOL. THEY'LL BLOW THIS WHOLE PLACE TO COVER THEIR TRACKS.
THEN WE HAVE TO GET OUT OF HERE!
BOTH OF YOU... YOU SHOULD RUN. BUT I'M NOT LEAVING WITHOUT MINHO.
KLANG

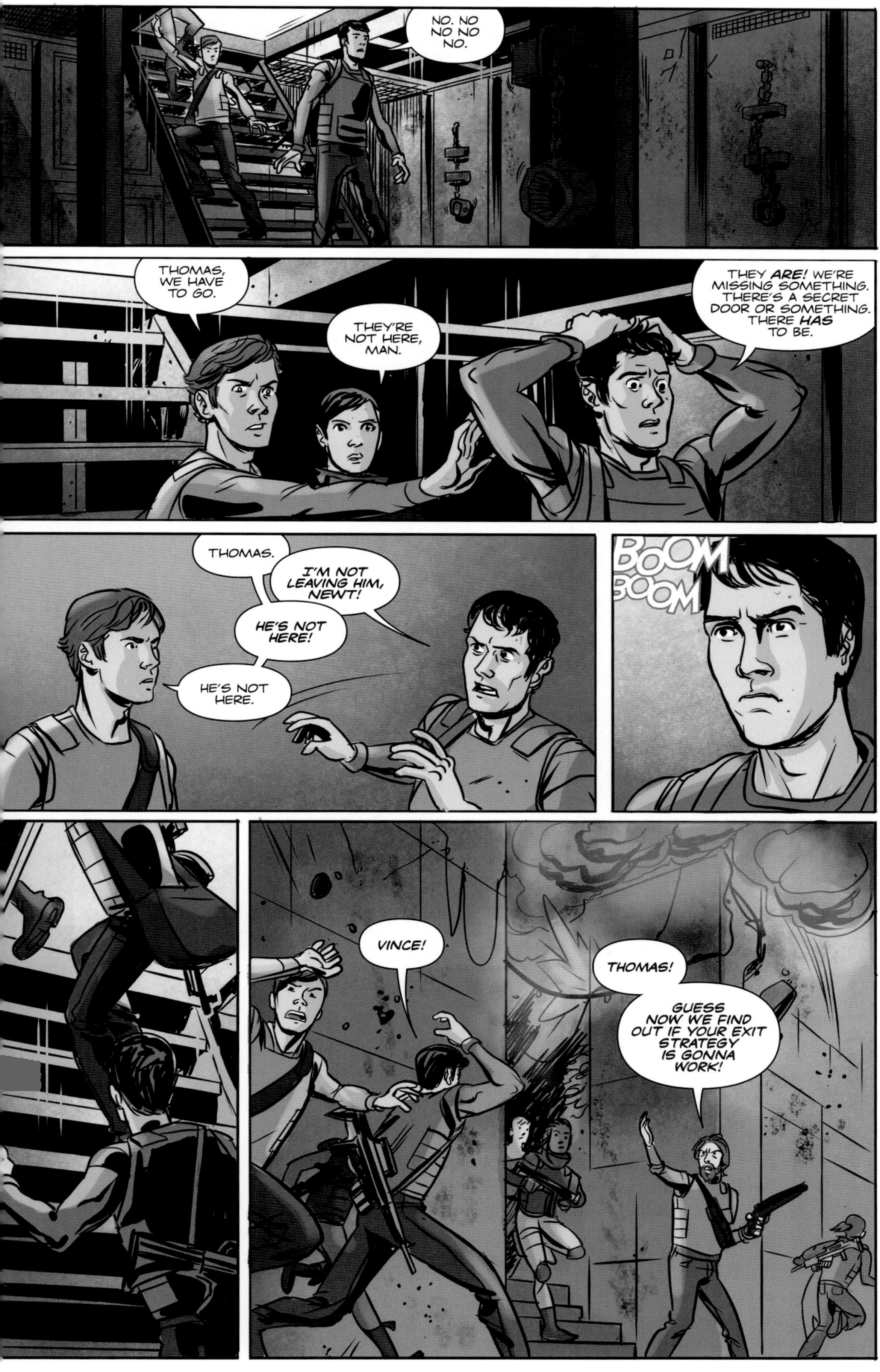
NO. NO NO NO NO NO.
THOMAS, WE HAVE TO GO.
THEY'RE NOT HERE, MAN.
THEY **ARE!** WE'RE MISSING SOMETHING. THERE'S A SECRET DOOR OR SOMETHING. THERE **HAS** TO BE.
THOMAS.
I'M NOT LEAVING HIM, NEWT!
HE'S NOT HERE!
HE'S NOT HERE.
BOOM
BOOM
VINCE!
THOMAS!
GUESS NOW WE FIND OUT IF YOUR EXIT STRATEGY IS GONNA WORK!

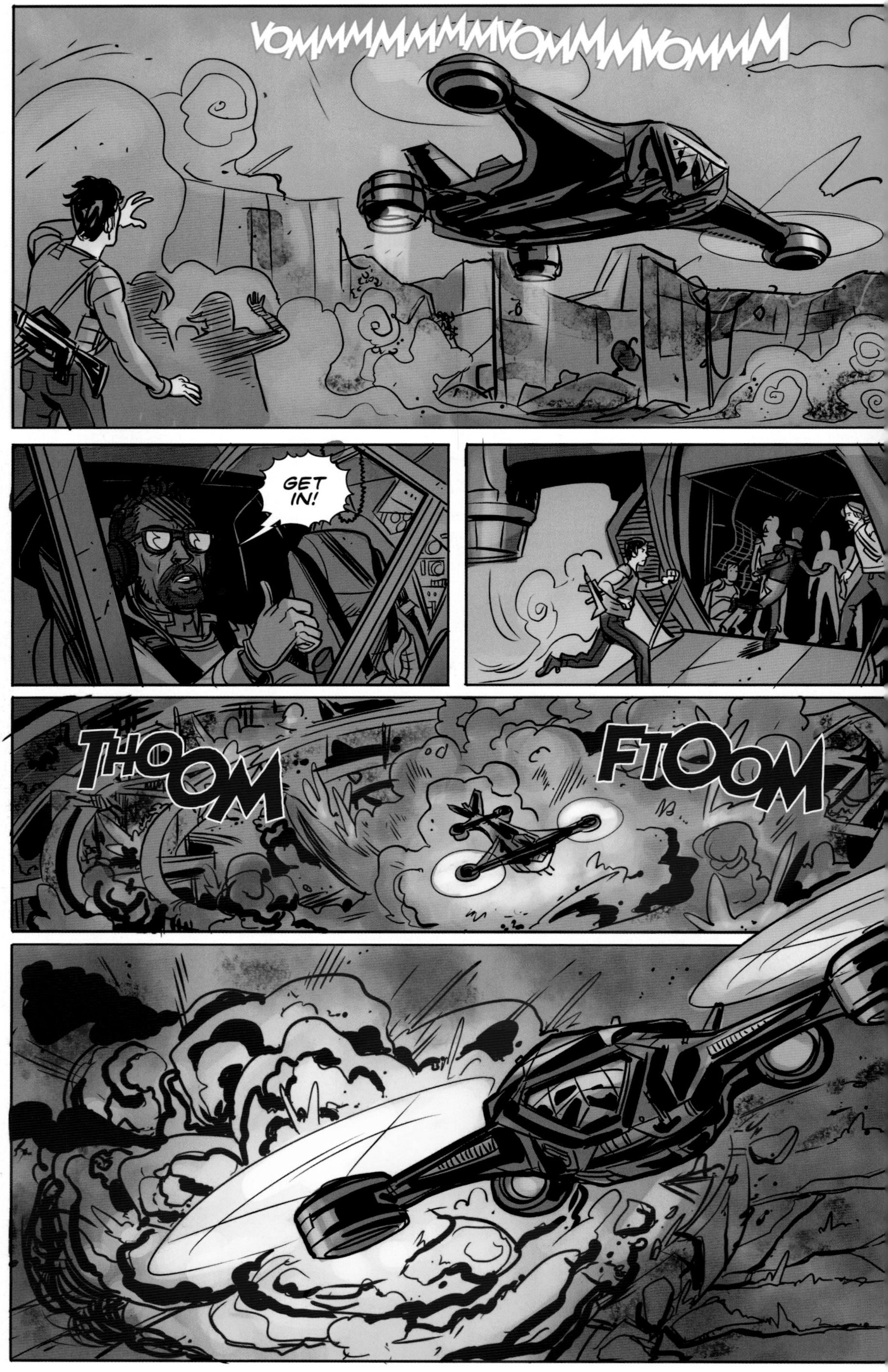
VOMMMMMMMVOMMMMVOMMM
GET IN!
THOOM
FTOOM

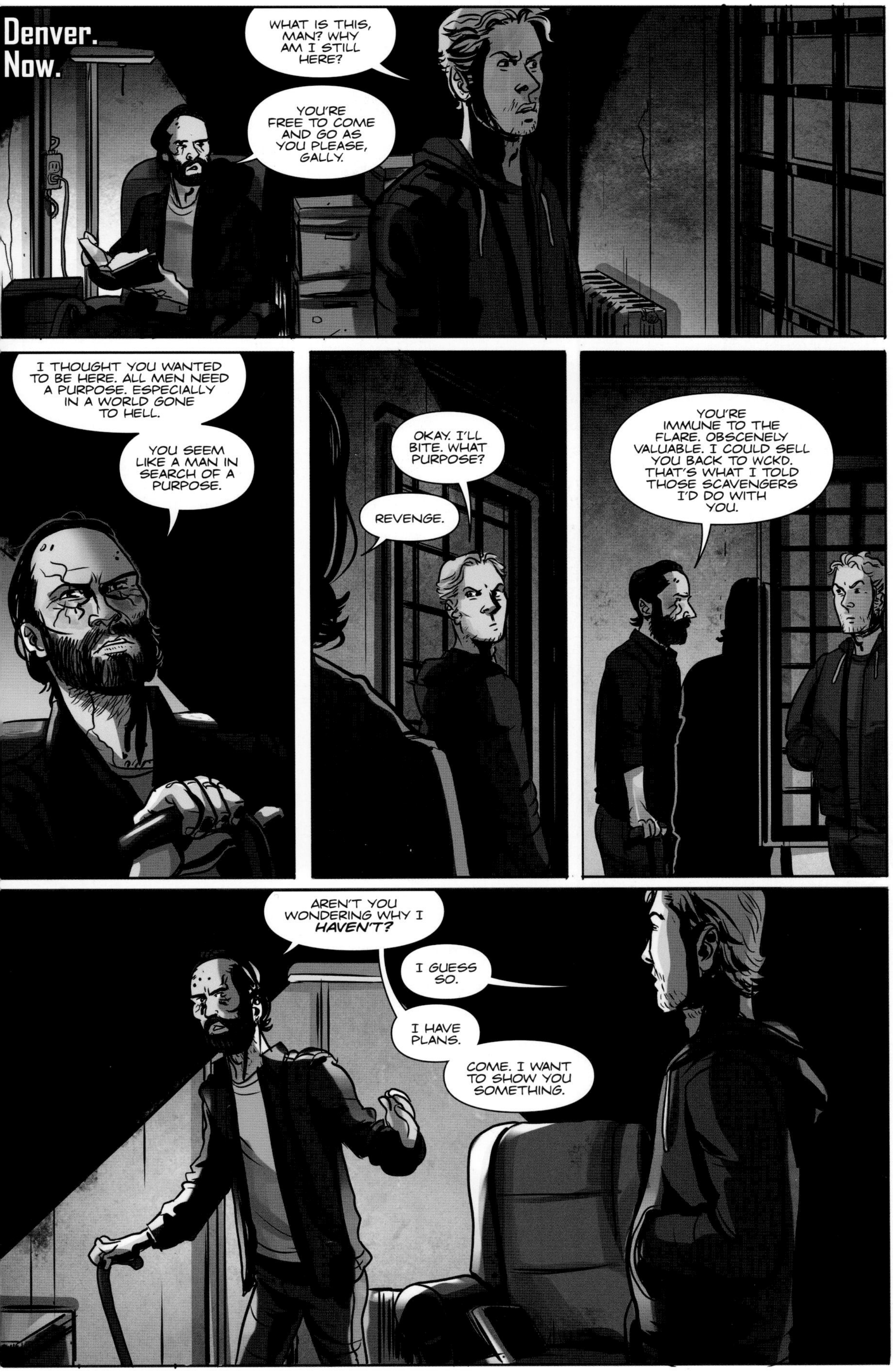
Denver. Now.
WHAT IS THIS, MAN? WHY AM I STILL HERE?
YOU'RE FREE TO COME AND GO AS YOU PLEASE, GALLY.
I THOUGHT YOU WANTED TO BE HERE. ALL MEN NEED A PURPOSE. ESPECIALLY IN A WORLD GONE TO HELL.
YOU SEEM LIKE A MAN IN SEARCH OF A PURPOSE.
OKAY. I'LL BITE. WHAT PURPOSE?
REVENGE.
YOU'RE IMMUNE TO THE FLARE. OBSCENELY VALUABLE. I COULD SELL YOU BACK TO WCKD. THAT'S WHAT I TOLD THOSE SCAVENGERS I'D DO WITH YOU.
AREN'T YOU WONDERING WHY I *HAVEN'T?*
I GUESS SO.
I HAVE PLANS.
COME. I WANT TO SHOW YOU SOMETHING.

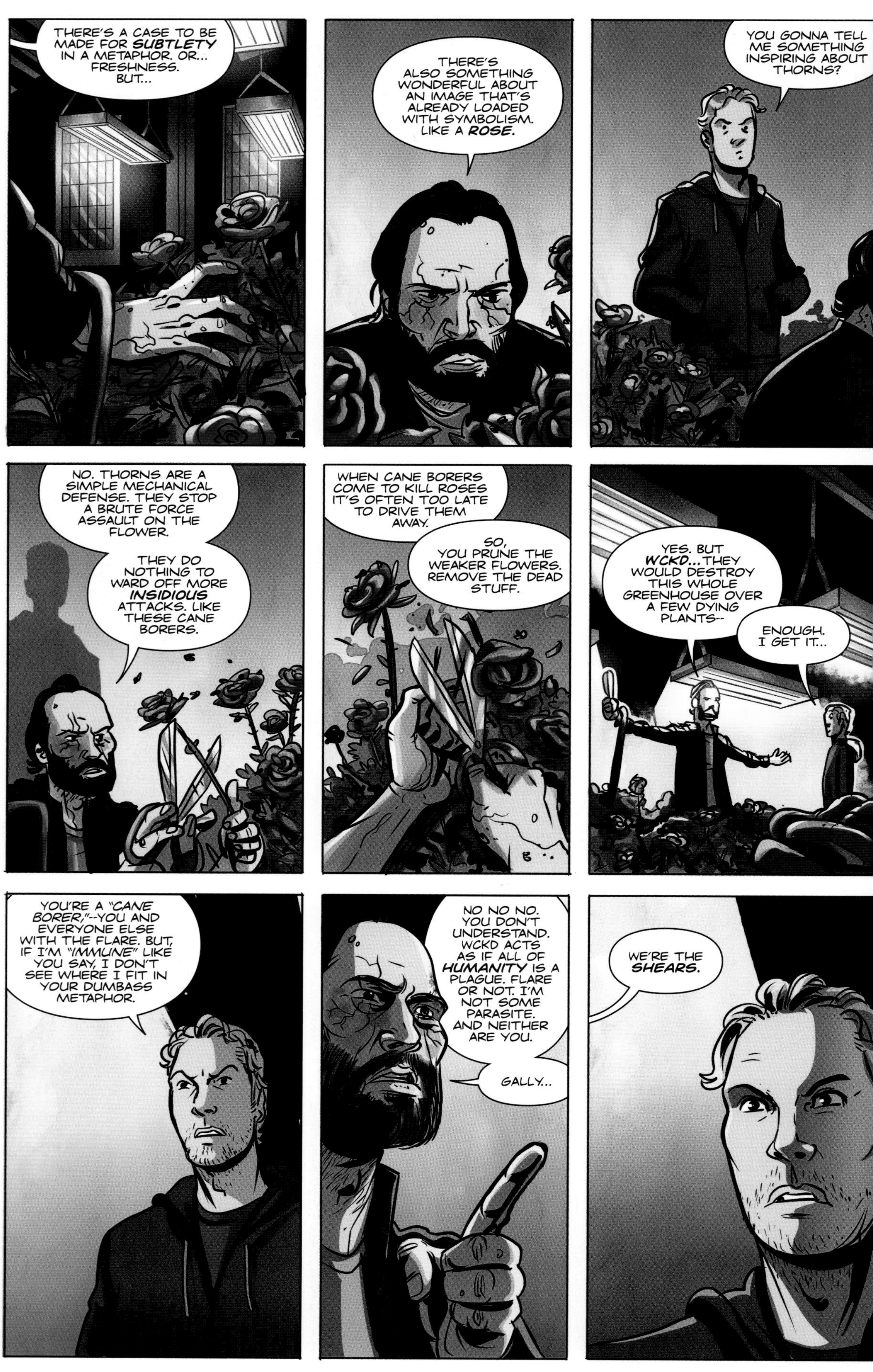

THERE'S A CASE TO BE MADE FOR SUBTLETY IN A METAPHOR. OR... FRESHNESS. BUT...
THERE'S ALSO SOMETHING WONDERFUL ABOUT AN IMAGE THAT'S ALREADY LOADED WITH SYMBOLISM. LIKE A ROSE.
YOU GONNA TELL ME SOMETHING INSPIRING ABOUT THORNS?
NO. THORNS ARE A SIMPLE MECHANICAL DEFENSE. THEY STOP A BRUTE FORCE ASSAULT ON THE FLOWER.
THEY DO NOTHING TO WARD OFF MORE INSIDIOUS ATTACKS. LIKE THESE CANE BORERS.
WHEN CANE BORERS COME TO KILL ROSES IT'S OFTEN TOO LATE TO DRIVE THEM AWAY.
SO, YOU PRUNE THE WEAKER FLOWERS. REMOVE THE DEAD STUFF.
YES. BUT WCKD... THEY WOULD DESTROY THIS WHOLE GREENHOUSE OVER A FEW DYING PLANTS--
ENOUGH. I GET IT...
YOU'RE A "CANE BORER,"--YOU AND EVERYONE ELSE WITH THE FLARE. BUT, IF I'M "IMMUNE" LIKE YOU SAY, I DON'T SEE WHERE I FIT IN YOUR DUMBASS METAPHOR.
NO NO NO. YOU DON'T UNDERSTAND. WCKD ACTS AS IF ALL OF HUMANITY IS A PLAGUE. FLARE OR NOT. I'M NOT SOME PARASITE. AND NEITHER ARE YOU.
GALLY...
WE'RE THE SHEARS.

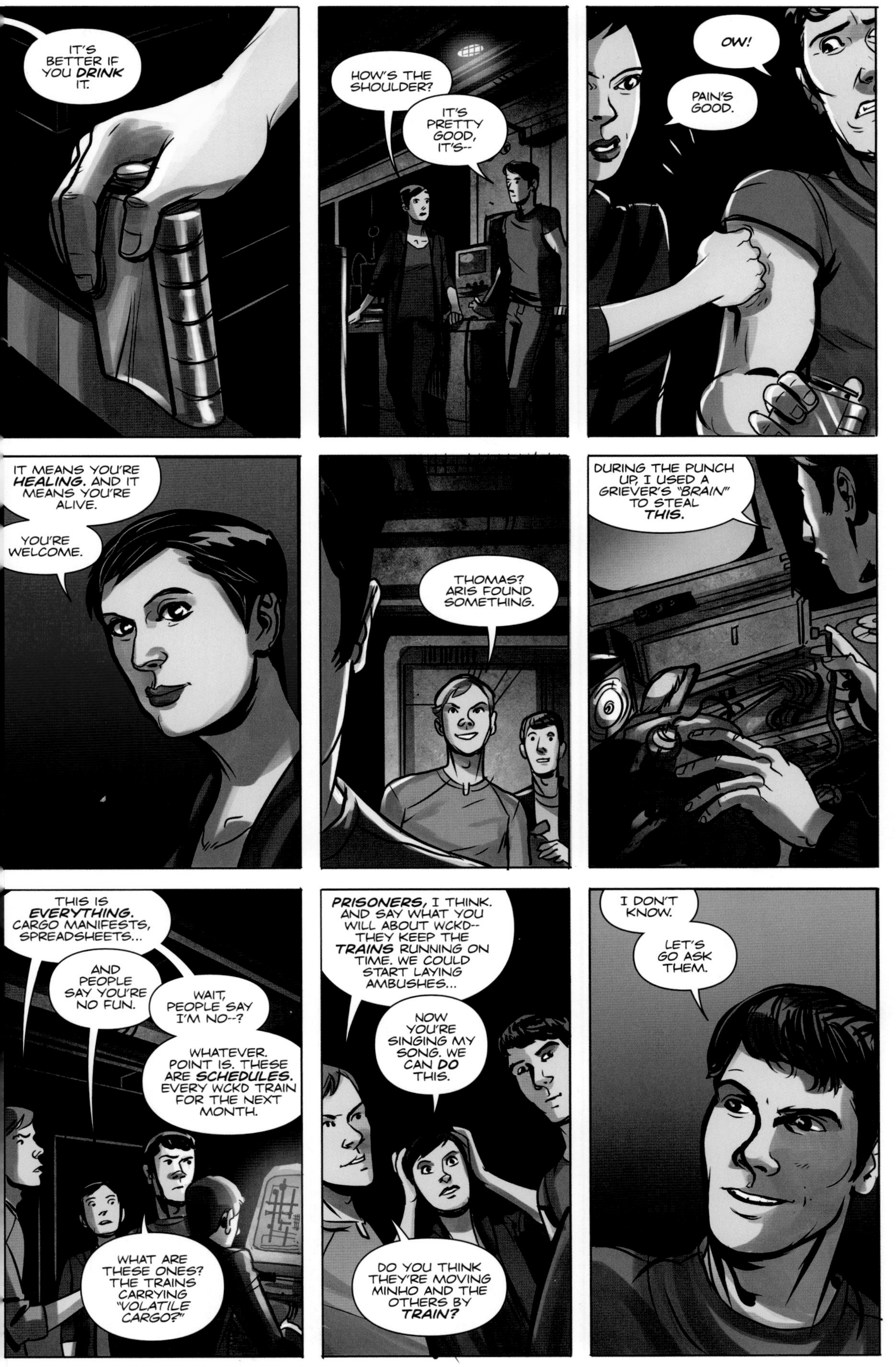

IT'S BETTER IF YOU DRINK IT.
HOW'S THE SHOULDER?
IT'S PRETTY GOOD, IT'S--
OW!
PAIN'S GOOD.
IT MEANS YOU'RE HEALING. AND IT MEANS YOU'RE ALIVE.
YOU'RE WELCOME.
THOMAS? ARIS FOUND SOMETHING.
DURING THE PUNCH UP, I USED A GRIEVER'S "BRAIN" TO STEAL THIS.
THIS IS EVERYTHING. CARGO MANIFESTS, SPREADSHEETS...
AND PEOPLE SAY YOU'RE NO FUN.
WAIT, PEOPLE SAY I'M NO--?
WHATEVER. POINT IS. THESE ARE SCHEDULES. EVERY WCKD TRAIN FOR THE NEXT MONTH.
WHAT ARE THESE ONES? THE TRAINS CARRYING "VOLATILE CARGO?"
PRISONERS, I THINK. AND SAY WHAT YOU WILL ABOUT WCKD-- THEY KEEP THE TRAINS RUNNING ON TIME. WE COULD START LAYING AMBUSHES...
NOW YOU'RE SINGING MY SONG. WE CAN DO THIS.
DO YOU THINK THEY'RE MOVING MINHO AND THE OTHERS BY TRAIN?
I DON'T KNOW.
LET'S GO ASK THEM.

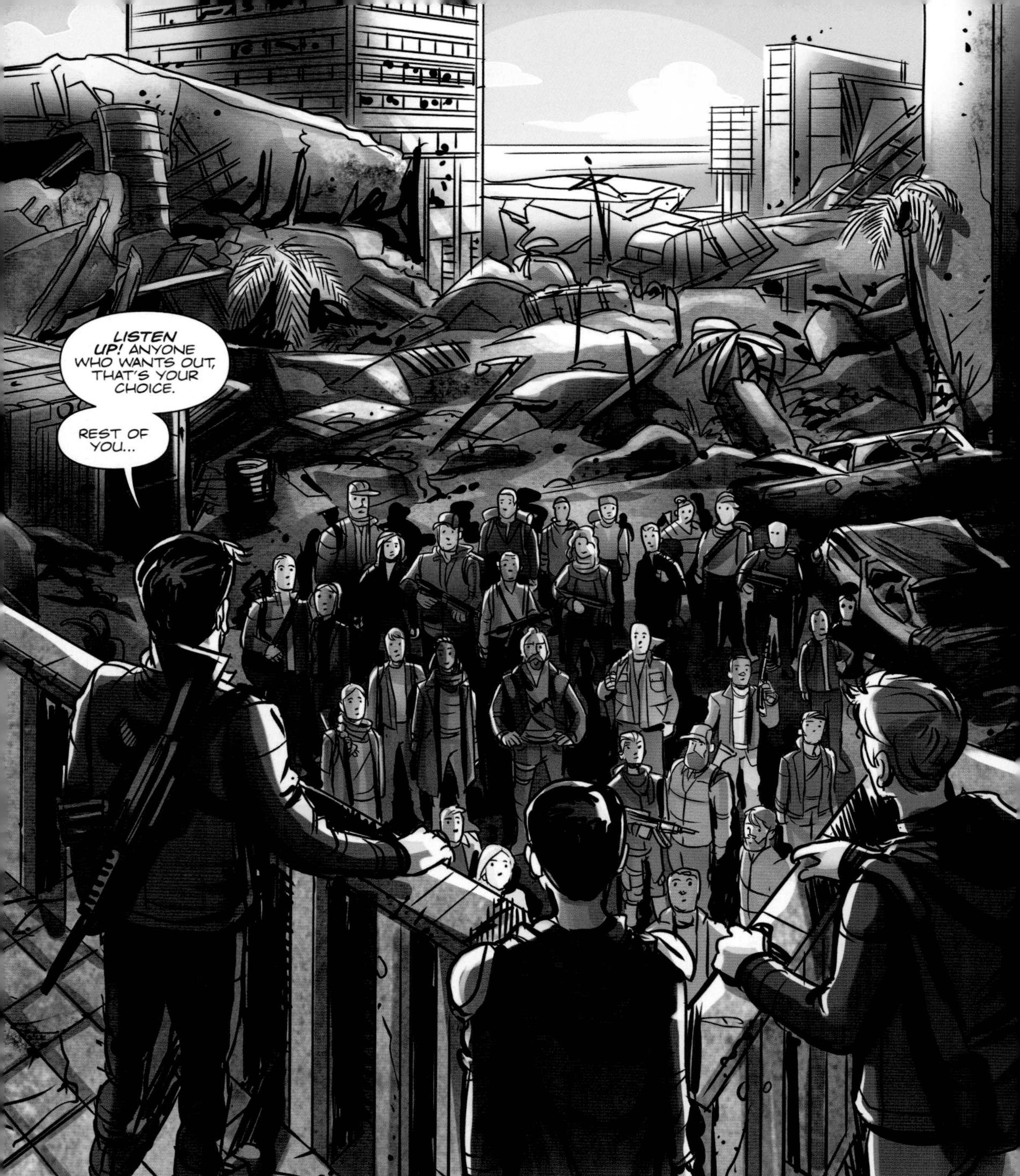
LISTEN UP! ANYONE WHO WANTS OUT, THAT'S YOUR CHOICE.
REST OF YOU...

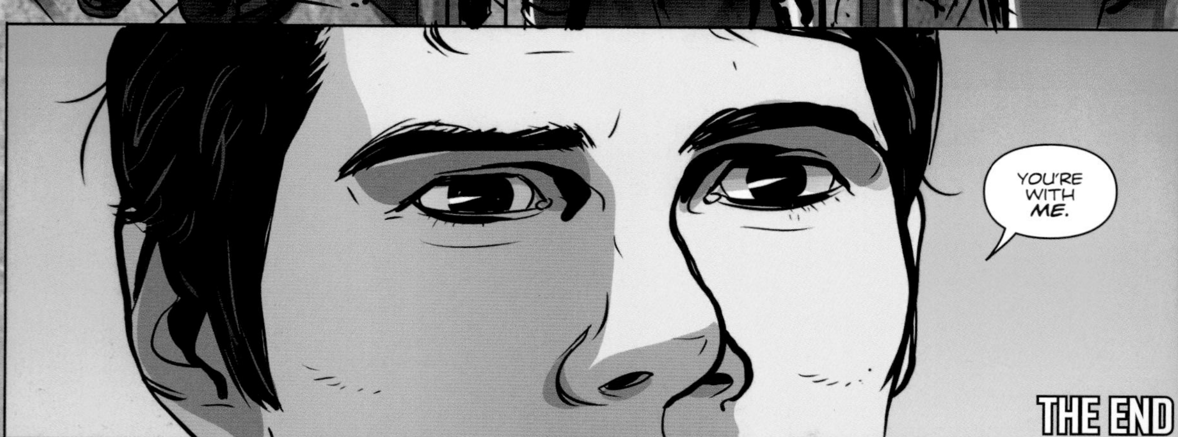
YOU'RE WITH ME.
THE END

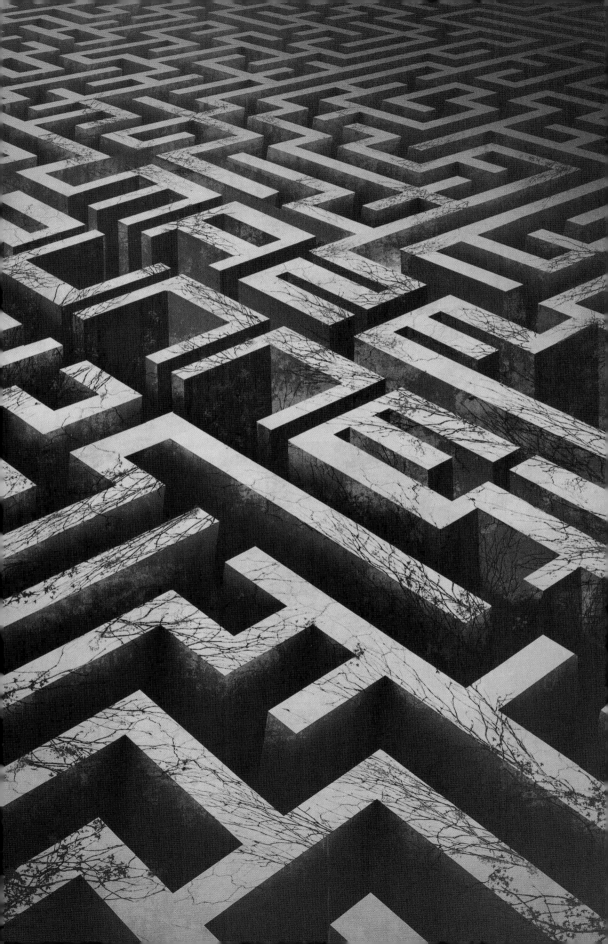

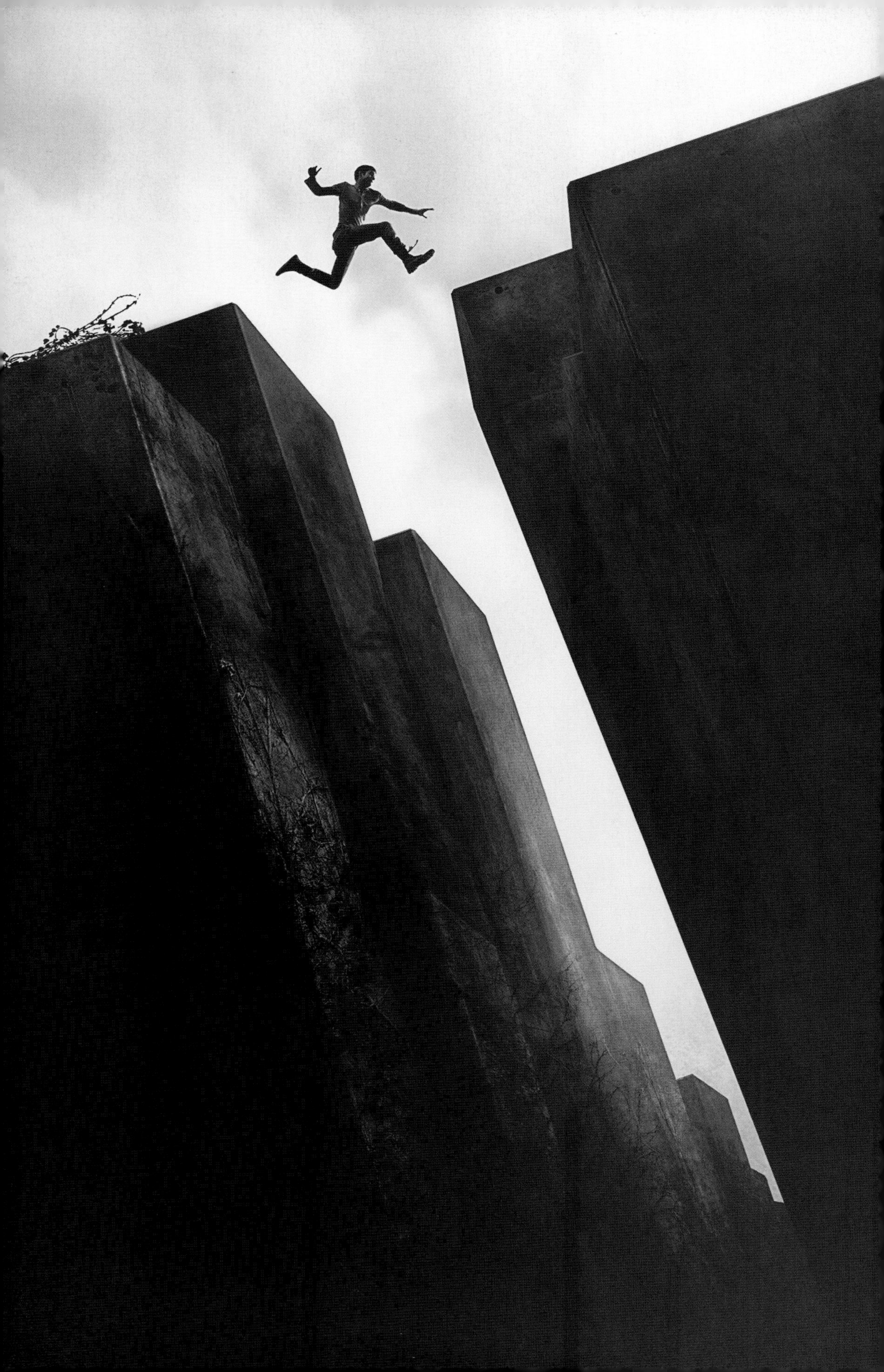

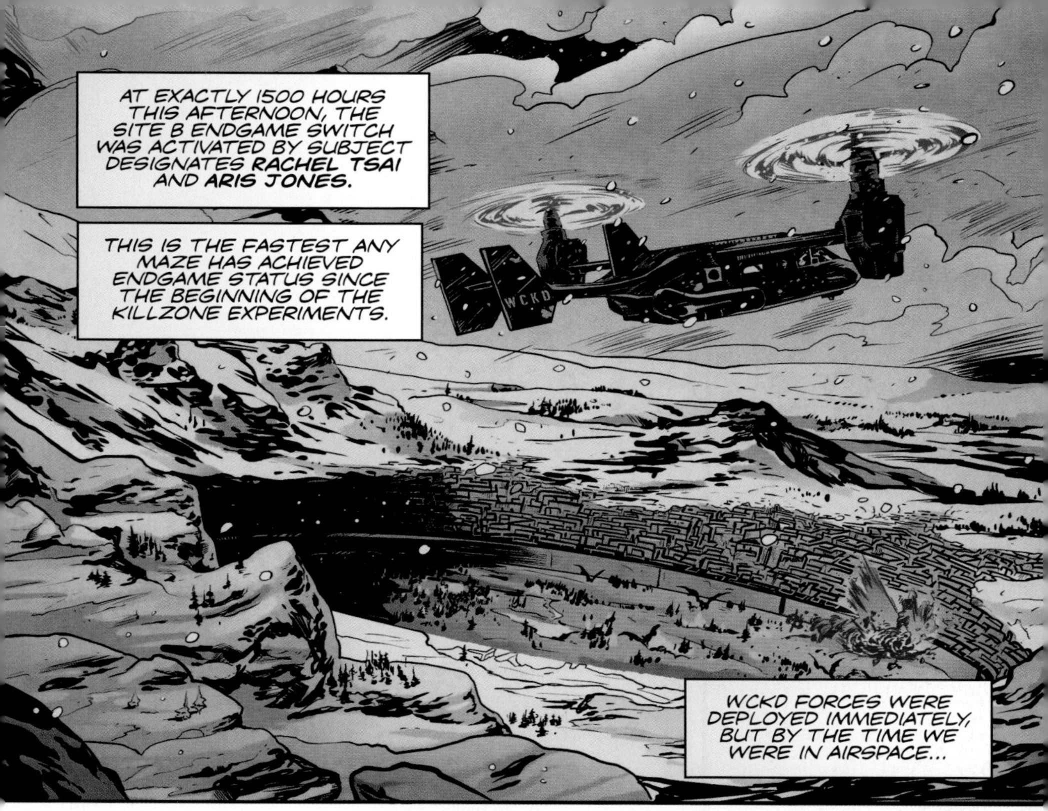

AT EXACTLY 1500 HOURS THIS AFTERNOON, THE SITE B ENDGAME SWITCH WAS ACTIVATED BY SUBJECT DESIGNATES RACHEL TSAI AND ARIS JONES.
THIS IS THE FASTEST ANY MAZE HAS ACHIEVED ENDGAME STATUS SINCE THE BEGINNING OF THE KILLZONE EXPERIMENTS.
WCKD
WCKD FORCES WERE DEPLOYED IMMEDIATELY, BUT BY THE TIME WE WERE IN AIRSPACE...

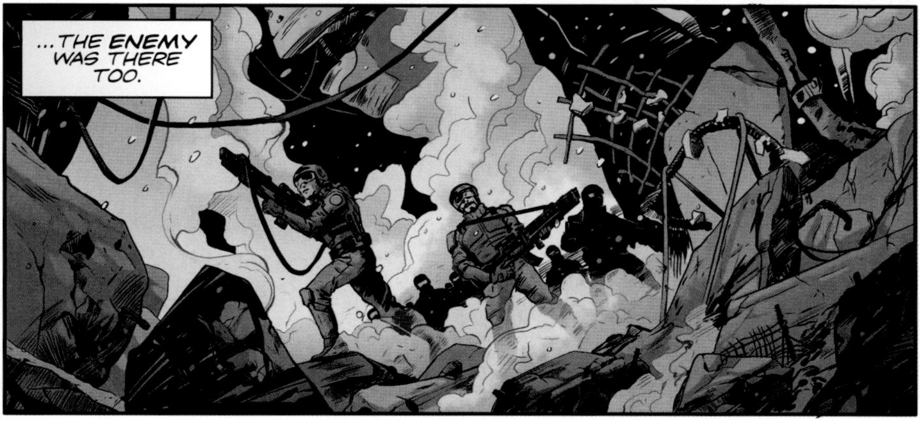

...THE ENEMY WAS THERE TOO.

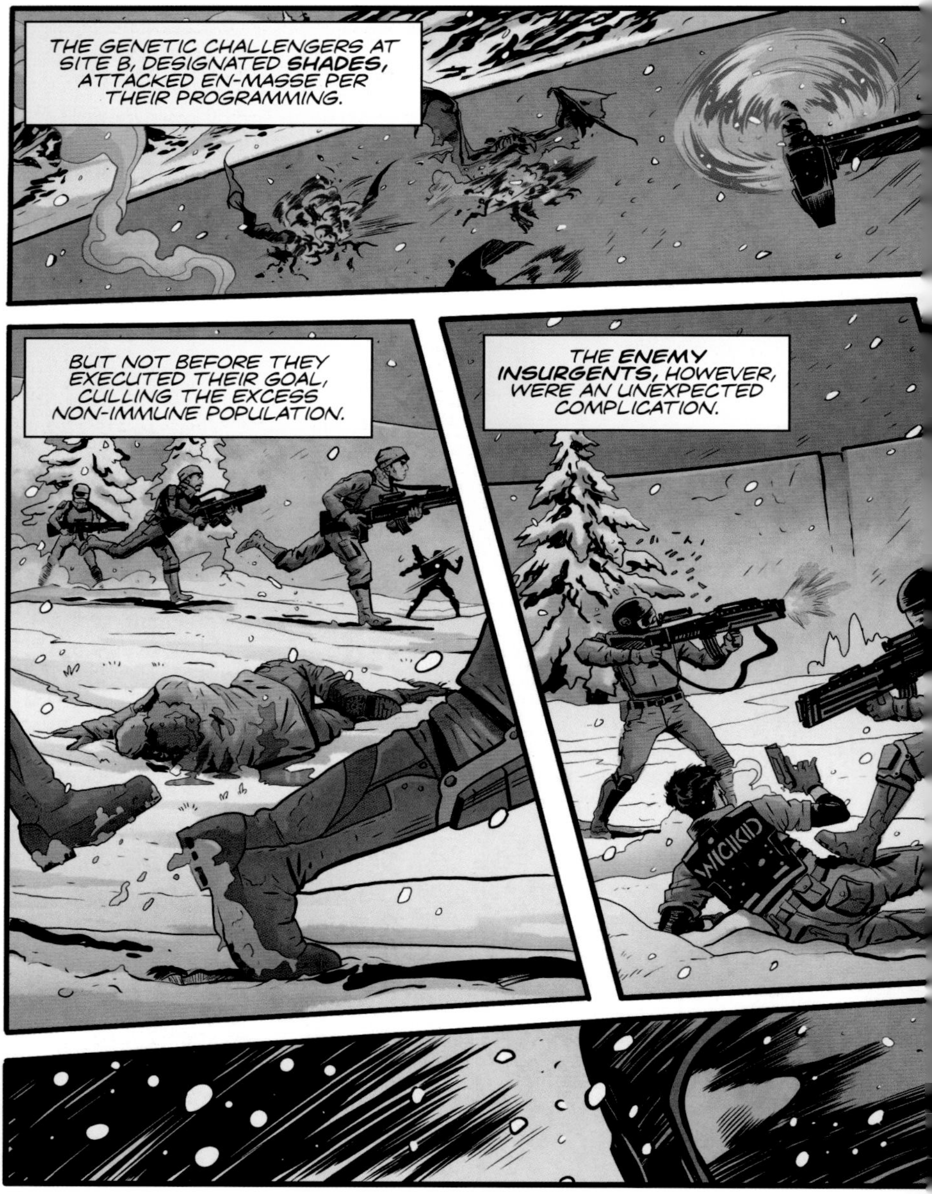
THE GENETIC CHALLENGERS AT SITE B, DESIGNATED **SHADES**, ATTACKED EN-MASSE PER THEIR PROGRAMMING.
BUT NOT BEFORE THEY EXECUTED THEIR GOAL, CULLING THE EXCESS NON-IMMUNE POPULATION.
THE **ENEMY INSURGENTS**, HOWEVER, WERE AN UNEXPECTED COMPLICATION.
WICKID

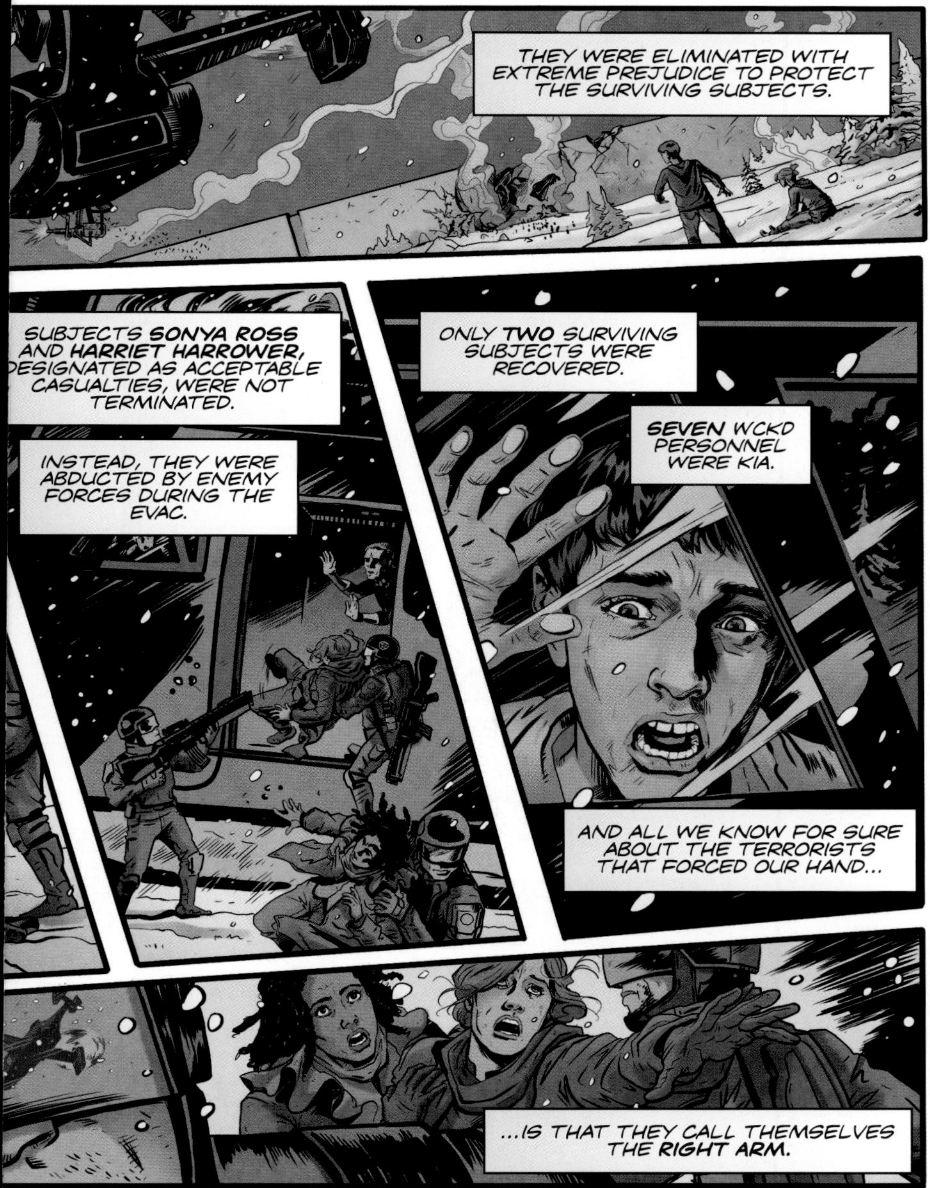
THEY WERE ELIMINATED WITH EXTREME PREJUDICE TO PROTECT THE SURVIVING SUBJECTS.
SUBJECTS SONYA ROSS AND HARRIET HARROWER, DESIGNATED AS ACCEPTABLE CASUALTIES, WERE NOT TERMINATED.
INSTEAD, THEY WERE ABDUCTED BY ENEMY FORCES DURING THE EVAC.
ONLY TWO SURVIVING SUBJECTS WERE RECOVERED.
SEVEN WCKD PERSONNEL WERE KIA.
AND ALL WE KNOW FOR SURE ABOUT THE TERRORISTS THAT FORCED OUR HAND...
...IS THAT THEY CALL THEMSELVES THE RIGHT ARM.

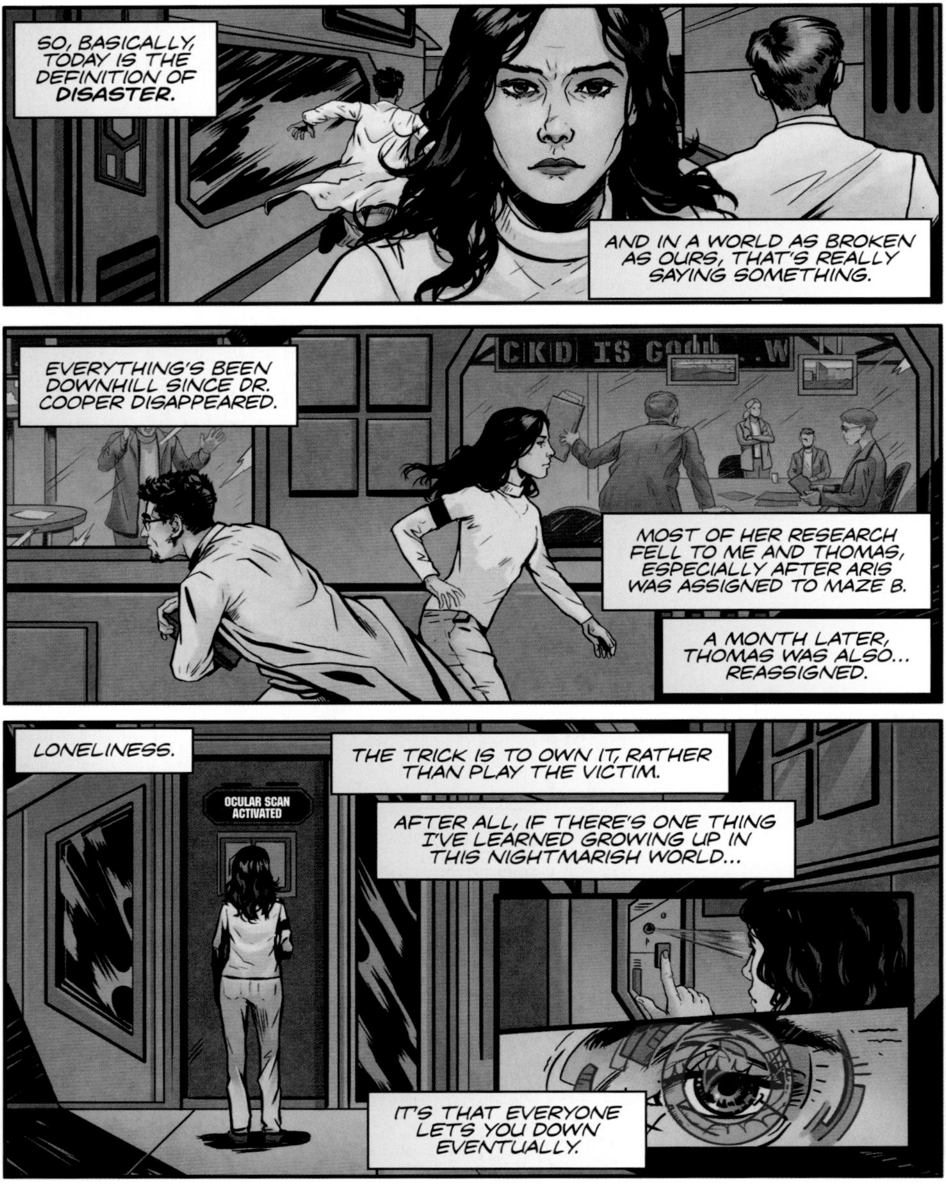
SO, BASICALLY, TODAY IS THE DEFINITION OF DISASTER.
AND IN A WORLD AS BROKEN AS OURS, THAT'S REALLY SAYING SOMETHING.
EVERYTHING'S BEEN DOWNHILL SINCE DR. COOPER DISAPPEARED.
MOST OF HER RESEARCH FELL TO ME AND THOMAS, ESPECIALLY AFTER ARIS WAS ASSIGNED TO MAZE B.
A MONTH LATER, THOMAS WAS ALSO... REASSIGNED.
LONELINESS.
THE TRICK IS TO OWN IT, RATHER THAN PLAY THE VICTIM.
OCULAR SCAN ACTIVATED
AFTER ALL, IF THERE'S ONE THING I'VE LEARNED GROWING UP IN THIS NIGHTMARISH WORLD...
IT'S THAT EVERYONE LETS YOU DOWN EVENTUALLY.

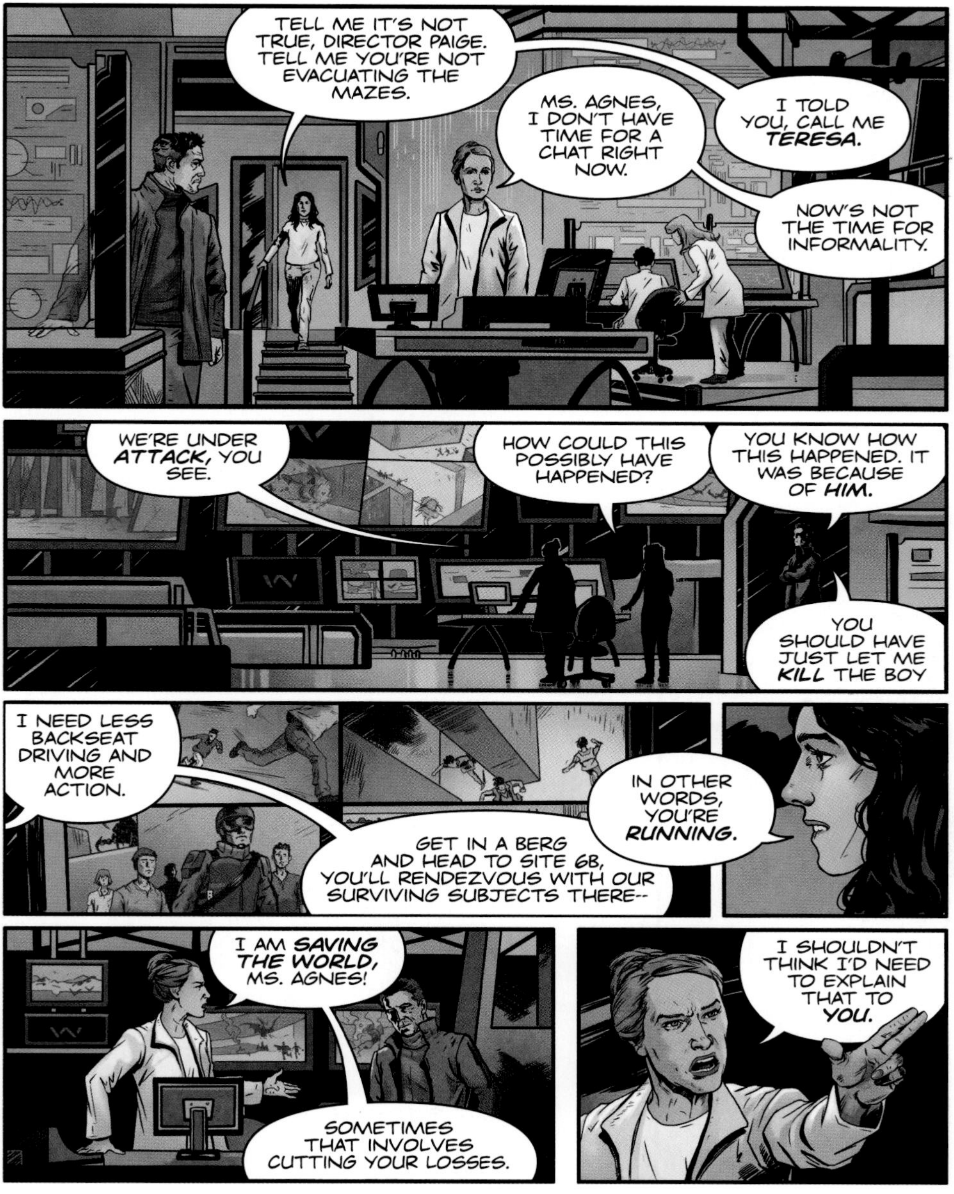

TELL ME IT'S NOT TRUE, DIRECTOR PAIGE. TELL ME YOU'RE NOT EVACUATING THE MAZES.
MS. AGNES, I DON'T HAVE TIME FOR A CHAT RIGHT NOW.
I TOLD YOU, CALL ME TERESA.
NOW'S NOT THE TIME FOR INFORMALITY.
WE'RE UNDER ATTACK, YOU SEE.
HOW COULD THIS POSSIBLY HAVE HAPPENED?
YOU KNOW HOW THIS HAPPENED. IT WAS BECAUSE OF HIM.
YOU SHOULD HAVE JUST LET ME KILL THE BOY
I NEED LESS BACKSEAT DRIVING AND MORE ACTION.
GET IN A BERG AND HEAD TO SITE 6B, YOU'LL RENDEZVOUS WITH OUR SURVIVING SUBJECTS THERE--
IN OTHER WORDS, YOU'RE RUNNING.
I AM SAVING THE WORLD, MS. AGNES!
SOMETIMES THAT INVOLVES CUTTING YOUR LOSSES.
I SHOULDN'T THINK I'D NEED TO EXPLAIN THAT TO YOU.

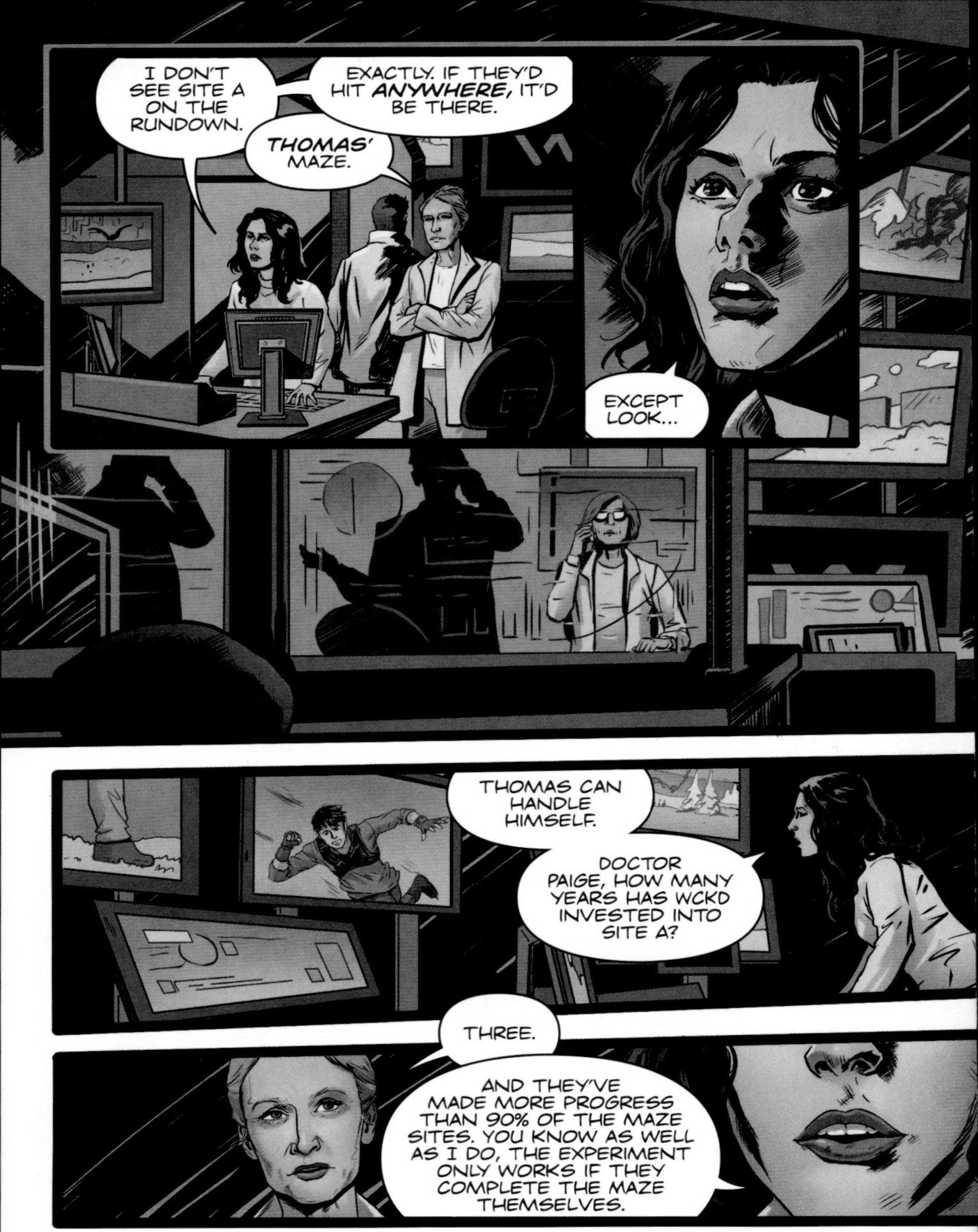
I DON'T SEE SITE A ON THE RUNDOWN.
THOMAS' MAZE.
EXACTLY. IF THEY'D HIT ANYWHERE, IT'D BE THERE.
EXCEPT LOOK...
THOMAS CAN HANDLE HIMSELF.
DOCTOR PAIGE, HOW MANY YEARS HAS WCKD INVESTED INTO SITE A?
THREE.
AND THEY'VE MADE MORE PROGRESS THAN 90% OF THE MAZE SITES. YOU KNOW AS WELL AS I DO, THE EXPERIMENT ONLY WORKS IF THEY COMPLETE THE MAZE THEMSELVES.

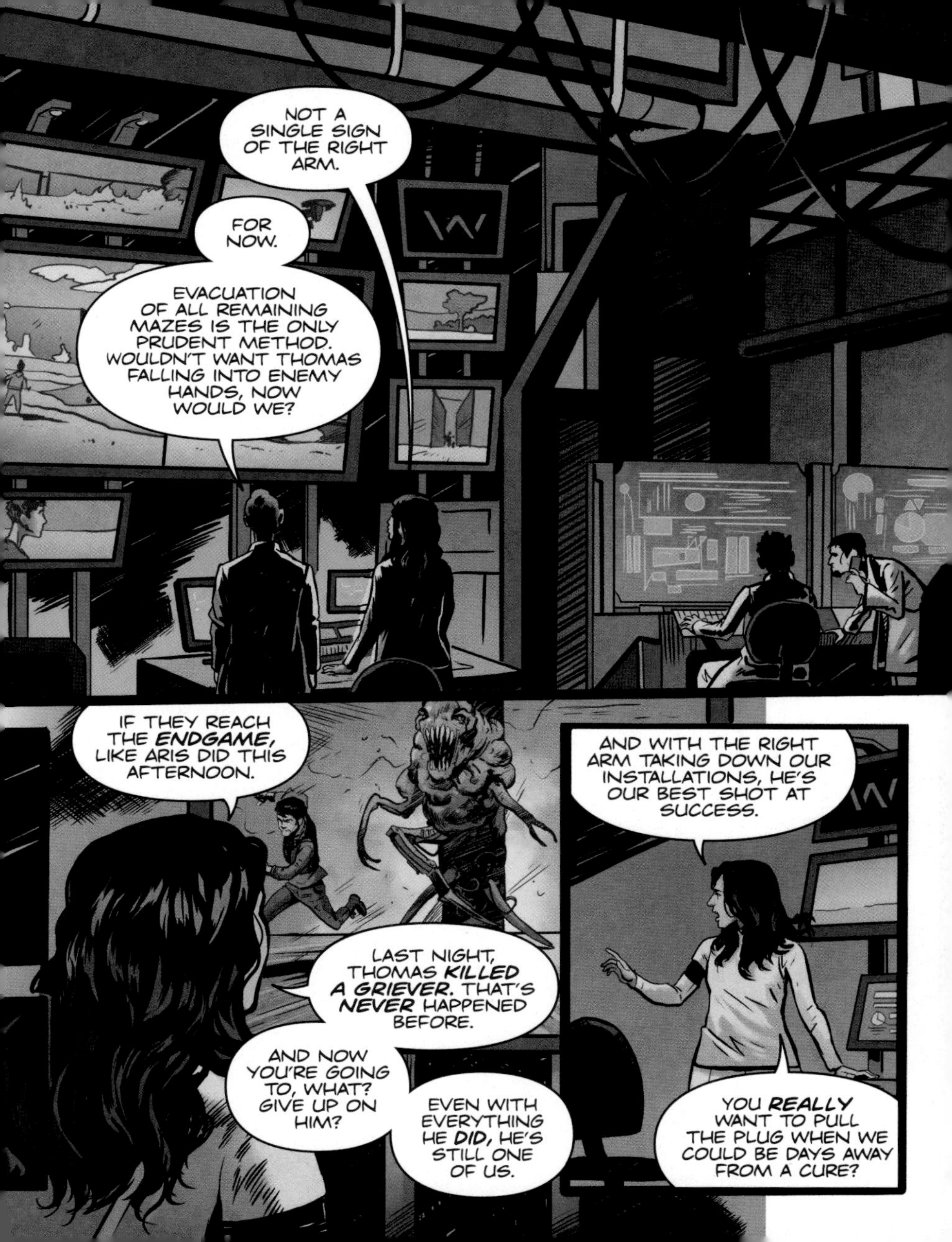
NOT A SINGLE SIGN OF THE RIGHT ARM.
FOR NOW.
EVACUATION OF ALL REMAINING MAZES IS THE ONLY PRUDENT METHOD. WOULDN'T WANT THOMAS FALLING INTO ENEMY HANDS, NOW WOULD WE?
IF THEY REACH THE ENDGAME, LIKE ARIS DID THIS AFTERNOON.
LAST NIGHT, THOMAS KILLED A GRIEVER. THAT'S NEVER HAPPENED BEFORE.
AND NOW YOU'RE GOING TO, WHAT? GIVE UP ON HIM?
EVEN WITH EVERYTHING HE DID, HE'S STILL ONE OF US.
AND WITH THE RIGHT ARM TAKING DOWN OUR INSTALLATIONS, HE'S OUR BEST SHOT AT SUCCESS.
YOU REALLY WANT TO PULL THE PLUG WHEN WE COULD BE DAYS AWAY FROM A CURE?

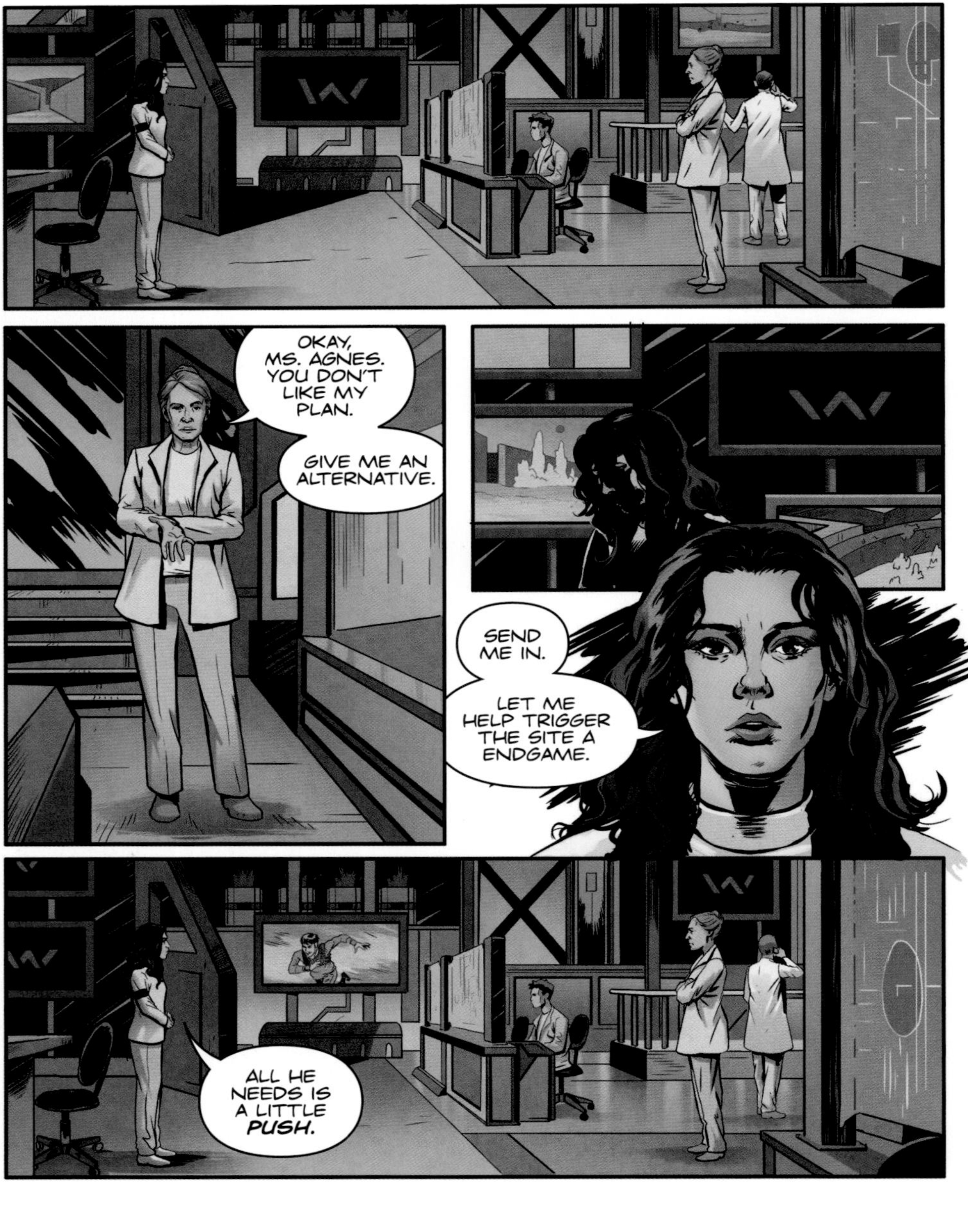
OKAY, MS. AGNES. YOU DON'T LIKE MY PLAN.
GIVE ME AN ALTERNATIVE.
SEND ME IN.
LET ME HELP TRIGGER THE SITE A ENDGAME.
ALL HE NEEDS IS A LITTLE *PUSH.*

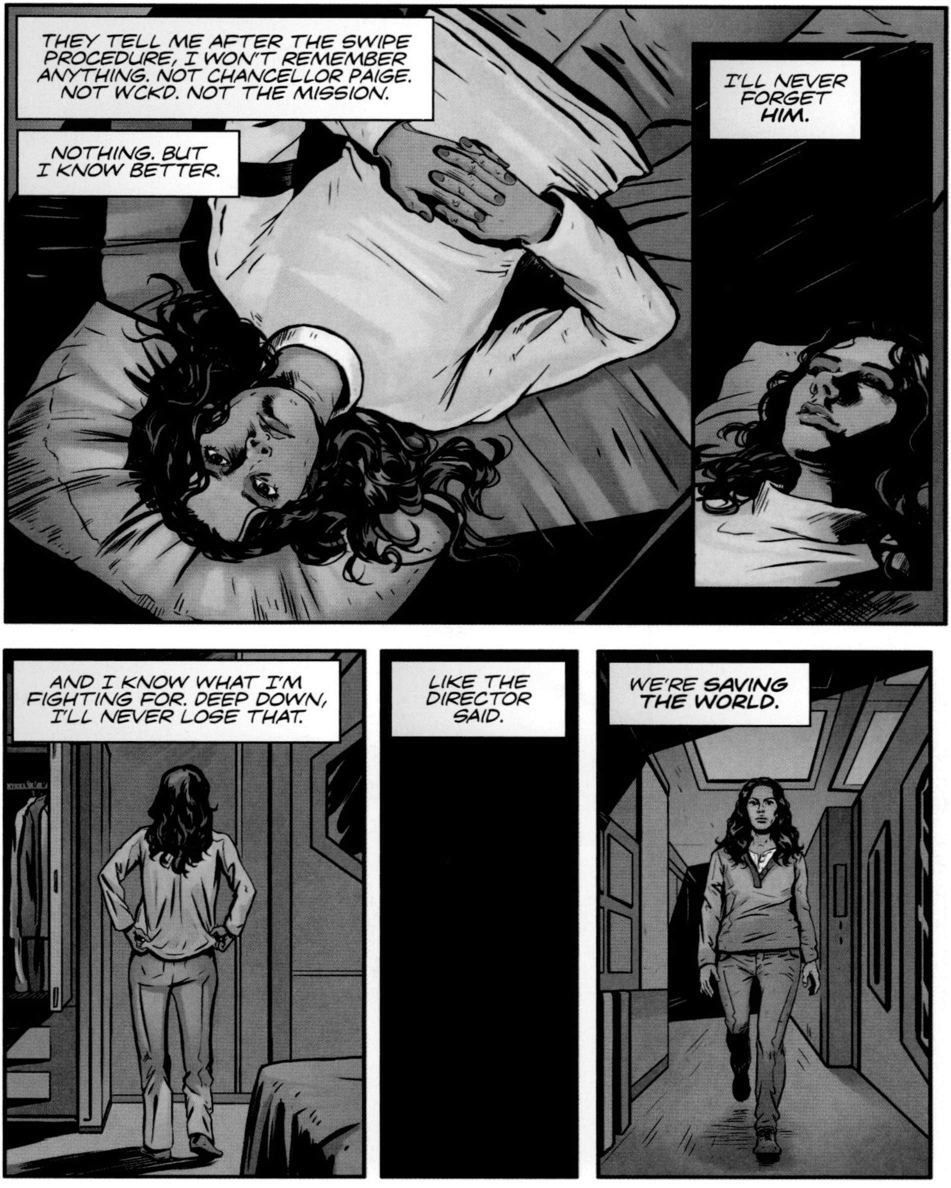
THEY TELL ME AFTER THE SWIPE PROCEDURE, I WON'T REMEMBER ANYTHING. NOT CHANCELLOR PAIGE. NOT WCKD. NOT THE MISSION.
NOTHING. BUT I KNOW BETTER.
I'LL NEVER FORGET HIM.
AND I KNOW WHAT I'M FIGHTING FOR. DEEP DOWN, I'LL NEVER LOSE THAT.
LIKE THE DIRECTOR SAID.
WE'RE SAVING THE WORLD.

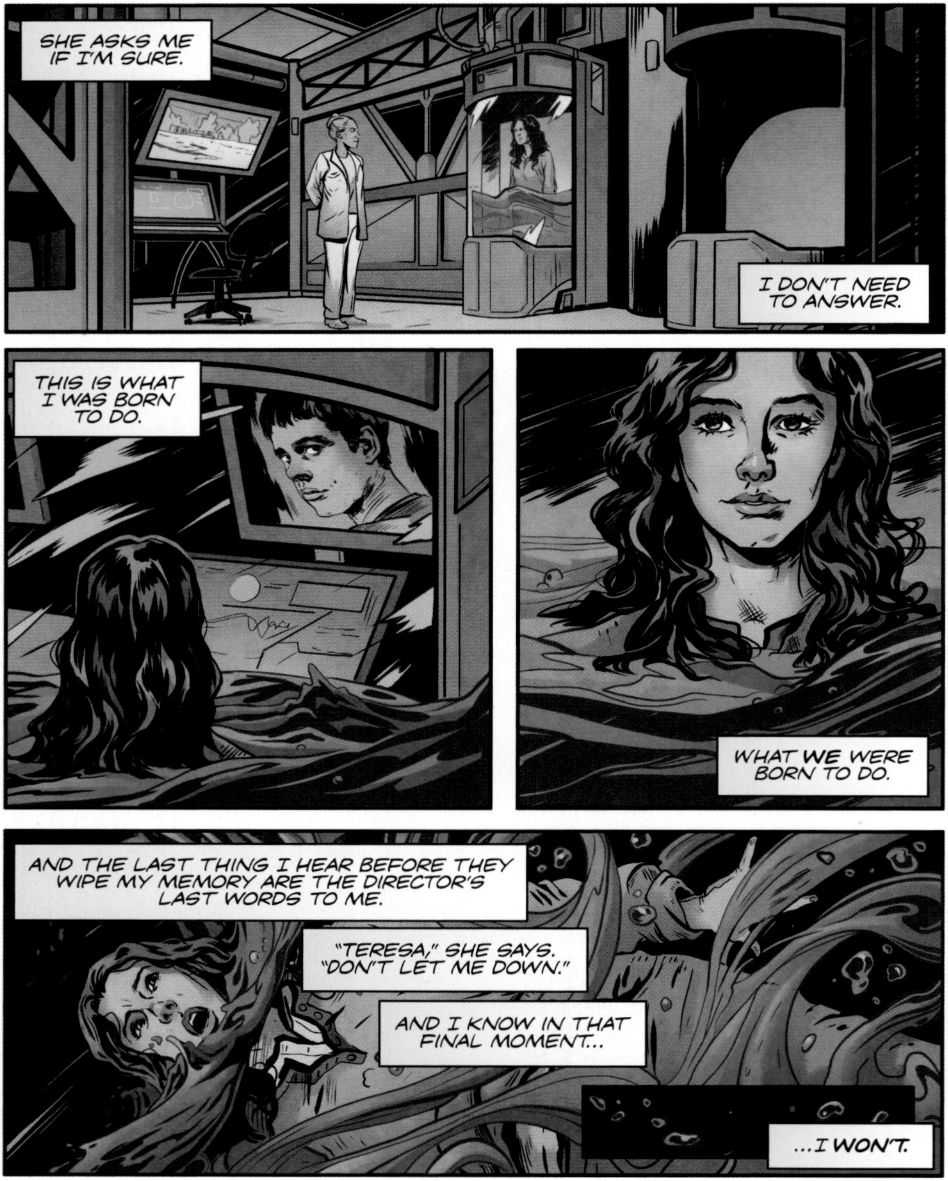
SHE ASKS ME IF I'M SURE.
I DON'T NEED TO ANSWER.
THIS IS WHAT I WAS BORN TO DO.
WHAT **WE** WERE BORN TO DO.
AND THE LAST THING I HEAR BEFORE THEY WIPE MY MEMORY ARE THE DIRECTOR'S LAST WORDS TO ME.
"TERESA," SHE SAYS. "DON'T LET ME DOWN."
AND I KNOW IN THAT FINAL MOMENT...
...I **WON'T**.

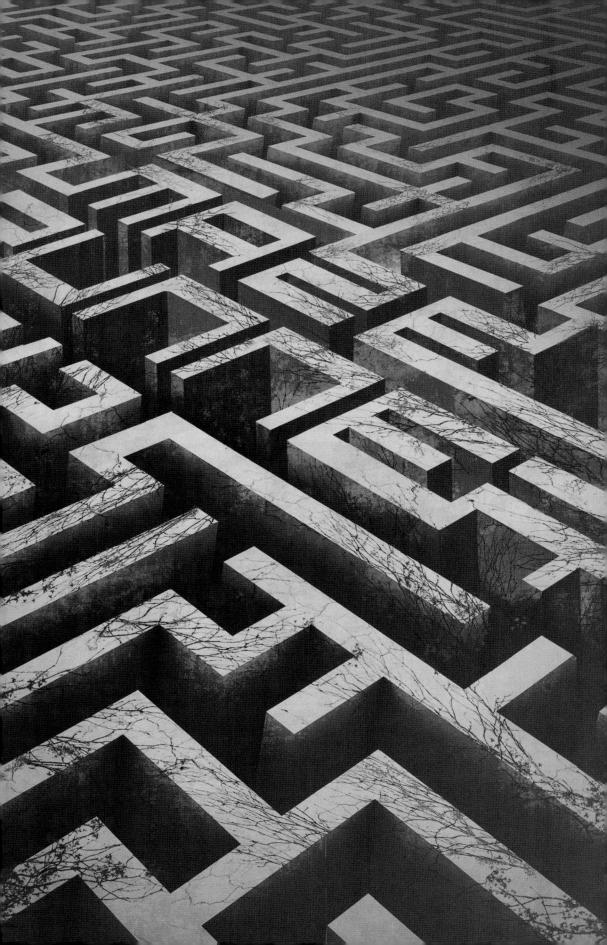

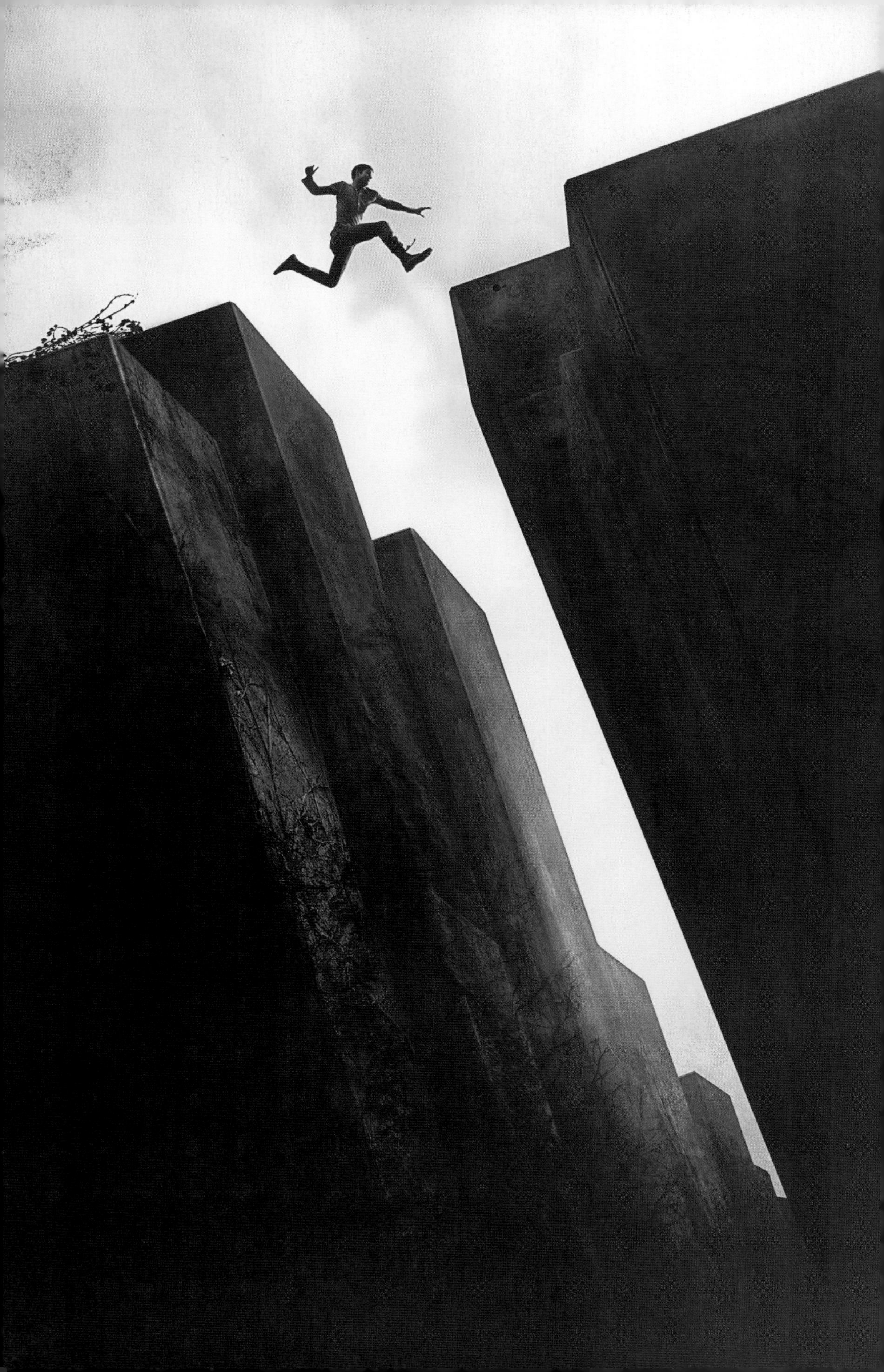

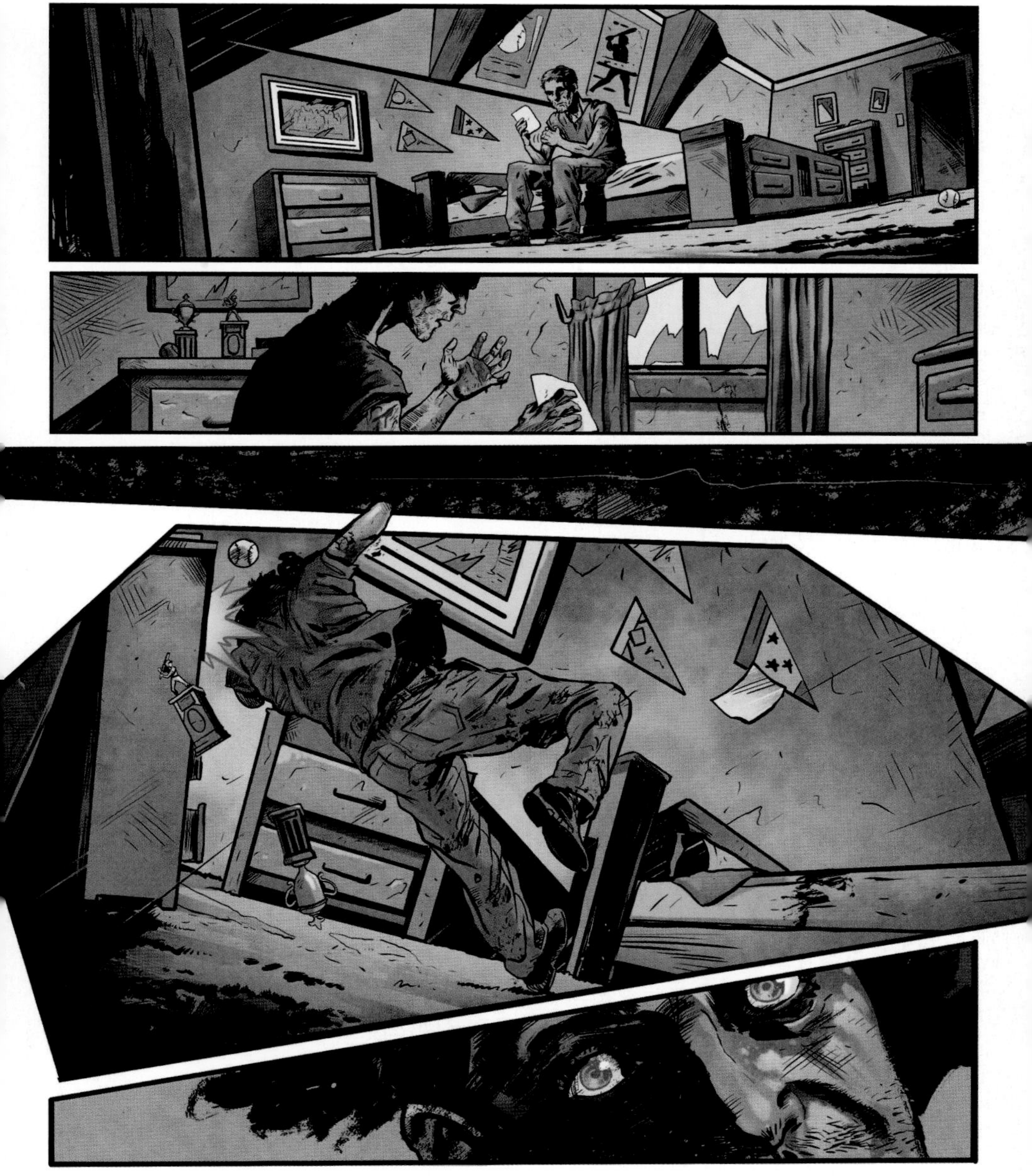

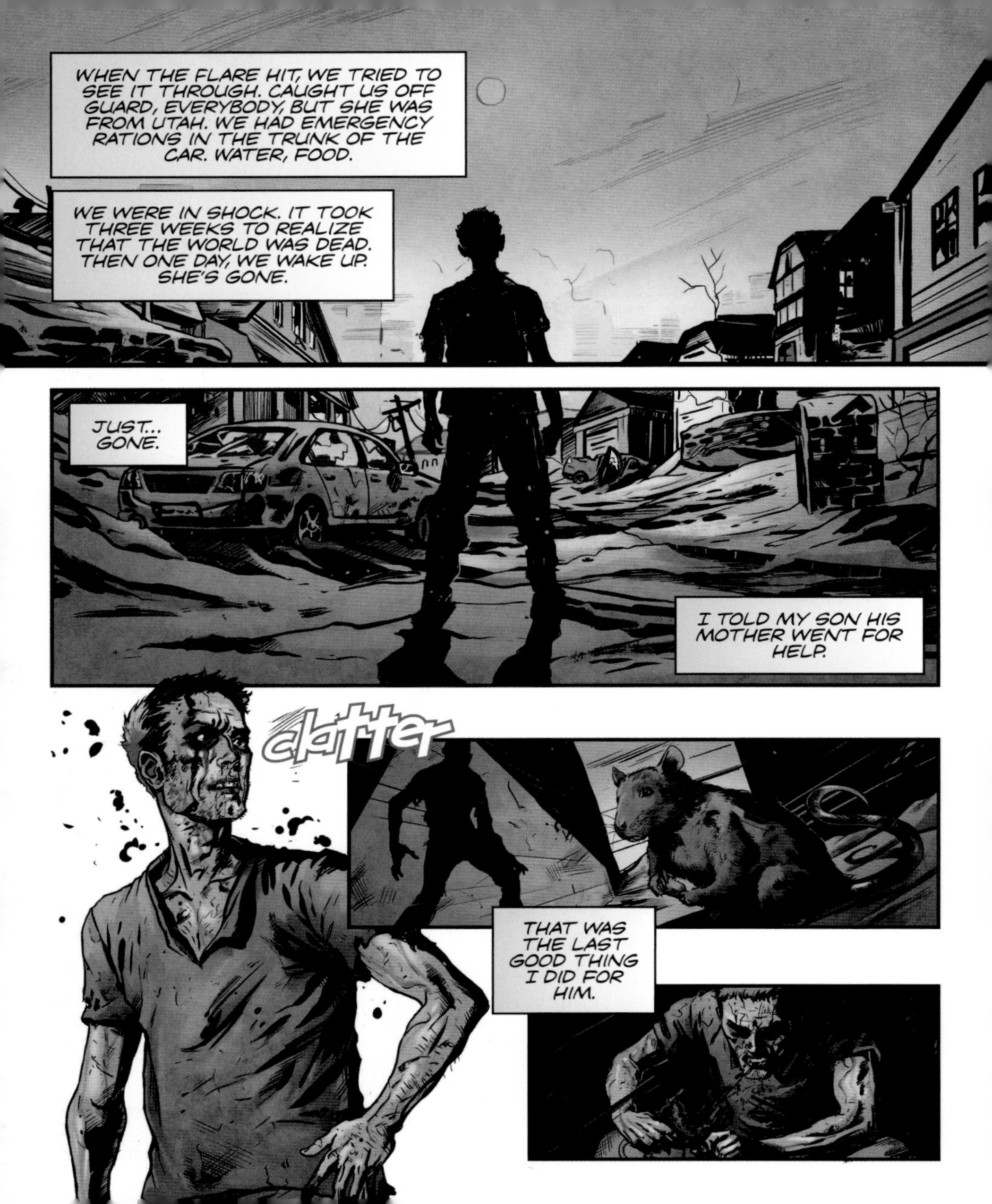
WHEN THE FLARE HIT, WE TRIED TO SEE IT THROUGH. CAUGHT US OFF GUARD, EVERYBODY, BUT SHE WAS FROM UTAH. WE HAD EMERGENCY RATIONS IN THE TRUNK OF THE CAR. WATER, FOOD.
WE WERE IN SHOCK. IT TOOK THREE WEEKS TO REALIZE THAT THE WORLD WAS DEAD. THEN ONE DAY, WE WAKE UP. SHE'S GONE.
JUST... GONE.
I TOLD MY SON HIS MOTHER WENT FOR HELP.
clatter
THAT WAS THE LAST GOOD THING I DID FOR HIM.

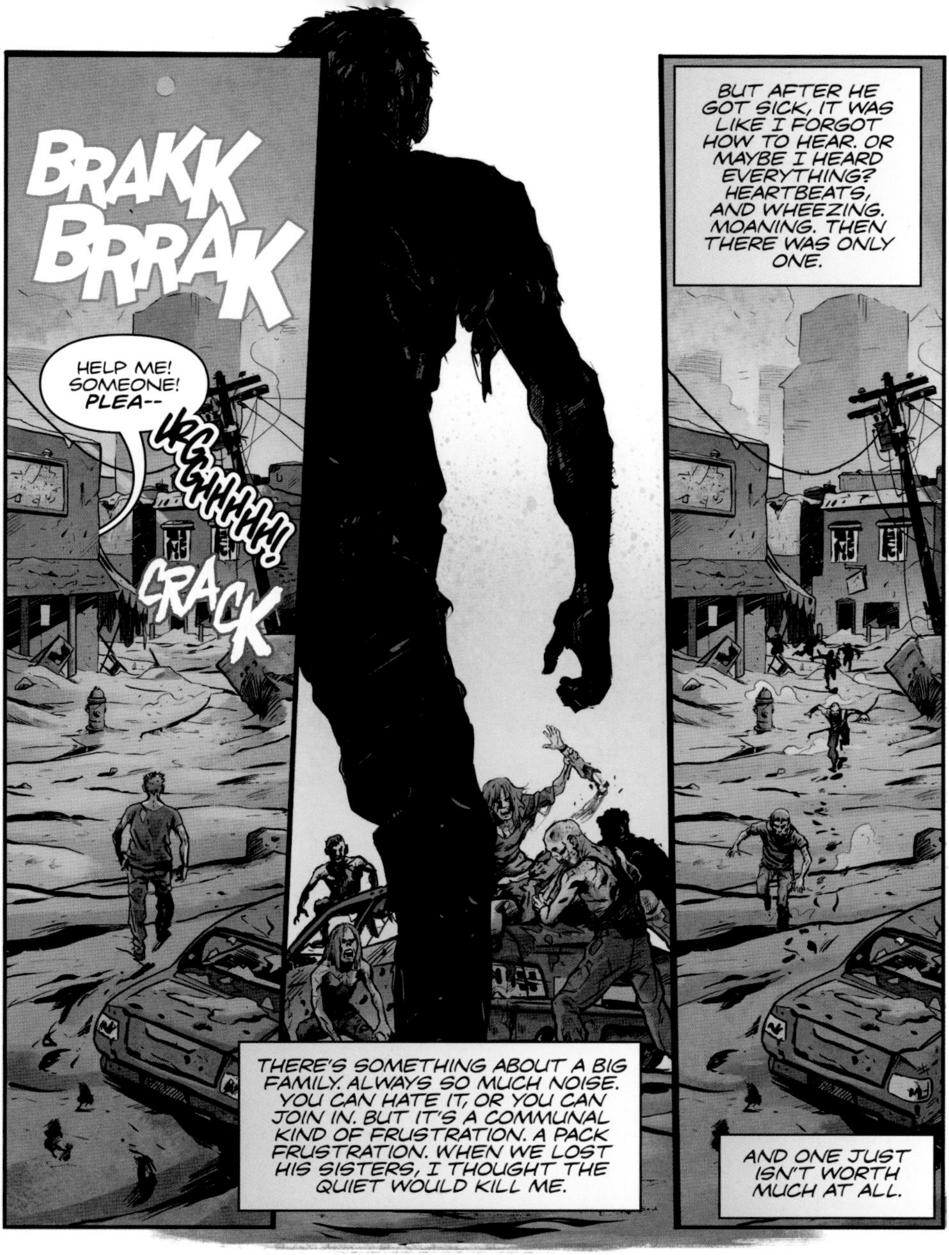
BRAKK
BRRAK
HELP ME! SOMEONE! PLEA--
URGHHHHH!
CRACK
THERE'S SOMETHING ABOUT A BIG FAMILY. ALWAYS SO MUCH NOISE. YOU CAN HATE IT, OR YOU CAN JOIN IN. BUT IT'S A COMMUNAL KIND OF FRUSTRATION. A PACK FRUSTRATION. WHEN WE LOST HIS SISTERS, I THOUGHT THE QUIET WOULD KILL ME.
BUT AFTER HE GOT SICK, IT WAS LIKE I FORGOT HOW TO HEAR. OR MAYBE I HEARD EVERYTHING? HEARTBEATS, AND WHEEZING. MOANING. THEN THERE WAS ONLY ONE.
AND ONE JUST ISN'T WORTH MUCH AT ALL.

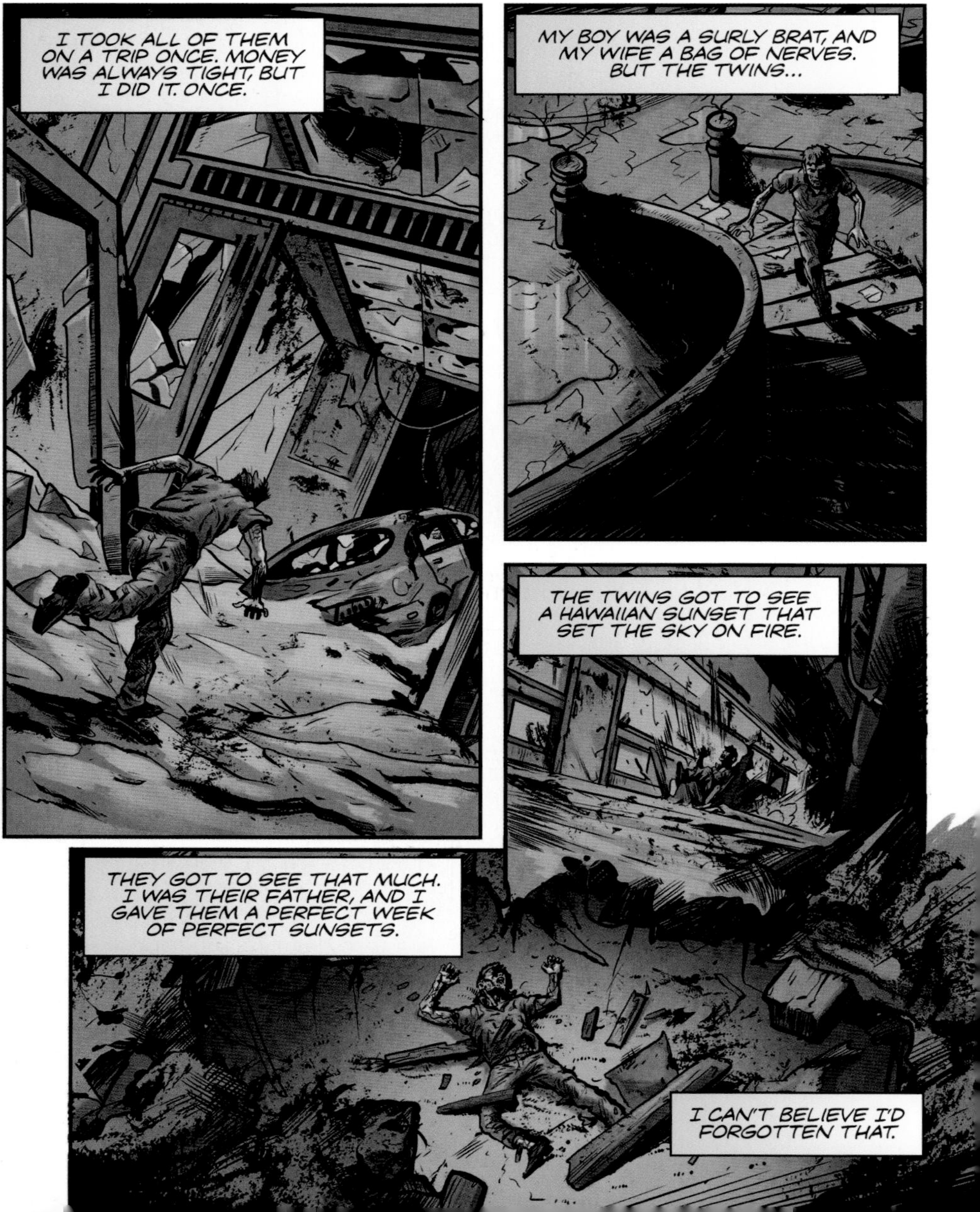
I TOOK ALL OF THEM ON A TRIP ONCE. MONEY WAS ALWAYS TIGHT, BUT I DID IT. ONCE.
MY BOY WAS A SURLY BRAT, AND MY WIFE A BAG OF NERVES. BUT THE TWINS...
THE TWINS GOT TO SEE A HAWAIIAN SUNSET THAT SET THE SKY ON FIRE.
THEY GOT TO SEE THAT MUCH. I WAS THEIR FATHER, AND I GAVE THEM A PERFECT WEEK OF PERFECT SUNSETS.
I CAN'T BELIEVE I'D FORGOTTEN THAT.

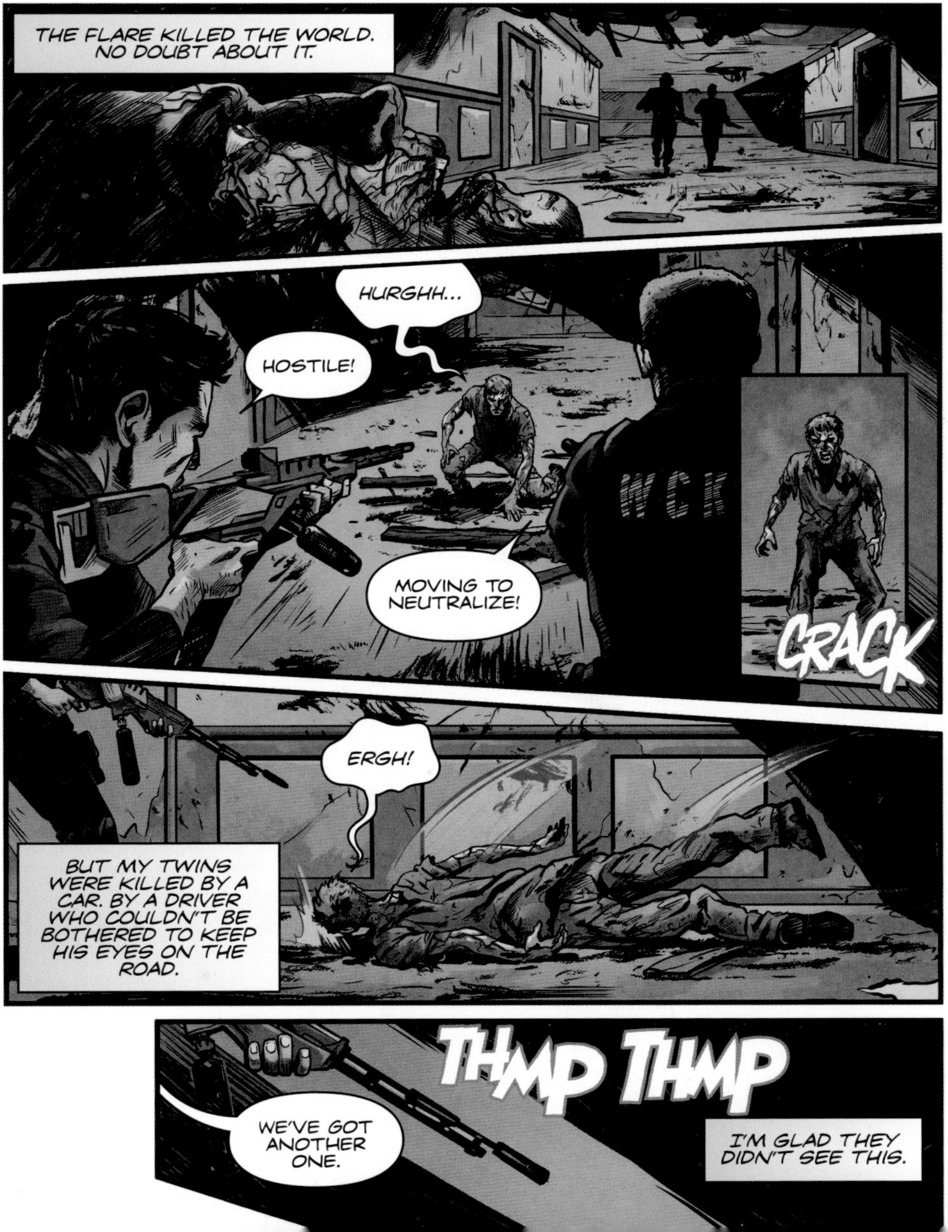
THE FLARE KILLED THE WORLD. NO DOUBT ABOUT IT.
HURGHH...
HOSTILE!
MOVING TO NEUTRALIZE!
WCK
CRACK
ERGH!
BUT MY TWINS WERE KILLED BY A CAR. BY A DRIVER WHO COULDN'T BE BOTHERED TO KEEP HIS EYES ON THE ROAD.
THMP THMP
WE'VE GOT ANOTHER ONE.
I'M GLAD THEY DIDN'T SEE THIS.

WHICH BRINGS ME HERE.

STRAPPED TO A TABLE. TABLE. **TABLE.** DIDN'T KNOW THAT WORD A MOMENT AGO.

WHAT'S HAPPENING TO ME?

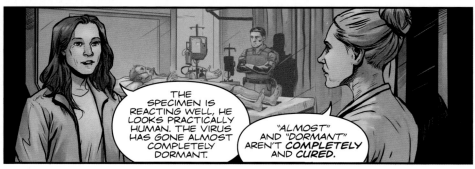

THE SPECIMEN IS REACTING WELL, HE LOOKS PRACTICALLY HUMAN. THE VIRUS HAS GONE ALMOST COMPLETELY DORMANT.

"ALMOST" AND "DORMANT" AREN'T **COMPLETELY** AND **CURED.**

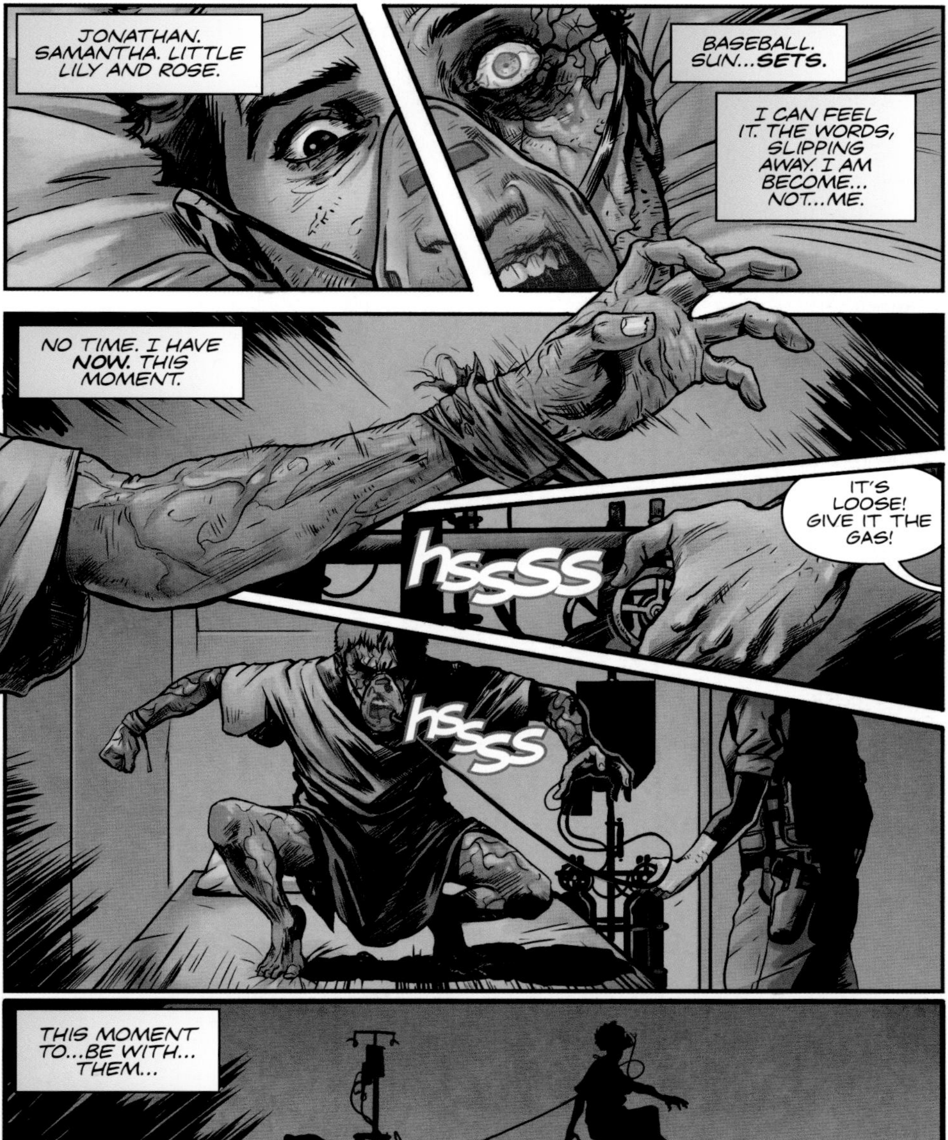
JONATHAN. SAMANTHA. LITTLE LILY AND ROSE.
BASEBALL. SUN...SETS.
I CAN FEEL IT. THE WORDS, SLIPPING AWAY. I AM BECOME... NOT...ME.
NO TIME. I HAVE NOW. THIS MOMENT.
IT'S LOOSE! GIVE IT THE GAS!
hsssss
hssss
THIS MOMENT TO...BE WITH... THEM...

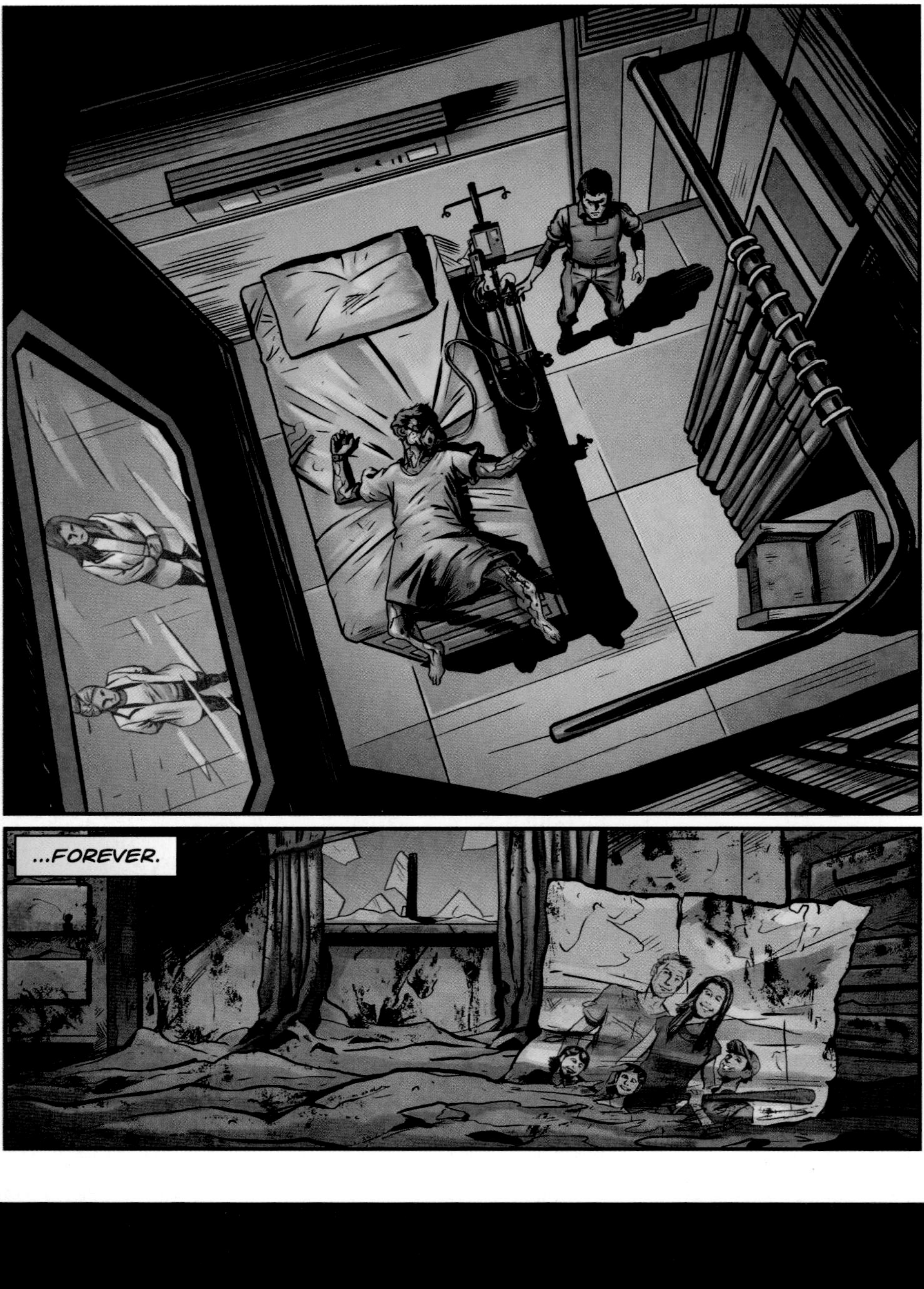
...FOREVER.

DISCOVER
VISIONARY CREATORS

THE WOODS
JAMES TYNION IV • MICHAEL DIALYNAS
VOL. 1
THE ARROW

"The Spire is fantastic! My kind of genre free-for-all."
—BRIAN K. VAUGHAN (Saga)
THE SPIRE
SIMON SPURRIER
JEFF STOKELY
ANDRÉ MAY

MARK WAID · PETER KRAUSE
IRREDEEMABLE
AFTERWORD BY GRANT MORRISON

J.G. JONES
MARK WAID
STRANGE FRUIT
Foreword by ELVIS MITCHELL

MICHAEL ALAN NELSON
DAN MORA
GABRIEL CASSATA
HEXED
THE HARLOT & THE THIEF VOLUME ONE

ABNETT & CULBARD
WILD'S END
FIRST LIGHT
JEFF LEMIRE

BOOM! STUDIOS

AVAILABLE AT YOUR LOCAL COMICS SHOP AND BOOKSTORE

To find a comics shop in your area, call 1-888-266-4226

WWW.**BOOM-STUDIOS**.COM

James Tynion IV

The Woods

Volume 1
ISBN: 978-1-60886-454-6 | $9.99 US
Volume 2
ISBN: 978-1-60886-495-9 | $14.99 US
Volume 3
ISBN: 978-1-60886-773-8 | $14.99 US

The Backstagers

Volume 1
ISBN: 978-1-60886-993-0 | $14.99 US

Simon Spurrier

Six-Gun Gorilla

ISBN: 978-1-60886-390-7 | $19.99 US

The Spire

ISBN: 978-1-60886-913-8 | $29.99 US

Weavers

ISBN: 978-1-60886-963-3 | $19.99 US

Mark Waid

Irredeemable

Volume 1
ISBN: 978-1-93450-690-5 | $16.99 US
Volume 2
ISBN: 978-1-60886-000-5 | $16.99 US

Incorruptible

Volume 1
ISBN: 978-1-60886-015-9 | $16.99 US
Volume 2
ISBN: 978-1-60886-028-9 | $16.99 US

Strange Fruit

ISBN: 978-1-60886-872-8 | $24.99 US

Michael Alan Nelson

Hexed The Harlot & The Thief

Volume 1
ISBN: 978-1-60886-718-9 | $14.99 US
Volume 2
ISBN: 978-1-60886-816-2 | $14.99 US

Day Men

Volume 1
ISBN: 978-1-60886-393-8 | $9.99 US
Volume 2
ISBN: 978-1-60886-852-0 | $9.99 US

Dan Abnett

Wild's End

Volume 1: First Light
ISBN: 978-1-60886-735-6 | $19.99 US
Volume 2: The Enemy Within
ISBN: 978-1-60886-877-3 | $19.99 US

Hypernaturals

Volume 1
ISBN: 978-1-60886-298-6 | $16.99 US
Volume 2
ISBN: 978-1-60886-319-8 | $19.99 US

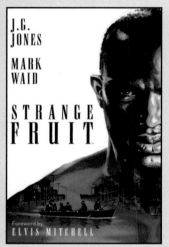

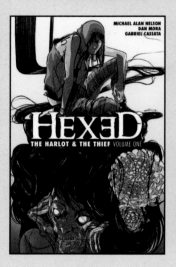

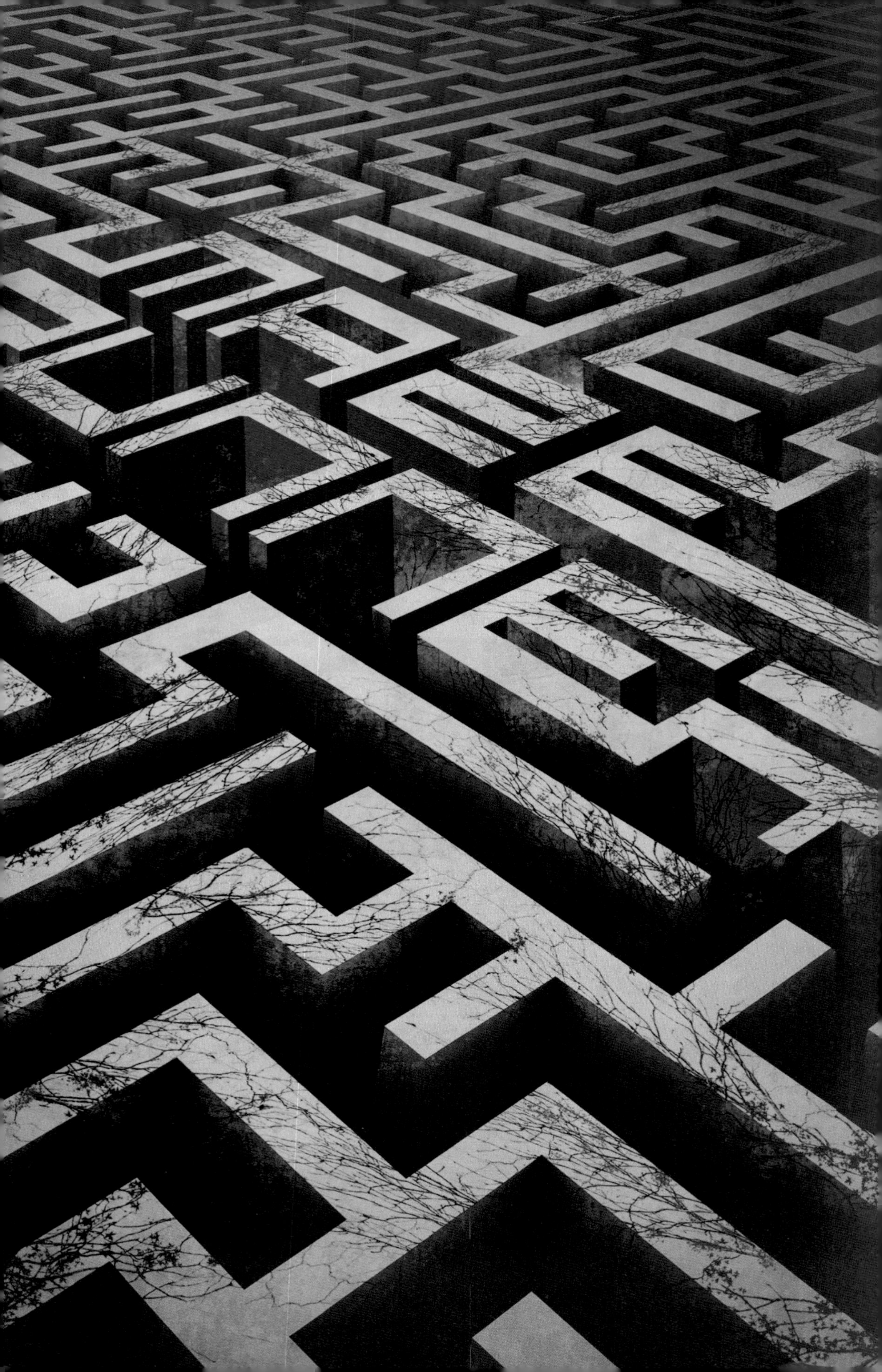